THE MAN DIED

The playwright and poet Wole Soyinka was born in Nigeria in 1934. The son of a schools' master, he attended the universities of Ibadan and Leeds, and spent eighteen months studying the theatre in London. He was attached to the Royal Court Theatre, where his play 'The Invention' was produced. In 1960, he returned to Ibadan to study indigenous drama forms at University College. He then became Director of the School of Drama at the University of Ibadan. At the beginning of the Nigerian Civil War, Wole Soyinka was arrested by the Federal authorities and imprisoned. In 1969 he was released. He holds an honorary Doctorate of Letters from Yale University, and has been accorded major literary prizes in England, including the highly prestigious John Whiting Award. His published works include *Collected Plays*, the work of criticism MYTH, LITERATURE AND THE AFRICAN WORLD and the childhood memoir AKÉ.

Wole Soyinka

THE MAN DIED

Prison Notes

Spectrum Books Limited
Ibadan • Owerri • Kaduna • Lagos

This edition published by
Spectrum Books Limited
Sunshine House
1, Emmanuel Alayande Street
Oluyole Industrial Estate
PMB 5612
Ibadan, Nigeria

in association with
Safari Books (Export) Limited
Bel Royal House
Hilgrove Street
St. Helier, Jersey
Channel Islands, UK

First published by Rex Collings 1972

Reprinted 1988 (twice), 1990, 1993

ISBN: 978-246-012-5

Printed by Intec Printers Limited, Ibadan

this book is deservedly

DEDICATED

to 'LAIDE

who rejected compromise and demanded

JUSTICE

Ten Years After

Seinde Arigbede did not die. In the course of his duties as a medical doctor, however, he was caught up in the violence unleashed on the citizens of Ondo by the Nigerian state after the disputed 1983 elections, and nearly perished. An eye-witness account from a citizen who managed to escape alive from one such exercise of 'peace-keeping' by this Special Field Force arm of the Nigerian police was published in *The Guardian* (Nigeria) of 24 September, 1983. *The Guardian* is an independent newspaper which has built up a reputation for carefully investigative, non-hysterical reporting.

The circumstances would have amazed even Franz Kafka, even without the physical degradation. Hardly believing that it was indeed happening to him, Dr Arigbede was taken to an empty cell, where he was hung up by the wrists and left dangling, his feet away from the ground, from specially fixed ceiling hooks. Between beatings and other forms of torture the question was incessantly put: Where is the training camp? In the progress of his ordeal he could hear the cries of others subjected to even worse treatment – as he was later to discover – in their own cells. He conceded that, unlike others, he did not undergo the agony of having broomstick switches driven up his penis!

Dr Arigbede, however, like others in my own class, can raise effective voices and stir up officialdom in an emergency – sometimes. His wife, Aduni, moved with desperation in every possible direction and, through intervention from higher police quarters, Seinde's ordeal was ended after a week. He lost the use of both hands for some time; one is now more or less fully recovered. The fate of the other is still much in doubt, despite daily physiotherapy.

At the time of writing this, Dr Arigbede is still trying to identify his torturers who, he discovered were students of Political Science at the University of Ibadan. Both the army and the police (including the National Security Organization) send their men on special courses (Psychology, International Relations, Law, Sociology Political Science, etc., etc.) at all the universities – there is nothing hidden or improper about this. It is, however, the first-known instance where our universities have actually been educating torturers. A more hideous obscenity has yet to be imagined in the system of power controls which make it actually possible, even probable, that a student in one's class will one day be his torturer, or that a student patient at a university hospital, will one day drive electrified needles beneath the nails of his erstwhile physician or push broomsticks up his genitals!

Frequently one is compelled to ask: What sort of society is one a part of? What community of the intelligentsia is it that accepts, without a squawk, the disappearance of a trade union leader without trace? What sort of labour solidarity is exhibited when the Secretary-General of the huge army of the Post and Telegraph Workers is allowed to die like a dog in the dungeons of Dodan Barracks, without a voice raised in protest, or a demand for explanation? I have moved back now ten years, to the events preceding and provoking *The Man Died*. Gogo Chu Nzeribe was arrested for some undisclosed offence during Gowon's regime, and imprisoned in Dodan Barracks where he died. Among the various versions of his death, the most credible appears to be that Gogo Nzeribe was starved to death. He was arrested for some reason that remains totally impenetrable and brought out daily for flogging. One day he fought back, and this resulted in orders that he should be permanently locked up in a solitary cell and 'forgotten'. I am inclined to this version because it was provided by a highly placed officer in the police shortly after my own release and enquiries. The details of Gozo Nzeribe's death are, however, irrelevant; what matters always is the criminal complicity of his own peers, through silence, and the failure of self-asserted progressive voice of the nation's intelligentsia to ask questions, the failure to understand that such events are habit-forming in the psychology of power, and that the boundaries of the geography of victims eventually extends to embrace even those who think they are protected by silence.

Or shall we simply avoid the troublesome 'Left', whose 'extremism' is conveniently accused of being the cause of its own woes? Let us turn then to the respectable bastion of Establishment, the Civil Service. We can hardly hope for any aspect of government with less 'subversive' complications, least of all when it is the Medical Department in question, and the victim is the Head of the Federal Medical Services, the late Dr Adeyemi Ademola. This civil servant was mysteriously gunned to death at his Ikoyi home by three armed intruders – a bare two-minute drive from the residence of the then head of state. The assassins did not even make any pretence at being robbers. They were a well-briefed assassination squad who carried out their operation with military precision and vanished thereafter, not a trace of them uncovered (or looked for!) anywhere. The administration of General Yakubu Gowon made no effort to stem the heavy tide of speculations, fuelled by the fact that this politically innocuous but conscientious doctor had been conducting a sensitive autopsy at the time of his death on a highly placed military brass, the head of one of the Armed Forces Divisions. The papers went suddenly silent. No commission of enquiry into this wildly sensational murder of the highest medical officer in government employ, no public appeals for information or clues. Those with whom I spoke soon after my release from detention shushed me up in fear – not even the fact that this doctor was the brother of the then Chief Justice of Nigeria, Justice Adetokunbo Ademola, was sufficient to jolt the police from an unbelievable inertia, to prompt that force into any special activity towards uncovering the perpetrators of the notorious crime. As for the victim's own trade union, the prestigious Medical Association of Nigeria, it was as if Dr Ademola had been struck off the Medical Register in ignominy, – for the unspeakable crime of being murdered in the line of duty.

I understand and sympathize, therefore, with the reaction of squeamishness to the language I employ on those who are ultimately guilty of these and a thousand similar crimes. It is only a camouflage for such critics' failure to find their own corresponding language – in an act or symbolic gesture – for these assaults, not even on their humanity, but on their civic being. Their courage, they feel, is called in question, which of course is far from being the intention, but their feeling is an admission of their own minds' unease.

If these and like crimes were complete in themselves, if they ended in their own occurrence and had no implications for the future beyond the unpleasant memory, we would be content to bury our dead, console the maimed and proceed with a calmed will into the future. But with the certain knowledge that such events are unresolved, and that their lack of resolution promotes their own kind a hundred-thousandfold, with increasingly sophisticated machinery of outrage and camouflage, in increased boldness and cynicism which only pauses when a people's will is wholly dominated, one recognizes the sanctimonious opiate inherent in popular slogans like 'Bygones is bygones'.

Those who are not dead to language must know that this is of the same order of pious platitudes as the much touted 'magnanimity' expressed at the end of the war in the words 'No Victors, No Vanquished', a sedation of political understanding, cunningly confected by those who know damned well who the vanquished were – no, not the Biafrans, but the deluded national polity, a people misled into making sacrifices for the true victors, the civilian and military collaborators in the entrenchment of an exploitative socio-economic mutuality. Even in totalitarian states, the time comes when past 'errors' are admitted, high-placed criminals unmasked and victims rehabilitated, mostly alas, posthumously! In Nigeria, we fail to establish a climate of enquiry which, even if they do not provoke immediate consequences, at the very least, by the vigour with which they are pursued and the manifested rejection of falsifications, ensures that such unresolved anomalies remain on 'HOLD', sinking finally into the armoury of public wrongs which will reinforce the channels to eventual change. The avoidance strategy of our intelligentsia, especially of the Left, which spends almost all of its combative energy berating the role of *denuciation* but upgrades the equally impotent and monotonous *discourse*; its negligible attention to a need to shore up the crumbling political will of the masses through self-identification on concrete, immediate issues would be merely pathetic, if one did not constantly recall cautionary precedents in the growth of Fascism in Europe, and the naked, undialectical terror which has erupted in other African nations, notably Uganda, Zaire, Malawi and Equatorial Guinea. As it is, such evasion becomes truly tragic. Any economic system can be imposed by fiat or habit once the political machinery is entrenched, without so much by-your-leave from ideological purists. Hindsight is not in question. The lessons of the Iberian peninsula – both Portugal and Spain – suffice to remind one that forty to fifty years is a long spell of political repression to pay as price for the incertitude of a 'correct' ideological victory.

When, some twelve years ago, I set out to recapture certain realities of experience in preventative detention, I most certainly made no claims that I was writing a political tract. I did not set out to write the history of Nigeria up to and including the Civil War, nor was I about to set down prescriptions for its political or economic salvation. That some background material would enter the narrative was inevitable – that is taken for granted. What I did not anticipate was that, in some 'enlightened' quarters, a sanctimonious reaction would be provoked for my failure to present an ideological blueprint for would-be revolutionaries or trace the course of Nigerian history for teacher and student historians. Such critics, of course, had no suggestions to offer for an apt language for a truthful representation of the obscenity that provokes certain experiences. Perhaps a little digression may help.

In the United States, the average viewer was appalled when, for the first time, the blood and marrow of soldiers in the Vietnam war was spattered on his screen, right in the snug Coca-Cola and popcorn cosiness of his living room. Suddenly, it was for real. The distanced reportage of a war with some alien, hardly human beings – 'gooks' was their name for the Vietnamese – was transformed into a grisly reality which exhibited, in colour, the innards of a son or husband as he was blown to pieces thousands of miles away. For the first time, the average American saw warfare as a human obscenity, and this specific war, more importantly, as an unjustifiable, indefensible species of that general obscenity that is human warfare.

A war photographer, David McCallum, introducing his

shocking images of the Vietnam war at a conference in Aspen, Colorado during that war, expressed his motivation as a driving need to capture, with his still camera, some measure of that same human self-destruction which so readily expresses itself in wars. In a different idiom, theatrical grotesqueries – verbal and imagic – were created around L. B. Johnson and Richard Nixon, the two presidents who inhabited the White House as Americans finally began to understand, and to reject the moral and ideological implications of the war, were also part of the totality of social mechanisms of expression whose cumulative effects led eventually to negotiations and the eventual end of the war. Of a more lasting value, however, is the change it wrought in the sensibilities of the average American, and the curbs (however temporary) it placed on obscene exercises of presidential power, such as the saturation bombing of North Vietnam in the name of peace.

When power is placed in the service of vicious reaction, a language must be called into being which does its best to appropriate such obscenity of power and fling its excesses back in its face. Criticism of such language is simply squeamish or christianly – language being expected to turn the other cheek, not stick out its tongue; offer a handshake of reconciliation, not stick up a finger in an obscene, defiant gesture. Such criticism must begin by assailing the seething compost of inhuman abuses from which such language took its being, then its conclusions would be worthy of notice. When it fails to do so, all we are left with is, yet again, the collaborative face of intellectualism with power – that is, the taking of power and its excesses as the natural condition, in relation to which even language must be accountable. But suppose we begin accounting all arbitrary power – that is, all forms of dictatorship – as innately and potentially obscene. Then, of course, language must communicate its illegitimacy in a forceful, uncompromising language of rejection, seeking always to make it ridiculous and contemptible, deflating its pretension at the core. Such language does not pretend to dismantle that structure of power, which can only be a collective endeavour in any case; it does, however, contribute to the psychological reconstitution of public attitudes to forms of oppression. Language needs to be a part of resistance therapy. When it plays such a role successfully in advance of the right circumstances for change, the political will escapes paralysis by the aura of sanctity which, the longer it lasts, power hypnotically exercises over all and sundry, but most especially the rationalizing, self-excusing intelligentsia.

The cold reality of power is, of course, that it has to be endured. Even when it is culpable and seen to be so, its effective reality is that it cannot be escaped for a duration, be this regulated by constitutional agreements,,or subject to abrupt termination by a contending interest. All that is left then to the populace over which it is made manifest, is an attitude towards it, outwardly expressed or internalized. It is this and this alone which constitutes the accessible arena of public-activity – for activity is acknowledged to be also of the mind as of public expression – media criticism, street demonstrations, civil disobedience, etc., etc. None of these various forms of overt activity occurs without prior preparation towards the destruction of the mystique, of the inviolability, and above all the impregnability of power. Let us make this concrete at the most seemingly ludicrous level.

I believe that from the moment that power is deemed culpable in any way, each family unit should, in place of, or after its regulation morning prayers, make a ritual of throwing their breakfast slop at a pinned-up photograph of the symbol of power before going out to earn a living under an insupportable system. Every morning, religiously. Or maybe also last thing at night, but certainly in the morning – as a self-reminder that the very act of going out to earn a living under the system, or studying under the system, is in itself an act of collaboration, a species of legitimization whose only excuse is an immediate lack of options. Their political being therefore succeeds in becoming a political mask, worn over a constantly hardening reality of their feelings, bound together in a secretive communal resistance. Some forms of this ritualistic therapy of power aversion certainly preceded the ecstatic acceptance of, or indeed participation in, the decapitation of 'divinely appointed' kings and despots whose carefully nurtured myths have, in the history of the world, regularly enslaved the minds of men and women with superstitious awe. If the execution of King Charles I of England, Louis XVI of France or the last Tsar of Russia barely months after the mere notion had been unthinkable were acclaimed by the populace in their times, the violent dethronement of modern-day despots on the African continent should be recognized as an inevitable development of its political sophistication and, all forms of preparatory exercises of the public mind towards 'willing' the 'hitherto unthinkable' seen as contributions towards the freeing of an enslaved public psyche. The language we use in addressing culpable power is, in itself, part of the needful preparatory activity towards this liberation of a popular political will; it is, shall we suggest, certainly more productive than splashing the image of power with breakfast slops each morning. One thing which even critics of this language in *The Man Died* cannot deny was the adoption of a number of phrasings, including the title, as referential points in the Nigerian public media, public lectures and even church sermons. Indeed, some of the twists in debates on current themes made simply to accommodate a borrowing from the text were often less than pertinent. Apart from the title itself, which has reappeared in more than a hundred guises, the other favourite, significantly, has been, accident of history', used in the book to describe the national repository or symbol of power. Obviously this language was not simply the language of one 'aggrieved' writer; it is the hidden language of an oppressed populace – the writer does no more than expose it, re-appropriating it for the commencement of the liberation therapy.

The wheel has come full circle and soon there will be need yet again for more than just this language of preparation. Clearly the events of 1983 have taken us beyond this stage. The incident described at the beginning of this introduction, the unheeded cries of the Academic Staff Union of the Universities of Nigeria, the National Association of Nigerian Students, Labour Unions, churches, mosques, obas and chiefs, market women, the threats of preventive detention laws and the many gestures in the direction of totalitarianism of the Right now render any personal testimonies superfluous. The madness of power, unchecked, is there for the world to see. And yet, the note is one of optimism. Why? Simply because the ethnic opportunism of 1965 and 1966 cannot be repeated. I believe that the stage of ethnic opportunism and therefore, of ethnic battlelines have been surpassed. There is a nationwide recognition of the deprived and their exploiters, of the oppressed and their oppressors, of the cynical and the derided.

The average Nigerian is aware of this. Even the sycophantic *Daily Times* was impelled to concede, after the elections, in a commentary carried on the front page with banner headlines:

Tremendous changes are already being noticed on the country's political map and, if events proceed at the current rate, they are bound to have salutary effects on the nation's body politic. One of the more easily remarkable changes is the gradual disappearance of the erstwhile ubiquitous myth of ethnicity.

But to quote the *Daily Times* would be really to advance the devil's own game. The *Daily Times*, alas, was only concerned to provide a cloak of political advance to the fraudulent, reactionary victory which had just been pronounced by the National Party of Nigeria, to cover a vicious, murderous 'victory' in the garb of political virtues. Words fail to convey the gall of this reversal of realities which steals not only the votes of the populace, but appropriates to itself a progressive reality which was popularly expressed as belonging to the opposition parties. Far more thought-provoking and significant is the statement by the Academic Staff Union of Nigerian universities which explicitly identifies the 'dismemberment forces' of the nation and therefore represents and implicitly conveys that reality of political development which poses a permanent threat to the dismembering powers. At a meeting in Jos, Plateau State, after the elections, the Union declared (*National Concord* 12 September, 1983 Report):

That the Federal government was deliberately and systematically creating an atmosphere in which it could unleash a state of violence and terror on a specific segment of the country's population; that the Federal government was violently repressing the views of dissent, and had, by so doing, created an atmosphere of restive and uneasy calm in a particular part of the country; that the Federal government – as well as some state governments were sponsoring acts of violence, while the Federal government itself was provoking some people who were already aggrieved over the outcome of what it called "the bungled Federal elections"; that the Federal government was deliberately dividing, isolating and deliberately repressing a section of the country, and was making an unsubstantiated allegation that that part of the country was planning to destabilise the rest of the country".

The ASUU also accused the Federal Government of setting up the police, soldiers, tanks, barricades and other instruments creating a siege of terror in a part of the country.

My purpose with this quote is to call attention to the self-identification of organizations like present-day ASUU with every part of the nation without discrimination. It is a departure from the standard, rhetorical beatitudes of the virtue of 'oneness'. To identify, in such unambiguous terms the enemies of that oneness is an act of courage, but it is one which is only possible if it happens to translate accurately the mood of the nation, against which a minority, but one with a reckless concentration of power, is ranged. That minority sector is merely perpetuating the legacy of Gowon's regime which sought to isolate the same region referred to in ASUU's statement, when that head of state would flippantly refer to it as 'The Wild, Wild West' at the slightest sign of agitation against injustices. The horrendous massacres of 1966 took place in other parts of the country, everywhere but in the 'Wild, Wild West', yet these only earned from the humourist the responses already detailed in Chapter 15 of this book. So who then are the true nationalists? Who are the committed patriots? It cannot be at one and the same time the 1983 ASUU and the Federal Government of Nigeria 1983, any more than it can be, at one and the same time, the Labour or student unions and the military regime of the 1960s. A choice of allegiances is constantly unavoidable, and that choice carries with it the unvarnished exposure of the opportunism of the divisive and diversionary tactics of our unabashed, even self-glorifying reactionaries.

And so, ten years after *The Man Died*, it is possible

to claim that there has been a positive, nationalist shift in the political group comprehension of the Nigerian people. This is not to dismiss the powerful influential voices which insist: it is still better for everyone to go his own way. Even some progressive voices have been lately heard in this vein; disillusioned, they see no way out of the blind alley into which the country has been pushed by the recent (1983) elections. They are reacting, ironically, to their traditional enemies, that unrepentant group of 'dismemberers' who, while noisily applauding the concept of Nigeria as One, nevertheless indicate to the rest, by their words and deeds, that Nigeria can remain a single entity only on the condition that power is retained permanently in the hands of those who belong to a particular section of the country. See, for example, the arrogant pronouncements of Federal Legislator Malam Muazu Babangida Aliyu, reported in *Nigerian Tribune* of 29 September, 1983. For all its potential for harm, however, this group is a minority, located almost exclusively in the ruling party of Nigeria, the Nigerian People's Party. Its current ascendancy is foredoomed, and from within. This alas, appears to represent the lonely consolation eagerly embraced by most Nigerians in their present shell-shocked condition. What many have failed to consider is how much of the country the NPN may pull down about our ears as their centre caves in and their party disintegrates.

Despite the apparent success of reaction, optimism remains. How does one explain such irrationality? After all, despite violent responses here and there, the NPN still remains in strutting, arrogant and vengeful power: poised to turn the rampant misgovernment of the past four years into child's play during its next mandate. The monetary outlay for this recent seizure of power, running into billions of naira, must be recouped. Loyal servants must be rewarded with positions, no matter their mediocrity in ideas or performance. These and others must come somehow from an already depleted treasury and a bankrupt economy – so where does this professed optimism in the future manifest itself?

Ironically, the answer is to be found in the violence, not just violence itself, but the nature of violence that was offered back to the oppressors. For 1983 was, depressingly, only a replay of 1965 when elections were similarly rigged. This time, however, the people *did not identify their enemy with any single geographical sector of the country*! The depressing feature of the responsive violence in 1965 was that, in many instances, the enemy was identified with one section or another with the consequences of a deep ethnic mistrust which carried over into, and coloured the botched military coup of January 1966.

Of course, when we speak of this shift, this positive advance in political consciousness which is very discriminating in its identification of national enemies, we have to continue to caution against the increasingly desperate activities of that handful of political leadership who are determined that the retrogressive status be maintained. Their tactics vary from crude tribal demagoguery to economic red herrings. They do not hesitate, for instance, to explain away the widespread poverty in the nation as selective deprivation which is limited to their section of the country only and thus a direct consequence of the monopoly of national resources by yet another section of the nation. In 1982, a brief respite was bought by an external shift in their sectionalizing through the inhuman expulsion of millions of aliens, the Ghanaians being the worst sufferers in the unprecedented exodus. The last of such scapegoats having departed, there had to be recourse to internal villainy for the consolidation of the geographical bases these politicians represent. That they have failed so far was decidedly proved when the people were robbed of their hopes for a change of government in the most cynical non-election in the brief history of national existence. Then the masses turned on the representatives of the party in power, whoever they were. Unlike the case of 1965, not one attack took place on 'alien quarters' within any community.

Violence in politics takes many forms. All dead-end approaches to political goals – that is, political acts which create a cul-de-sac for all participants in the political process, including even those who initiate the process, constitute a violence which in itself breeds counter-violence. The nature of the violence can be purifying or it can be obscene. The violence which preceded, accompanied and was the predictable aftermath of Nigeria's 1983 elections, was ironically, a gross obscenity. The first thing to note is that it was unleashed by the party which was already in power. The purpose was to cow the populace into retaining the status quo, terrorizing voters away from manifesting their political allegiances. One example: in Ondo State, one of the staunchest, if not indeed the most implacable base of opposition to the National Party of Nigeria, three leaders of the main opposition party, the UPN (United Party of Nigeria) were killed, gangland-execution style, in their own homes. The assassins went coolly from one house to the next on a given list and shot down their victims in front of their families. Seven were on the list; three were not at home when the killers called, and one escaped with gunshot wounds. This event took place months before the election. It was calculated either (i) to initiate a violent reaction which would give the incumbent president occasion to use his emergency powers, cancel the elections and impose his own administrator, or (ii) to serve as an unmistakeable warning to the opposition. If popular leaders could be shot down with such impunity, what chance have the faceless followers? Such, in identical or qualitatively similar details were the acts of violence unleashed on the people of Nigeria. The 'luckier' opposition party activists were simply arrested at whim, taken to remote police cells, where they were starved, tortured and forgotten.

Perhaps the Right-wing death squads of El Salvador may have a thing or two to teach our newly created para-military police units – if so, it cannot amount to much. These creatures were paraded on television and introduced by the Inspector-General of Police, Sunday Adewusi, as something worse than psychopathic killers, who would be unleashed on the people at the first sign of trouble. They did, in the event, live up to their promise; the 'dialectic of fists and pistols' of the Spanish Phalangists had been modernised into a dialectic of horsehide whips, tear-gas and sub-machine guns'. Did not the incumbent president himself, Alhaji Shehu Shagari announce to the nation that these creations of his head had been ordered to 'shoot at sight'? They did better. They shot out of sight, pumping live ammunition into densely populated quarters, blowing away unseen lives with a strange mixture of disdain and relish. Nothing that Eisenstein could have composed matched the horror of the pictures in places like Odo-ona (Ibadan, Oyo State), Oke-Igbo (Ondo State) as innocents were brought out dead from the broken sanctuary of their own homes.

Let this fact remain to warn of what is yet to come: the atrocities committed by Sunday Adewusi's para-military agents, often side by side with the thugs of the ruling party who were sometimes attired in police uniforms – a fact belatedly admitted by Oyo State Commissioner of Police, Alhaji Omolowo, beggars anything perpetrated by the army during its thirteen-year rule, always excepting, of course, the period of the Civil War itself and the specific genocidal acts already dealt with in *The Man Died*. More armour is seen patrolling the townships and villages today than at any time during even the Civil War. The level of contempt for civilian life has finally reached its nadir, and torture has been institutionalized to such an extent that even provincial police stations now have their own torture cells. It is for this reason that I have eliminated from this edition some now superfluous details and comments on the atrocities committed by the army against innocent Nigerians; that dismal record has been more than beggared by this civilian government, and there is worse to come.

I believe, however, that the will of our people cannot be broken. The current phase of despondency is understandable; one does not see the tentative foundations of one's nation smashed repeatedly by juggernauts out of control without an acute sense of futility. Yet the alternative, to abandon one's goals is such a negation of existence that one can only view it as worse than physical annihilation. Our people have just undergone a savaging, contemptuously inflicted upon them for no other reason than their resolve to change a government by peaceful means. It is therefore only appropriate that I adopt as epilogue, a warning which, since the elections, served as a banner on successive issues of one of the Nigerian dailies: THOSE WHO MAKE PEACEFUL CHANGE IMPOSSIBLE MAKE VIOLENT CHANGE INEVITABLE.

WOLE SOYINKA,
October 1983

Contents

The Unacknowledged

Between the lines of Paul Radin's *Primitive Religion* and my own *Idanre* are scribbled fragments of plays, poems, a novel and portions of the prison notes which make up this book. Six other volumes have been similarly defaced with my writing. For fear of providing a clue which would lead to a reconstruction of the circumstances and the certain persecution of probably innocent officers, I cannot even provide the titles of these books much less indicate at which periods of my imprisonment they were smuggled in to me one by one. After the indescribably exquisite pleasure of reading, I proceeded to cover the spaces between the lines with my own writing.

The books came from among several which were addressed to me in prison from several sources. At the beginning such contributions were brusquely returned (see letter overleaf); afterwards they were simply left to gather dust and cobwebs in Lagos and Kaduna prison offices. Books and all forms of writing have always been objects of terror to those who seek to suppress truth. Yet in spite of the most rigorous security measures ever taken against any prisoner in the history of Nigerian prisons, measures taken both to contain and destroy my mind in prison, contact was made. But no matter how cunning a prisoner, no matter how ingenious – and the definition of a prisoner's nature is animal cunning – the humanitarian act of courage by the exception among his gaolers plays a key role in his survival. I cannot yet repay this debt by public acknowledgement. Even in the two years at which I have been at liberty I have not dared contact such individuals knowing that the largest security force on the continent is still very closely interested in my personal relationships. To all such, patience. In the continuation of the efforts to defeat and destroy all such evil, this debt will finally be settled.

WOLE SOYINKA

Tel. 24871/20

P.H.Q. No. 17034/53/80.
HEADQUARTERS OFFICE,
PRISONS DEPARTMENT,
PRIVATE MAIL BAG 12522,
LAGOS, NIGERIA.
28th February, 1968.

Sir,

Concerning Wole Soyinka:
Civil Detainee.

I am directed to refer to your letter of 24th January, 1968, and to inform you with regret that correspondence with the above-named detainee is not allowed.

I am therefore returning herewith your letter and the Penguin Book "Four Greek Poets".

Yours faithfully,

Akinola Ajoni

(E. A. AJONI)
for DIRECTOR OF PRISONS.

/JJA.

1

A Letter to Compatriots ...

... prompted by two items on my table at this moment. One is the latest copy of the journal *Transition* which has recently been resurrected in Accra: the other a cablegram from home. The message on the latter is a simple one: The Man Died.

It is the former, however, a letter from a victim of the current Greek fascism which has created the greater intrusive shock. It is always a shock to encounter duplicated experiences in another being especially such experiences as reproduce near identical sensations, thoughts, reactions and even expressions in the other man. For intimately felt experiences it is even a little frightening. One *knows* of course. Indeed it is the certitude of an indestructible continuum of ordeal-survival-affirmation, constantly reinforced by the knowledge of predecessors in this cycle which sustains a prisoner in his darkest moments and which, his liberty regained, urges on him a pledge and a duty to all victims of power sadism in and outside of his own country.

The author of this letter is a professor in Greece, George Mangakis, at present a captive of fascist dictators.* I quote some passages from his letter to reinforce certain very simple truths of a prisoner's precarious existence in isolation. It seems to me that testimonies such as this should become a kind of chain-letter hung permanently on the leaden conscience of the world. To defeat, to uproot in entirety any concepts of and pretension to a mitigating base for inflicting atrocities on the human mind, it is essential that the extent

*George Mangakis is now at liberty.

of this unnatural strain be fully grasped. After that, there can be no pleas, no arguments. Each individual will make only a simple act of choice – do I say *yes* to this or *no*?

The Greek prisoner writes:

> Among so many other things, the anguish of being in prison is also a deep need to communicate with one's fellow human beings. It is a need that suffocates one, at times.
> Self-defence. That is why I write. That is how I manage to keep my mind under control. If I let it loose, unsupported by the frame of written thought, it goes wild. It takes strange sinister by-ways, and ends up by begetting monsters.
> ... we need somebody else's mind in order to keep on working terms with our own. We also need moments devoid of thought.

I testify to the strange, sinister by-ways of the mind in solitary confinement, to the strange monsters it begets. It is certain that all captors and gaolers know it; that they create such conditions specially for those whose minds they fear. Then, confidently, they await the rupture. It is necessary to keep in mind always that we know only of those who have survived the inhuman passage.

This book has taken many forms and shapes. The question of what to include, what suspend, what totally erase, all influenced by problems of expediency, of my continuing capacity to affect events in my country, of effecting the revolutionary changes to which I have become more than ever dedicated, consideration even of my own safety, a reluctance to break the last restraints on a régime whose knowledge of guilt compels it to remain by force in descredited power ... all these have changed the format, title, conception of this book at least a dozen times. Only last week, I had split it into two parts, one to be kept in suspension, a kind of Sword of Damocles waiting for the precisely just moment of political retribution. And this morning, the title was still *A Slow Lynching*.

Sometime this morning however the other item arrived, a cable bearing the very simple words: *The Man Died.*

I was struck first by the phrasing. It sounded weird, yet familiar. Its familiarity was that of the ending to a moral tale, a doggerel – 'the dog it was that died', a catechumenical pronouncement, the eyes of a surgeon above the mask, or the surprise of a torturer that misjudged his strength. I heard the sound in many different voices from the past and from the future. It seemed to me that this really is the social condition of tyranny – the man died, a dog died, the matter is dead.

The man dies in all who keep silent in the face of tyranny.

The dog of this immediate death was a journalist, Segun Sowemimo. He was brutally beaten, he and other colleagues, by soldiers on the orders of a Military Governor of the West. The reason? An imagined slight. But at least he was fortunate – to start with. He had the help of his trade union and as his condition worsened, the Governor was compelled – all at the expense of the State, yours and mine, not at a punitive cost to the Governor and his men – to fly him to England for treatment. But gangrene had set in and the affected leg had to be amputated.

I followed his case with interest. I looked for Mr Sowemimo in London but found that he had been flown back to Nigeria. I sent word to a colleague to trace him and send me news of him. His reply is contained in the cable beside me at this moment: The Man Died.

This evening I recognized in it the only title for this book. I recognized also that I moved long ago beyond compromise, that this book is *now*, and that only such things should be left out which might imperil those on whom the true revolution within the country depends. My judgement alone must serve in such matters, and my experience which, it strikes me more and more, is unique among the fifty million people of my country.

I must quote George Mangakis once more, and in so doing, confess that it not only gives contemporary expression to our own present fate but that it also performs for me a therapy. It rescues words from a debasement to which they were constantly subjected by my gaolers, a debasement which, as the relevant section of the book will show, constituted one of the gravest challenges to my egoist survival after the escape fantasy spun by would-be assassins. When I secretly began to write in gaol I observed for instance how my mind turned and twisted to find substitutes for one harrowing word, adopting even the extreme dodge of changing whole passages, entire sequences of action to avoid the concept of such an emotion as 'humiliation'. This word 'humiliation', the reality of the emotion, the actuality of it at this moment is restored and acknowledged at last in its rightful context, as the only dignified feeling for all who are not prenatally injected with hormones of subservience and servility. George Mangakis writes:

When a dictatorship is *imposed* on your country, the very first thing you feel, the very first day – and it is a feeling that has a totally spontaneous immediacy, free from all mental elaboration – the first feeling is humiliation. You are being deprived of the right to consider yourself worthy of responsibility for your own life and destiny. This feeling of humiliation grows day by day, as a result of the oppressor's unceasing effort to force your mind to accept all the vulgarity which makes up the abortive mental world of dictators. You feel as if your reason and your human status were being deeply insulted every day. *And then comes the attempt to impose on you by fear, acceptance of various barbarous actions of theirs that you hear about, or that you actually see them commit against your fellow human beings.* You begin to live with the daily humiliation of fear, and you begin to loathe yourself. And then, deeply wounded in your conscience as a citizen, *you begin to feel a solidarity with the people to whom you belong.*

I experience this solidarity only with such of my people as share in this humiliation of tyranny. I exclude and ignore all others. Whatever the factors that made a dictatorship inevitable in the first place, those factors no longer exist. The present dictatorship is a degrading imposition. It is additionally humiliating because, in my knowledge and yours, this dictatorship has exceeded a thousandfold in brutish arrogance, in repressiveness, in material corruption and in systematic reversal of all original revolutionary purposes, the worst excesses of the pre-1966 government of civilians. This is a shameful admission but it is the truth. I address this book to the people to whom I belong, not to the new élite, not to that broad stratum of privileged slaves who prop up the marble palaces of today's tyrants. I testify from my personal experience and in so doing accuse them of the crime of war profiteering. I do not mean in material terms – that fact is too well known, too easily absorbed into the shock system of a materialist society. There is, however, another form of profiteering, a greater humiliation which appears too tenuous to challenge the will of a war-weary people, and this is power profiteering from the common disaster and mutual sacrifice of war. And the greatest insult to a people's intelligence is if, as the supreme irony, such power profiteers are not free of a measure of culpability in the fundamental causes of the war itself. My testimony is that only the degree remains arguable; the fact of guilt is obvious and self-acknowledged by today's power profiteers. Their present excesses and mutual condonement of crime have made necessary the uncompromising contents of this book, for the first step towards the dethronement of terror is the deflation of its hypocritical self-righteousness.

It is only the first step. In any people that submit willingly to the 'daily humiliation of fear', the man dies.

14 December 1971

Ibadan-Lagos

2

My arrest and my framing were two entirely different affairs. The one was prompted by the following activities: my denunciation of the war in the Nigerian papers; my visit to the East; my attempt to recruit the country's intellectuals within and outside the country for a pressure group which would work for a total ban on the supply of arms to all parts of Nigeria; creating a third force which would utilize the ensuing military stalemate to repudiate and end both the secession of Biafra, and the genocide-consolidated dictatorship of the Army which made both secession and war inevitable.

I was framed for my activities in gaol. I was framed and nearly successfully liquidated because of my activities inside prison. From Kiri-kiri I wrote and smuggled out a letter setting out the latest proof of the genocidal policies of the government of Gowon. It was betrayed to the guilty men; they sought to compound their treason by a murderous conspiracy.

I stated at the beginning that my arrest and my framing were two different affairs; this is not fundamentally true. It is true only in so far as at the time of my arrest, and until that letter was betrayed into the hands of those whom it accused, there was little thought in the mind of my captors beyond keeping me out of circulation. On the essential level however, the two acts of violence, the arrest and the frame-up stem from the same source of corruption. More importantly, the letter from prison was for me validation of the political stand which led to my arrest. I recognize today that it was this challenging fact of direct, immediate and continuing confirmation of the rot of power at the source which imposed on me the further duty of communicating the latest proof of the moral basis of our stand to my colleagues at liberty. It enjoined on us a continued commitment to all feasible acts which would demonstrate an ethical absolute even in the midst of the war. (For by now, with the invasion of the Mid-West we were faced with the realitv that this had become another civil war which would be fought to the end.)

It is appropriate therefore that the text of the letter should serve as preface to this book, for its subject matter made the secession, the war, and bred the current norm of brutalized instincts in a people who now flock in their hundreds of thousands, women and children, beggars and élitist vacuity to picnic at the public executions of proven, semi-proven and unproven felons. The deeper subject-matter of the letter – justice – resumes a debate that has been covered only thinly by the crust of blood. That crust is worn daily thinner by the continued tread of oppressive boots. It sums up the colossal moral failure within the nation, a failure that led to secession and war. Its truth is simply that then as now, the nation was humiliated by a treason promoted, sustained and accentuated by forces that lacked purpose or ideology beyond self-perpetuation through organized terror, the failure to:

acquire an extraordinary historic acuity of vision and see with total clarity that humiliated nations are inevitably led either to a lethal decadence, a moral and spiritual withering, or to a passion for revenge which results in bloodshed and upheaval.

I have quoted Mangakis for the last time. The following is the text of the leter that still lies hidden in the secret cabinets of today's national saviours:

In Durance Vile (Sept. 1967)

When some years ago, the bodies of three Civil Rights workers, one of them a black man, were recovered in the Deep South of savage America, we, like millions of black people all over the world, experienced a disgusted conviction that only the fact the other two were white (and rich) induced the massive effort to discover their fate and compelled the futile attempt to bring their murderers to justice.

The wheel has come full circle for us. Let me remind you of the affair of the Ibo photographer Emmanuel Ogbona who was abducted from his studio at Odo Ona, Ibadan, sometime last year, murdered and thrown into the bushes some miles away. Two soldiers of the 3rd Battalion, Ambrose Okpe and Gani Biban, were later charged with his murder and brought before the court in Ibadan. Try to recollect the mysterious delays in the trial of these men, the barely disguised obstructions and manoeuvrings which would have done credit to any Klan-impregnated court south of Alabama. We marvelled briefly when finally the public prosecutor announced that 'acting on instructions' he had no choice but to withdraw the case. The army authorities, he reported, had decided to deal with this matter themselves. This was the moment when we should have spoken and acted; as usual we decided on that common salve of timid consciences – 'to wait and see'. With that event not only the Courts of Justice of the Western Region, but the very pretence of law and justice in the entire federation were subverted to the doctrine of justifiable genocide!

And now hear the sequel. For nearly six weeks I have lived in close company with two products of what Hannah Arendt (*Eichmann in Jerusalem*) described by that strange expression – the banality of evil. I found myself (Fate, do you call it?) lodged here – of all the cell-blocks in Nigerian Prisons – immediate neighbour to those accused soldiers, compelled to listen, observe, and have confirmed beyond all questioning my insistent arguments about what happens to human beings and to a nation when any group within that nation is tacitly declared to be outside the law's protection and is fair game for any man with the slightest grudge of fanatical inclination that turns to homicide. This is not the place to be more explicit, especially about the proud, boastful confession of guilt that comes from one of these two men. Suffice it to say that three days ago, these two – well, we must continue to call them suspects – were triumphantly released from their token confinement.

There will be time later to deal with this and much else that we have seen take place in this nation during the past year whenever (if ever) quiet reigns again. Some things, however, need not, should not wait one moment longer. It is necessary even as this unholy war is prosecuted that one spot exist which boldly declares itself opposed to a pernicious doctrine which, by the very nature of the present struggle, may turn into a downright genocidal epidemic. Moreover, unless we are singularly shortsighted and confess no further interest in the kind of society that must be raised on the ashes of this one, it is obvious that certain foundations must be laid right now whose ideals will at least rescue our struggle from the common exercise of butchery and bestiality, and from their origin and cause of human damnation. A beginning must be made somewhere, so let it be made by us in the West. You must of course expect the deliberate misinterpretations of those murderers by consent within the Western Region, and their blood-stained allies in other regions. Sooner or later they will be shamed into following such an obvious example. I suggest:

First and foremost, that the judiciary of the West be declared independent. I do not know what this implies in our relationship with the Federal Courts nor do I particularly care. I only demand that one way or the other, the Western Judiciary place itself in such a position that no power within or without the region can ever again interfere with its judicial processes and render it, as it is today, accomplice by default in the doctrine of justifiable genocide.

Two: That some form of law be passed in the region which makes it a crime for any man or group to molest or in any way interfere with another for reasons of tribe, or practise any form of discrimination based on tribe. (Add religion etc. etc. if you wish to make it comprehensive.)

Let me repeat: What has happened in the case of Emmanuel Ogbona is only one example of the thousand blatant horrors of genocide, acceded to by the Judiciary of the West,* backed by other forces and authorities who must be named, denounced and forced to stand trial some day, whose philosophy poisons the hope of this country's future and condemns a large section of its people to casual and premeditated murder and mutilation in the name of unity. Be honest and ask yourselves, of what use is a Code of Conduct when the army is infested with self-confessed murderers who – because their victim was Ibo – are treated even in their brief confinement as Very Important Prisoners, let out for regular airings in the guise of 'investigations', and treated with deference and priviledge even by the most senior staff of the Prisons? The 'Code of Conduct' against the thousands, tens of thousands of boastful presences of the kind? And within a largely illiterate soldiery? I call that Hypocrisy!

For a contrast, I have selected a news item from the *New Nigerian* of 30 January 1967:

No. 330 NEW NIGERIAN Monday 30 January 1967 Page Five

MAN TO HANG, EIGHT OTHERS JAILED FOR KILLING A BOY

One man was sentenced to death and eight others, among them a Native Authority policeman, received various terms of imprisonment ranging from 10 to 3 years at the Sokoto High Court for murdering a boy and unlawful assembly in Sokoto last year during the disturbances. The men were Mailayi (death sentence), Liba Mamman, and Usman Sokoto, 10 years each, Alkali Tangaza, Duniya Mamman Wurno, Altine and Zagi had five years each and Balarable Dogon Daje (3 years).

Usman was a sergeant in the Sokoto N.A. police.

*I have since my release discovered that the Western Judiciary protested in very strong terms to Gowon over his decision to spring the accused from justice. I consider this event comparable (except that it is a hundred times worse) to the directive of Richard Nixon releasing Calley, the mass-murderer of My Lai, from custody pending his appeal.

According to the prosecution, between September 29 and October 1 last year, Mailayi and some others raided a house at Gayu Quarters in Sokoto where a government prison warder, Mr Joseph Uche, an Igala, lived.

Mailayi and his gang, the prosecution said, thought Uche was an Ibo. When they did not find him but his younger brother Ojibo Uche who was asleep, Mailayi struck him on the head and a warder, Maikawa, cut the boy's throat with a knife.

Sergeant Usman, the court held, did not take part but was believed to be present at the scene.

The Judge, Mr Justice Holden, told the convicted men that they could appeal if they so desired. The High Court has adjourned indefinitely.

The juxtaposition of these two sample events, even without the reminder of its large-scale horror context, the most comprehensive, undiscriminating savaging of a people within memory on the black continent, destroys the hypocritical disclaimers of the régime. It states one simple truth: that at the very least the *machinery of justice* existed all through and after the Northern massacres and that the lack or the prevention of their exercise was a deliberate, selective decision of Yakubu Gowon's government. Either this decision represented the will of the people of Nigeria or else the government of Yakubu Gowon is guilty of conspiring to defeat the will of the people. I deny the former. This leaves me no choice but to accuse Yakubu Gowon and his government of treason, of falsification of the Nigerian popular will.

But perhaps it is a dead subject. Better still, perhaps it never happened. Perhaps some fifty thousand Nigerians were not butchered and brutalized, and a population shift of a million and a half people did not take place. Perhaps if the butchery did take place it was not *planned*, and perhaps the machinery to halt it did not exist. And yet again, perhaps the civil war that resulted did not owe part of its origin to the deliberate subversion of the machinery of equity and justice by the historical throw-ups that had taken power. Perhaps this event of genocide had nothing to do at all with the Ibo secession.

Finally, perhaps it *cannot*, it is *unthinkable* that it will, ever happen again.

I prefer however to follow my own observation of human impulses, not blind myself to the actualities of history, crushing in its catalogue of brutish repetitiveness. The words of David Astor on the anniversary of the Warsaw Ghetto uprising are very simply to the point:

> Mass exterminations are themselves related to lesser killings ... if you understand the processes which produce a lynching you are more likely to be able to fathom the processes which underlie the greater perversions of moral sense ... this wider study is more likely to prepare us and our children to defeat future symptoms of this disease in whatever forms they appear ...
>
> We must learn more of the fatal, fearful process of thought which makes people feel not only justified, but that they have a duty to destroy others. We cannot tell what may excite this process of mass psychology. Its next form may not be racial or religious but political (as has happened before in times of revolution or civil war ...)

Indonesia ... Asaba. My Lai. Pakistan ... ASABA!*

But this book is not about genocide, it is very much about a lesser lynching. In relative importance – except inasmuch as it is the admission of guilt by the lynch-gang – all that need be said on the subject is virtually contained in this section. The rest is mostly private conversation with a handful of individuals – that self-generating community of victims who have been or who are yet to find themselves in a battle not merely for a held idea but more critically for an integrated

*And now Burundi.

survival. It is not a textbook for survival but the private record of one survival. And perhaps at the least it will refresh the world conscience on the continuing existence of the thousands of souls held under perverted power whose survival necessitates the self-infusion of inhuman acts.

3

MY return from Enugu* was followed by a serious manhunt organized by the Army Intelligence and the Gestapo from Lagos. I ensured that I fell into the hands of neither, submitting finally to arrest at the hands of a uniformed policeman outside the gates of the University of Ife. After the arrest I developed one major concern – to delay my transfer to Lagos long enough to organize a number of elementary precautions. A tussle for my body began, engineered with a swiftness which baffled and angered Lagos. The military governor of the West was brought into it, a precious twenty-four hour delay was gained, but finally after much telephone negotiations, dodges and guarantees, it was agreed that I be escorted by a very high police official into Lagos for an interview with Gowon. The agreement was worked out between the Governor of the West and Gowon. We would drive straight to Dodan Barracks, Gowon would ask me one or two questions on my activities and I would be returned to Ibadan the same day.

I had been in the 'E' Branch before, always in the perennial pursuit of my passport towards which the Security police had developed a possessive attachment since my early innocuous brushes with governments from about 1962. Periodically we even developed a peaceable *ménage à trois*. By giving sufficient notice of my intention to travel I was, in return for a statement of intent and a search at the airport going and coming, right down to my balls, permitted the use of this much pawed, submissive teaser which I continued to insist was my inalienable right. The *modus vivendi* did not

*See Section 23

always hold. Something about the barely disguised smugness of power in the knowing faces of the 'E' branch has a way of breeding aggressiveness even in the most phlegmatic resolve. The psychological trickbags were all too evident even in the supposedly neutral waiting-rooms where I waited to see the officer in charge of my case. Often they had no names. It was S7 or E5, yet this numerical entity appeared humanly dressed, all set to charm, to play ignorant, all set to flash out some ridiculous scrap of information which he expects you to deny. Yet always wholly ignorant about why, about just what purpose the harassment served since any political subversive knows better than to carry incriminating documents on him at the airport, knows better than to have his entry and exit in a tabooed – that is, communist – country stamped on his passport, knows only too well that the most respectable overseas address which he can offer to the 'E' Branch is any address in good old United Kingdom. But those were merely useful preparations: the crippling mind-scattering impotence that came from those encounters, the knowledge that one individual could hold the power to limit you in your movements, all in his own right, without the need to justify his action to you or to the society of which you are both a part, that such a power exists to stultify your private life by circumscribing your movements and jeopardizing your livelihood.

The silent barrier of 'E' Branch closed behind me. I was led into an office to wait. There were movements. I sensed a galvanization of that department right from our entry. Then I heard voices. The Commissioner from Ibadan appeared to be receiving a tongue-lashing from a creature whom I was later to know even better. The Commissioner was reiterating the terms of his mission and the Lagos man was telling him that he took no orders from anyone in Ibadan, however highly placed. The voice was violent, filled with its own sense of power. Then the voices were cut off as a door was slammed.

Seconds later a big slob of a gorilla looked into the office where I sat, eyed me all over as one would an insect destined for pinning and formaldehyde, overwrought still with the power excitement of his triumph and fulfilment over the Ibadan man. I had no doubt at all that this was the hectoring voice. He didn't say a word. Perhaps the venom of his encounter with Ibadan still oozed and an object was needed for the overflow, perhaps he thought to frizzle me in the dying embers of his indignation, or perhaps he really intended – at such speed did he wrench the door open barely checking his headlong charge by hanging to the doorknob – perhaps he did intend to soften me up with those well-known disorientating tactics of sudden whirlwind violence: all these possibilities were there in his abrupt entry. The apparition, frightening in its suddenness – and he was indeed like an escaped, harassed gorilla – this apparition materialized, hung by the doorway and stared. My involuntary start brought under control, I had no chance but to stare right back at him, first inquiringly – no need to antagonize these wild apes – then, since I encountered only venom, with an abrupt change to some expression which I hoped registered acceptance of whatever challenge he was there to pose. With equal abruptness he vanished, swinging by his hairy forearms, I supposed, into the ceiling fan. Certainly some force whirled him into oblivion before my eyes and it was difficult to imagine that his speed was unaided.

Later I learnt his name – Yisa Adejo, an Assistant Commissioner.

Next, the Ibadan Commissioner came in, apologetic. We were not going to Dodan Barracks, the matter seemed to have been taken out of his hands . . . he went on and on, barely coherent from emotional exhaustion. I assured him I had guessed all that from the voices. Just then a young man came in. Cocky, self-assured, I put him down at first glance as one of those untried replacements for the Ibo exodus from professional positions. Out to prove himself, no question of that. His manner towards the Commissioner, his superior by several ranks was deliberately arrogant. I demanded from this new creature why I was at the Security Branch instead of Dodan Barracks. He raised his eyebrow as if he had never heard the term. I repeated my formalistic protest and it made him snap back:

'And what have you got to say to the Head of State? Do you think you can demand to see the Head of State like that?'

'I have an appointment. He is expecting me now.'

'I don't know anything about that. I have been asked to ask you some questions. Anyone can simply walk here and say that he has an appointment with the Head of State.'

I turned to the Commissioner. Jerked from a daze which still hung over him he mumbled a confirmation of my claim. The young official merely repeated –

'I've said I don't know a thing about that. Anybody can claim appointments with the Head of State.'

Angry now with the man's off-handedness I said, 'You are not suggesting your superior officer is lying I hope. He's just told you that I do have an appointment.'

D. looked up inquiringly, feigning – it was obvious – ignorance. Only then did the Commissioner introduce himself, telling the whole story in a garbled manner that left me tired of the scene. Gracelessly, the young cock muttered some kind of apology ... it was not unusual for them in 'E' Branch not to know regional commissioners by face, he had been away from the country for some time – all this with a casual condescension. I looked wearily at this Deputy Commissioner ... oh go away man, go away to your wife and family... He left finally, guiltily, apologizing to me till the last moment for the change of programme:

'Take it cool please, just do what you can to co-operate, I am sure you will find you are in safe hands.' I felt sorry for him.

The young man seemed to have taken the advice for himself. He 'took it cool'. He even apologized for the recent scene, explained how sometimes official orders did overlap. Security had already requested Ibadan police to pick me up and bring me in for questioning so the business of Dodan Barracks was a development they could not be expected to know anything about. Introducing himself – 'by the way I am D.' – he promised to get in touch with Gowon's *aide-de-camp* to find out what was going on. I watched his little comedy of telephoning. Naturally the *aide-de-camp* is not available, but of course a message is left for him to call D. back first thing. 'Lucky thing,' he remarks, 'I know him personally, in fact I expect him here any time this afternoon.'

The apologies are by no means over. D. apologizes that he has not yet read my books though he has heard so much about me. 'A hateful job this, hardly time for leisure and for doing things for the sheer pleasure of it.' Altogether a good half-hour before getting down to business. Cigarettes? I choose to smoke one of my local 'murada'. D. lights his own cigarette and offers me a light. Then casually, 'While we are waiting for that call to come through from the *aide-de-camp* suppose we talk over one or two things?'

'When did you last see Ojukwu?'

'About eight days ago.'

The question had come into the smoothest 'abrupt' technique. The silence, then stammering, that followed my reply could only have come from his astonishment. Clearly he had expected a denial. Or at least some hedging. He gave himself time to reconsider his approach by permitting, at the first opportunity, the interrogation to digress along somewhat inconsequential channels. Then back to the theme.

'Why did you go to see him?'

'It's obvious isn't it? You must have read my article in the papers.'

'Oh yes.' And opening a drawer in the desk he brings out a folder. It is full of clippings. 'Yes, I read them. And the replies too. What did you think of the replies to your article?' The tone was one of relish. It had a note of admire-us-wasn't-it-neat? which made sense some moments later.

'They seem to have come from a very frantic propaganda machine,' I replied. 'Most of the names attached to those letters are false. Seventy-five per cent of the letters were written by the same group of hacks.'

'What makes you so sure of that?'

'I was struck by the sameness of style, I even recognized the style.'

'Oh, yes of course, you are a literary man.'

'Yes. Literary style is rather like what fingerprint is to you. Or a burglar's method of operation. In fact the same collective hand was obvious in the letters written against Tai Solarin* also. Shall I tell you who wrote them?'

'Who?'

I mentioned the group by name. He smiled, putting the file away.

'Well, I can't say anything about that. It does not matter anyway...'

*One of the handful of outspoken columnists in the Nigerian newspapers and Principal of the unique secondary school, *Mayflower*, Ikenne. A 'regular customer' of the police.

But it did. Mallam D. had too little of self-possession – at that stage – to withstand even the minor shocks of a seeming breach in Security. It was printed all over his face – how did I know? What else did I know of this group's activities for the military régime? I felt I ought to keep him off-balance for a little longer – it was only a temporary tiny advantage in the skirmishing, but it was a moment for prodding at real or imagined weaknesses, guilty conscience or ambition in the adversary. How 'in' for instance was Mallam D., how high up in the overall intentions of the men who ordered my arrest and worse?

'Tell me,' I asked, 'Why was Lagos so anxious to liquidate me?'

'What do you mean?'

'Soldiers were sent to Ibadan to kidnap and do away with me. They were ordered to hunt me down at all costs.'

'What makes you think the Army wishes to kill you?'

I lied. 'I met a friend of one of the officers sent from Lagos. He warned me.'

D. said, heatedly: 'He was talking nonsense. What happened was that we asked the Army to arrest you, that's all.'

'Did you have to send a special squad from Lagos?'

'I have no idea whether or not a special squad was sent from Lagos. We asked for your arrest, maybe that's what you heard about. Why should anybody want to kill you?' He washed off the idea as preposterous with a sudden vigorous gesture. 'Anyway, you are safe here with us.'

'I hope so,' I said, and watched him feel for the reins of his role, resolve not to permit any further dangerous disruption of his set course.

But I managed to prolong this state of reversed roles a while longer: 'The plot was beautifully coordinated. It began with those "spontaneous" replies to my article. Two of the letters, using exactly the same phrases, accused me of calling the Army in the West an army of occupation. I know your department has a thick scrapbook of everything I have ever written or am alleged to have said. Tell me if I have ever made such a statement?'

'People write all sorts of things. I mean, you must admit you made many people angry with your article.'

'The inclusion of that lie was deliberate. It served to whip up the hatred of Northern soldiers and officers. And the nerve they had to bring up my condemnation of genocide in the North! I would have thought they would be glad to forget it – except of course that the immediate purpose was more important.'

D. unexpectedly made an admission: 'There was no plot. You should have seen some of the other things which were scheduled to appear. Some of them were even more revolting. Terrible. I went to the *Morning Post* myself and told them it was too much. It was already set but we had it removed.'

This was a development unknown to me, the Gestapo's control even on 'Letters to the Editor'. I wondered if he felt that his admission did suggest an admission also of those lies. D.'s eyes occasionally turned shifty, looked at you under covert eyelids, embarrassed by thoughts other than those of immediate things. I could not decide anything until suddenly, as if in an effort to convince himself of the justness of any tactics, he exploded:

'But what gives people like you and Tai Solarin the right to think that you know everything? What makes you think from your ivory towers that you have solutions to the problems of the country? When the government has already laid down a policy, what makes you think you know better? You are intellectuals living in a dream world, yet you think you know better than men who have weighed out so many factors and come to a decision.'

'No, it is you in this sixth-floor citadel who have no knowledge of reality. The two examples you accuse, Tai and I and a number of others are closer to the hard realities than any régime or its functionaries living half their days in fear of subversion and *coups*.'

'But you are also against other intellectuals. Others who approve the stand of the government.'

'Such as who?'

He hesitated. 'Well, the Committee of Ten. They are intellectuals same as you.'

'Are they?'

'Well why not?'

'They are not intellectuals. And they lack any sort of conviction. Or commitment. Except of course playing games in the corridors of power. Why do you take such objects seriously?'

'What have they done wrong?'

'Debased what little intellect they ever had to start with, that's all. Ever since the old Akintola days. You forget what their role was during that period?'

'That time is past. Everyone is now joining together to place their talent at the disposal of the country. One of them is a member of the Cabinet.'

'Yes, you picked the slimiest of the bunch didn't you?'

'Femi Okunnu? What do you have against him?'

'Are you serious?'

But he missed the contempt in my voice completely. 'Of course. We want to know what you think, not only of official policies but of the people who formulate or execute those policies.'

'This is part of the interrogation?'

His protest was energetic. 'No, no, it is wrong of you to

think of all this as interrogation. We want to be able to understand people like you. I want us to have a real discussion. It will help me. Why do you write the things you do? Why do you take your stands? What do you think of the way the country is going? And so on. I'll want to know what you think of the national figures – the Chief Justice for instance. Awolowo. Enahoro. Tarka. Even Gowon.'

'I have never met Gowon.'

'All right. Perhaps you will soon. In fact I am quite sure he will want to meet you. Depending also, I am sure, on how our own discussions come out.'

Slipped in very casually, but not so casually that the point should be missed, not so strongly that it meant bargaining.

'Anyway you haven't really told me what you have against the Committee of Ten.'

I shook my head. 'Let us say simply that I disapprove of power prostitutes.'

'I see. So who are the intellectuals you approve of? People like Tai Solarin I suppose?'

'Tai does not claim to be an intellectual. He is a dedicated and selfless social reformer whose thinking is original but sometimes confused. The country could do with a lot more confused but original thinkers like Tai.'

'But not with the Okunnus? You think Tai Solarin should be a Commissioner instead of Okunnu.'

Again I sighed. 'Tell me, do you know anything of Femi Okunnu? Do you know anything of the Okunnu-types of the young opportunist bourgeoise?'

'No, tell me about them.'

I shook my head. 'You'll find out in time.'

'No, I want to know from you. We are asking you for your views.'

'No,' I repeated. 'I'd rather not talk of him. Let me just

say that when you choose that type to be part of a team for formulating national policies it's no wonder you expect and demand yesmanship from the intelligentsia.'

Abruptly D. asked, 'What do you know of the Third Force?'

Obviously there would be no more digression that afternoon.

4

I AM seated in a spare office – on the floor above the interrogation office. Mallam D. my interrogator fusses nervously about: what I would like you to do for me Mr Soyinka is simply set down all the things you have told me, everything about your activities to stop the war, how it all began, how much you have done, the people you have talked to or still plan to contact ... you know, all the details and any other thing you may have overlooked. I am sure your case will be cleared up in no time at all, just help me by putting it all down and then maybe we can take up one or two points in it ...

Can I have a typewriter? My handwriting is so bad ...

It was the first thought at that point; nothing in my handwriting. And no signatures on anything. Even without formulating clear possibilities of danger, the risks could be reduced by making it all machine clinical. A hurried flit to and fro offices and Mallam D. soon returned – no he could not find a spare typewriter. Doesn't matter I said, thinking, like hell it doesn't. So much bulk handwriting would yield plenty of practice material for an expert forger. I am not even thinking remotely of forgery for public consumption but of that cheap police trick – show a piece of 'confession' to some other unfortunate sod and break his morale that way ... 'here, read it yourself, he has implicated you in his statement. Why don't you tell your own side of it?'

Caution. Even breath is drawn cautiously, deliberately. From now on all is calculation. A quick glance round the room for hidden microphones, hidden spy-holes. Microphones! But you are by yourself man! So? A 'sympathetic' cell-mate might be added later. Well, time to look for microphones when that happens. In the meantime stick to composing your statement. Organize your thoughts, select what you want to say and set it down. No deletions after writing, that would only arouse suspicions. What did you delete? Why? The first session with Mallam D. is recognized for what it was – the preliminary skirmish. There is no such thing as an 'enlightened' interrogator. Methods differ that is all. Any system which allows for the machinery of secrecy against an individual is the method of the Gestapo. The Gestapo mind believes more in holding than releasing, in guilt than in justice. This building is Gestapo Headquarters, there is no other term, no other point of view for survival ... I begin to write.

The reminder was timely. Three men had just entered the room. At first I thought they had missed their way because they had with them heavy manacles and chains the like of which I had seen only in museums of the slave-trade. They looked sheepish and embarrassed and I half-expected them to turn round and disappear with an apology for intruding. But they had halted and were looking at me. One of them coughed and stammered out the news. They have been instructed to chain my legs together.

'Are you sure? I was put here to write my statement.'

There was no mistake. Yet it was not fifteen minutes since Mallam D. left me. Nothing of course had been said about chains. I held out my legs, the manacles were fastened, my legs went down of their new acquired weight.

Settling down again was not very easy. The feel of chains was a novelty of sensation to which I could not immediately adjust. I looked down on the odd objects with truly detached curiosity, raised the legs again to feel their weight, tried walking in them and performed a hundred other experiments. Walking was possible, or more strictly shuffling. Again a wave of unreality, I think I laughed aloud at this point. I bent down, picked up the loose chain and held it up. One foot six at the most.

I sensed a vivid contradiction in all this, a contradiction in my being, in my human self-awareness and self-definition. In fact one might say that never until this moment did that self-definition become so clear as when I viewed these chains on my ankles. The definition was a negative one; I defined myself as a being for whom chains are *not*; as, finally, a human being. In so far as one may say that the human essence does at times possess a tangible quality, I may say that I tasted and felt this essence within the contradiction of that moment. I was nothing new; vicariously, by ideology or from racial memory, this contradiction may be felt, is felt, with vivid sufficiency to make passionate revolutionaries of the most cosseted life. Abstract, intellectual fetters are rejected just as passionately. But in the experience of the physical thing the individual does not stand alone, most especially a black man. I had felt it, it seemed to me, hundreds of years before, as I believe I did experience the triggering of a surely re-incarnated moment when at school I first encountered engravings of slave marches in history books. Even when I met my first lunatics under the care of traditional healers, chained at the ankles to curb their violence, the degree of non-acceptance of such therapy bordered, I often think, on racial memory. Surely it cannot be a strictly personal experience.

That moment when the key was turned in the locks often comes back to me – I, seated on a straight-backed chair, the two men stooped down at my feet fastening the locks, the third man watching the dangerous animal in case he attacked – and it occurred to me, not then, no, only now, with the scene of the chaining passing before my eyes, that we were all black, that Mallam D., another black man, had given the order and fled, that I was not a 'convict' in a chain-gang in

South Alabama or Johannesburg but that this human antithesis had its enactment in the modern office of a modern skyscraper in cosmopolitan Lagos in the year 1967.

Well, just in case it *was* real, just in case other realities such as going to the toilet, stretching out my legs in the middle of sleep or jerking them involuntarily at night from a mosquito bite, just in case all these other hazards of existence would be manifested, would accentuate the feel of the pendants at my feet, I commenced without any internal debate a hunger strike. It was one obvious antidote to a mood which half-mocking, half-earnest raged: Ogun, comrade, bear witness how your metal is travestied! Well, the early chirurgeons bled the choleric; I have learnt to starve my violence into calm.

It worked. The very act of taking the decision not to eat brought the futile spasm of rage and the trembling under control almost at once. My mind was working again, dispassionately. Immediate aim. Far-reaching aim. Contingency. What effect must be produced in the Gestapo mind. I began work on the statement, a new motif being now dominant—the anticipation of a trial and the classic reversal of roles. Visions of Castro's *Historia me Absolvera*! The statement was a dense affirmation of my role in organizing lobbies to stop the supply of arms to both belligerents. I wrote in a vein calculated to prod them into bringing me to trial on the premise that my activities were anti-government, completed the essay in two or three hours, transferred to an armchair, took another look at the chains and tried to drop off to sleep.

A knock. The cook contracted out to the Gestapo for the feeding of the hundred inmates undergoing interrogation was on his rounds. Thank you, no. The guard outside the door thought that I would prefer a 'European' diet, the supposed ultimate accolade of VIPism to a prisoner or detainee. No? Not even a tin of sardines? Bread? Milk? I said, it's dangerous to feed chained animals, you know. I might get power and snap these trinkets.

Evening. 'E' Branch was overcrowded. Every office, the library, even some landings were used as interrogation rooms. All through the day Ibos and suspected sympathizers were brought in by the hundreds. Denunciation was easy and old scores were settled by a whisper to the police. Some, mostly non-Ibos, came in already defeated by terror, prostrating, pleading for a chance to make a defence. All evening I heard voices of new arrivals, men and women. The words were monotonous, the protests and counter-accusations: 'I never said so. Na lie. I no say dat kin' ting.' It was enough to accuse a man for expressing Ibo sympathy or damning the Army. Or telling the truth of a torture or murder which he had witnessed. It was sufficient to look disapproving on methods of terror.

Night. A weird, brief encounter. I had dozed off. Suddenly the door was flung open and a woman catapulted in. 'Stay there and shut up.' The officer gave orders for some others to be shut away in different offices. From her accent I knew she was Ibo. I had never witnessed such terror in a woman. It was some time before she was even aware that there was another being in the room. The shock – she was at first convinced that it was an officer, perhaps her appointed torturer – the shock took her to the opposite corner of the room from where she stared with huge panicked eyes and a quivering throat which barely stopped short of a shriek. Then her eyes came downwards and she saw the chains. I saw her body go lax, sympathetic. She came forward, her hand patting the table as if to engage some reassurance of concrete things. I watched her silently. She needed no further comforting from me; the sight of my chains had done more than words could have done for her, calmed her down. But then I saw yet a new change in her face. She stood suddenly still, unbelieving. Recognition. I saw it even before she spoke. Are you not . . . are you not Wole Soyinka? I nodded. From my face, to my legs, back to my face. A pause to take it in. Then she broke down in tears.

The guard – he must have gone off briefly to help with the new influx – looked in a minute and gasped. What is she doing here? He screamed down the corridor for the officer on duty. No one is supposed to go in the room with that suspect! When they all rushed in she had stopped crying. The duty officer was all regretful; he had not known there was anyone in there. They led the woman away, calmer, stronger. She turned round at the door, looked at me in a way to ensure that I saw it, that I knew she was no longer cowed, that nothing ever again would terrorize her. I acknowledged the gesture. I wondered if she knew what strength I drew from the encounter.

D. returned late the following morning. 'Why are you on hunger strike?'

'I am not on hunger strike.'

'No?' He looked puzzled. 'I was told you did not eat last night and you haven't eaten this morning.'

'Oh that! I've been misinterpreted. It's not a hunger strike at all.'

His immediate concern was touching. 'What's the matter? Are you ill?'

'No, I'm very well. Just a simple precautionary measure that's all.'

Outraged now: 'You are afraid of being poisoned.'

'If only you'd let me explain. It's these chains – oh not that I mind them – they are quite comfortable sitting down.

Unfortunately going to the lavatory is one walk a man can't avoid taking. I avoid that you see, or minimize it by not eating.'

'You can't do completely without eating.'

I pointed to the glass of water on the table. 'Just one of that a day. Quite sufficient. By tomorrow I should need to piss only once a day. After that maybe I won't need to go at all. The statement is on the table.'

He took my notes and went out. 'I'll see what can be done.'

Nothing that day. The chains stayed on the second night running. The third morning D. came in to ask some questions – so he said. He came in smiling. 'I hope you've begun eating now.'

'No. The situation has not changed.'

He looked down, saw or pretended to see the chains for the first time. Angry or anger-feigning he summoned the guard and demanded why they had not been removed. The guard explained that he had had no instructions.

'Go and fetch the keys and remove them at once!'

The guard disappeared.

'Sorry about this, Wole' – yes, it became Wole from this morning – 'I gave instructions about them last night. As soon as they have been removed and you've had something to eat I would like us to have another chat. I shall send someone for you.' The chains were removed but I had already passed that crucial stage which I like to refer to as the Battle of the Belly Bugs. Once that pinching feeling is past, fasting turns to floating. The exercise kept me evenly disposed, phlegmatic – I resolved to continue on a lower key, drinking a watered-down tin of milk a day. The guard sent someone to fetch it.

I never had the milk. An hour later D. stormed in, angry.

'How is it that the foreign papers are already carrying news of your arrest?'

I stared blankly. What was that to me?

'How could they have known and why all this publicity? They are already insinuating that you are being ill-treated. I hope you realize that all this publicity is not helping your case one bit. They simply make your position more awkward.'

'What case and what position precisely? If I am innocent of whatever you suspect me of, just what difference should foreign or local publicity make? Or are you now admitting that you presume me guilty already?'

'We are not presuming you anything . . .'

'Listen, I am not unknown. Even faceless burglars have the event of their arrest publicized. Are you claiming special privileges for the Nigerian Gestapo?'

'Nobody is claiming anything.'

Either he did not hear or had decided to ignore the Gestapo label. Control . . . control. . . . He too seemed to be offering himself the same advice.

'Look Wole, we know you are a world-famous figure, but these foreign papers are naturally mischievous. Any opportunity to slander the authorities . . .'

Young, intense, uncertain and a victim of the dilemmas of his position, he continued to talk himself out of his unreasonableness. He had after all charged into the room in a tone of accusation and condemnation. And breathing a kind of blackmail.

'I don't really know what you expect me to do,' I complained. 'I can't go out and talk to them. Of course you could always arrange a press conference and produce me . . .'

An hour later he gave orders that I was to be transferred to Kiri-kiri Prison.

5

CURIOSITY. Puzzlement. Recognition. The eyes of prisoners feed on the newcomer. I had spent time before in police cells, in makeshift custodies, never before within the full complex called prison. Adjustment was unconscious, my body rhythm was already slowed down. I slowed it down some more.

'I am anxious to send money to my family. Can the prison arrange for me to obtain a cheque?'

'No, you are a detainee. We must not do a thing without police approval. They are very strict about that.'

'Books?'

'You can have the books you brought in with you. There is also some kind of library in the Superintendent's office.'

Nothing is smoother than transition to prison routine. Its miniscule totality in duplicating outside life makes acceptance easier – for the first week or two. Like going into a retreat or a monastery. Again for a week or two. And there is human variety. I did not welcome the company. I badly needed to be alone with my thoughts. With only one exception they recognized this need and respected it.

A small block, ten to twelve cells, a population of just over thirty. It was known as the 'Back Cell', in reality the punishment block, but since the fashion of imprisonment without trial and the swelling of prison population, punishment cells all over the country have become the blocks for special detainees. Our population included a group of former Action Group 'stalwarts' who had trained in Ghana. With that political naiveté common to the moronic plagues who infest the corpse of meaningful power on the continent, the new régime in Ghana sent their photographs and personal data to the Nigerian Security after the fall of Nkrumah. They were rounded up in Nigeria and had now spent over a year in detention. One had gone peculiar in the head, spoke all the time to himself and uttered terrible oaths against unseen enemies. One day he ran berserk . . .

There was a convict too, a former NNDP official convicted of embezzlement in his grace-and-favour public office. A special class prisoner. A stool-pigeon too. I discovered that even before the others thought it necessary to warn me.

There was Tiger Pedro, self-confessed sex offender who insisted on narrating his life-story. I have a sensitive organ he would say, it's not my fault, that is how God created me. I know my weakness . . .

Apart from the NNDP embezzler there were two more special class inmates. Detainees both. Soldiers. One was a sergeant, one a mere corporal. Their standing in that block aroused immediate curiosity because they were given a special status, treated as Very Important Prisoners and with deference from officials. The other detainees and prisoners eyed them darkly yet enviously and with some fawning as the soldiers opened uncensored letters, returned from 'investigations' which lasted the whole day, reeking with drink and picking their teeth, as they returned with their pockets bursting with cigarettes, colanuts and a hundred other contraband items, as they bullied the prison officials and complained about the unsatisfactory implementation of a hundred other privileges . . .

From a warder I inquired if this was normal treatment for Army detainees. His answer was No. There were other army detainees both at Kiri-Kiri and at the Maximum Security. Excepting the officers, none of them enjoyed such privileges. But these two were the ones who had been whisked from a murder trial in Ibadan on orders from the Military on High.

Three days later and the Gestapo was again ready for me.

6

MALLAM D. now became hungry for names. Names, names, that luscious commodity of names made him suddenly, predictably ravenous. Yes, yes, the notes you have made for us are very interesting but you are not very forthcoming about names, are you, Mr Soyinka?'

I gently corrected this, pointing to the half dozen names mentioned in my notes.

'Ah, but they are all outside the country.'

'Not all. You did say that Aminu* has now arrived in the country.'

'Yes. But that is the other point. All the names you give us are names of people who have actually done nothing. At least according to you. They are people you recruited or tried to recruit into this movement of yours but according to you nothing really has been achieved. Are you suggesting that you have no resident Nigerians in this committee of yours?'

'Given time there would have been. But you arrested me before I got busy. The war broke out when I was abroad.'

'Nevertheless you did speak with people here.'

'Of course. I hold discussions with all sorts of people.'

'You haven't mentioned their names in your statement.'

'I don't find that necessary. I am referring to casual discussions.'

*Aminu Abdullahi, a Northerner, was one of the Nigerians whom I had tried to recruit in London for the anti-war movement. He was sent to Nigeria by an organization to try and obtain my release. He offered to go to Ojukwu during our London discussions, but we decided that this was too risky, he being a Northerner and the war having already begun. I went instead.

'All right. Let's have some of their names.'

'I don't see how I can give you such names. I argue with anybody on any topic. I express myself freely to anyone – in fact I have been told that is one of my troubles.'

'You are not expressing yourself freely to us.'

'Much too freely I'm beginning to think. Since it results in your insisting that I incriminate innocent people.'

'I did not ask you to do that.'

'It comes to the same thing doesn't it? I give you one name and you think you have to arrest them: what did you discuss with W.S. on such a day? Why?'

'Mr Soyinka '– we were back to Mister – 'I'm afraid you are not being very cooperative.'

'I am being more than cooperative.'

'You are not. I will give you another example. You say here that you formed a committee to campaign internationally against the importation of arms to Nigeria – you realize by the way that that is a very disloyal thing to do?'

'I don't accept that.'

'You don't think it helps the rebels? How is war to be fought without weapons?'

'The rebels would use the same argument with justice to prove my antagonism to their cause.'

'We are not particularly concerned with the views of the rebels.'

'I am. I have declared already that this war is morally unjustified.'

'Are you a pacifist?'

'Certainly not.'

'You would accept some other wars.'

'Depends. And always as a last resort.'

'What kind of wars would you support for instance?'

'Any war in defence of liberty.'

'And what of the Rivers people who have been forcibly

brought into the so-called Biafra? You think we have no obligation to give them their liberty.'

'I do not support Biafran secession, so I am clearly for the statehood of the minority groups.'

'How then do you want the secession brought to an end?'

'Not by this particular war.'

'How? Do you have any ideas at all beyond merely saying you don't support this and you don't support that?'

'If I did not have concrete and practical proposals I would not ask to see Gowon. Nor would I have gone over to talk to Ojukwu.'

'Well let's have them. Just what are these proposals?'

'I'll tell Gowon when I see him.'

'I'm afraid there is no guarantee of that. If you talk about them now I can relay your message and I have no doubt he will want to see you.'

'I've told you, I represent an independent group. My message was for Gowon and Ojukwu. I have no commission to speak to the Police on the subject.'

'All right Mr Soyinka, let's go back to your campaign to deprive the legitimate government of its means to end a secession which you say you disapprove of. Do you really claim the right to take it on yourself to embark on international diplomacy on this scale?'

'My experience has been an international one.'

'I see. This man you mention, the one who first put the idea in your head – that's a funny name.'

'It's Brazilian.'

'And you say he's a Nigerian.'

'Born and raised in Lagos.'

'I put it to you he does not exist.'

'He exists.'

'So this man hears you are in New York, gives you a ring, this totally unknown man . . .'

'I had met him before.'

'Ah yes, so you state here. A businessman. I thought you were an artist. Do you have much business with businessmen, especially sinister ones like this?'

'Sinister? I would have thought you'd be grateful to him and to me. He could have acted for the Biafrans but he didn't.'

'If his story is true.'

'I accepted his word. Why should he bother to contact me if it wasn't?'

'Perhaps he knows you are for the rebels.'

'Am I for the rebels?'

'That remains to be seen. This man comes to you, tells you a cock-and-bull story of Biafrans asking his help with armaments. In spite of the opportunity to make a good profit he refuses. You are suggesting to me that an American businessman would let an opportunity for profit slip by?'

'He's not an American.'

'American-trained then. He has business in the States, not so?'

'I know many loud-mouthed Nigerian patriots who would sell arms to Biafrans if they had a chance.'

'Perhaps your friend is one of them. He's a Nigerian too isn't he?'

'A month ago he was American.'

'Or a Brazilian; who knows? Tell me Mr Soyinka, did he contact you or did the initiative come from you?'

'I have already told you. My picture appeared in the *New York Times* as the result of a press interview. I was there in connection with a film. He traced my hotel and telephoned me.'

'Why?'

'I've told you. To see an old friend to discuss this encounter with Biafran agents.'

'He wanted your opinion?'

'Yes and I gave it. And he took it. We were both agreed on this one point, that for all we cared this particular civil war could be fought with bows and arrows. I phoned up some friends at the U.N. and they joined in the discussion. We set up a pressure group to lobby against all supply of arms to either side. The facts are there in my statement.'

'Ah yes, these two names not so? You see what I mean don't you Mr Soyinka? You are not cooperating. Every time we come to the question of names you offer us only the names of people we cannot reach. They are either non-Nigerians or they don't reside in the country.'

'But why do you want to reach them?'

'Why? Don't you want people who can corroborate your case?'

'I have a case? But you have accused me of nothing. If it is a crime to organize against the war I have admitted it. What is there to corroborate?'

'You can't seriously mean that you have no Nigerian accomplices.'

'Accomplices, Mallam D.?'

'You know what I mean – your fellow ... your supporters.'

'I'm afraid I have none here.'

'You are making things difficult for yourself. You're not cooperating at all.'

Enter on cue an old adversary, my prosecutor in the 65 radio hold-up trial, Ugowe.

Ugowe had a naturally tearful voice. His kindness sprang from a genuine Christian conviction although of course he could be ruthless and hard as his profession demanded. I had observed him off and on his police-being, and it seemed to me that he never completely lost a near-pious humaneness. One of the kind perhaps who has never played unfair with any accused. (D. in a moment of helpless confusion was to admit literally that he sometimes did.) Ugowe leant against the door listening for some moments to another few minutes of perfunctory interrogation. Clearly his entry was timed and he merely awaited the right cue to contribute his mission. At the beginning he was easy enough, speaking from an innate fellow-feeling, quite tearfully sentimental. He made a long plea for 'cooperation', reminding me of my family and children. Finally he moved on to the real purpose of his visit, skating thinly on the surface of 'reward' possibilities such as a ministry in the Government cabinet.*

It was a long lachrymose sermon, pious, well meaning, full of references to the recent treacherous activities of the Biafrans in coming into his own Mid-West region and causing destruction. He left me with those lofty thoughts, on which note Mallam D. also felt I ought to rest a while and had me escorted to my cell.

To ensure that I did not forget the set theme of meditation, three familiar figures entered the room. Chains.

'What is this again? I thought the question of chains was settled.'

'We have instructions to chain you, sir.'

'Mallam D. agreed no more chains.'

*This offer later took a more direct, overt shape in a bizarre night-visit by a high-ranking officer who claimed that he came directly from the top and was empowered to make the bargaining. On my side I would sign a statement that had I been sent to Enugu by a certain politician – who was in the civilian cabinet. This session – with the violence on me which resulted from his animal frustration – can only be recounted in full or not at all. The former is for the moment politically impossible. The idea was that this politician's resignation would then be forced, the cabinet would be reshuffled and a portfolio of Culture created for me.

'I'm afraid those are our instructions.'

'Whose instructions?'

'The officer on duty. He says those were Mallam D.'s instructions. In the evenings we are to keep you chained.'

'When the chains were removed they were left off the whole day.'

'Those are our instructions.'

The locks snapped about the ankles. Before D. arrived the following morning they had been taken off. I asked him what was behind it all. He looked surprised.

'Did they try to chain you?'

'Yes, in the evening.'

'Oh, but er . . . I thought you understood. The chains have to be left on in the evening. What time did they put them on?'

'Half-past five.'

'That's silly. I'll see they do it later. Half-past five is still daylight.'

'Just tell me, why do you find it necessary to keep me chained?'

'We received information that you might try to escape.'

'Escape? From the fifth floor of this fortress? Through where? And where did you come by such information?'

'Well, that was our information.'

'In that case I resume my fast.'

'As you wish. I don't advise it. It won't help you at all.'

Escape! Even at that stage they had begun to lay the groundwork.

The grilling lasted another two days, mounting into intensity. Names! Names! NAMES !!! The prepared catalogue of names passed in rapid succession. When did you last see X? What did you talk about? You said before, you saw him last in London. No I did not. D. checks the statement or pretends to, says a curt Sorry, admits even once or twice that he is beginning to get confused. Only a half truth. The other half of the time he indulges in the pastime of catching the suspect out. Deliberate falsifications, even insistence on his own version, then capitulation.

The confusionist tactics in which he was trained showed in every ploy, a mechanical technique which could nevertheless prove effective where the victim is himself playing by such rules of evasions and camouflage. I was not involved in camouflage but in the opposite. Again and again D. fell into his own traps, he had laid so many false trails that he no longer knew which was the path I claimed to have trodden. I watched his growing confusion and cautioned myself against a peril whose existence I was aware of only in theory. Sympathy.

To eliminate this danger, the mutual growth of sympathy between prosecutor and victim, I closely examined my relationship with D. I felt towards him, I acknowledged, a tenuous solidarity of our generation. He was young, lacked self-confidence and tried to make up for it by bursts of establishment and authoritarian passion. Incapable of any deep analysis he stuck to a solid kind of double-winched in-dogma; the dogma of power within the Secret Police and the dogma of power within the government. I never could make up my mind which in-ness was the stronger, the *cosa nostra* dogmatism of the Secret Service, or that lingering power aura, identified with the fact of successive North-led governments, which clung unfortunately still to many young Northerners of his age. (Aminu was perhaps the only Northerner of my generation I knew who was totally free of the reflection of this in-thing of divine power.)

I wondered if D.'s political confusion fitted him potentially for careful subversive nursing at some later stage, recalling how once he had suddenly held his head in his hands and said:

'Sometimes Wole, we have to do things which ... which we know are wrong. Really bad. But this is the set-up. You know, I began with Administration. I was sent to England to study Administration. Then somehow I got transferred to the Police. Maybe when the war is over I'll go back. There are things I have seen here which make me ... disbelieve in such a thing as justice.'

The fight against the tyranny of the early sixties was greatly assisted by policemen and officers who had uttered sentiments such as this. Or felt them. Some, whose positions made them crucial to the struggle had no more than a twinge of uneasiness. The task of conversion (or subversion from the Establishment's point of view) was then painstakingly embarked upon until yet another ally was acquired, another hole knocked in the rotted hulk of that régime. Sometimes such recruitment was finally achieved through their own self-interest; the prospect that the struggle might succeed created the need to play safe by occasionally obliging an anti-government group. But a core of altruistic hounds of justice remained then and today within the ranks not only of police, army, and civil service; and they form a firm independent sub-stratum of guts within the prurient flesh of successive governments. When they are not busy saving the lives of individuals by passing on details of coldly efficient plots for extermination, they compile dossiers of crimes, bestialities and material corruption by a swaggering, self-confident hierarchy. The majority of them even contribute independently, anonymously, prompted solely by disgust at what they have known, and a belief that their profession deserves better than to be an arm of the Nigerian Mafia. They snatch individuals known to them only by name from the brink of petty harassments, fiendish conspiracies at supposedly rarefied levels, and even calculated murder. Where they fail they record, waiting for the day when all such dossiers can be publicly displayed.

Giving all my attention to the many characteristics of D., his half-baked ideas, unresolved idealisms, expanding the glimpses which he had afforded me into his inner soul, recognizing even the enormous obstacle of his personal ambition, I began to muse on the possible sweet revenge of subverting this establishment man once the war was over and the conflict for the internal revolution was resumed. It was a rich idea and the imagined process of re-education and conversion occupied a night or two as I sat immobilized by my chains. Later events soon assured me he was a non-starter. Mallam D. will go on for ever, bulwark of the Cosa Nostra's *cosa nostra.*

7

IN the morning an officer brought in a new suspect, a male replica of that woman who had been thrust into my room during my first tenure of the office. He was ill, dispirited, he chain-smoked and his fingers shook. He dropped ashes all over himself. He eyed me cautiously from time to time but said nothing. Outside, the corridors trembled in the flurry of movements.

The sight of another suffering being creates an instant demand on one's own strength, deadens for the moment at least the anxiety of one's private situation. I resolved to speak to him and to take away his helpless fear.

'Why have they arrested you?'

He was a doctor from the University of Lagos Teaching Hospital, a Mid-Westerner. It was not three weeks since he returned from Moscow, a qualified doctor. First he had enormous troubles from the fact that he had studied in Moscow. Then, among other things, the Teaching Hospital instead of treating him like an intern, even placed him under the authority of the Hospital Matron. He did not stand for it. Relations between him and the matron worsened. He had a hyphenated name, which I cannot remember, but because it had an Ibo sound the Matron reminded him in his rebellious clashes with her that his position was very precarious. Finally they had a big public altercation; according to him she had countermanded his instructions on a patient. The following night the police came for him. Charges: reported for saying that he would not treat any soldier since they were all murderers.

Doctor X. swore that the Matron had denounced him; the police of course refused to reveal on whose word he had been arrested or bring him face to face with his accusers. He was flung into Ikoyi gaol where he became ill and cowed. After several days he was permitted a visit from his head of department. Either through him or through someone else he sent instructions to his family to insert an advertisement in the papers changing his name to a less Ibo-sounding one.

'Yes, I was advised that it was the only thing to do. It should come out in the papers today or tomorrow.'

I could not disguise my disgust. 'You changed your name because of these swine? You are a doctor, an intelligent man.'

His eyes swivelled straight to the door. 'Excuse me,' he said 'I would rather not continue this conversation. You seem to be assuming that I am against the government.'

'I don't care what you are,' I said, 'I am against any government which permits, under the guise of an emergency, the persecution of innocent men.'

'Well that's you. I haven't said anything and I don't really want to continue this talk.'

Then I understood his problem and laughed. 'Oh I see, you think I have been planted here to hear what you would say? I am not a police informer.'

He said nothing, continuing to smoke nervously.

'Perhaps you've run across my name during these last few days.' I introduced myself.

His reaction was predictable. 'Oh . . . I am sorry. I am not a political man at all. I am not interested in politics. But I do know your name.'

'Well don't be nervous of me. And don't mind anything I say. I've said worse things to my persecutors. They wouldn't believe me if I said or behaved differently.'

There was another nervous silence then he broke out. 'I've been very ill. At first they just wouldn't take me out for treatment. I couldn't eat the food and I think I must have picked up some virus, I was vomiting and running high temperatures. They brought me in for questioning today. It was a new man. He saw how ill I was so he's made arrangements for me to go to hospital.'

'Don't change your name.' I said.

'Oh but we've always wanted to change it in our family. You see, we're not really Ibos. We belong to the — family but you see our family moved and settled with the clan of —' I listened to the entire history of the clan, their migration, land disputes, intermarriages. My ears ached.

'Don't change your name,' I repeated. 'Wait for a more favourable moment. You see, these people despise intellectuals. If you change your name you are flattering their bestial egos . . .'

An inspector entered the room.

'Please get ready. You are to be taken back to prison.' Then he turned to my companion. 'The car is here. We take you to hospital after we have dropped Mr Soyinka at Kiri-kiri.'

It sounded too good to be true, but it was not quite good enough. If I also could go to the hospital I would have an opportunity to communicate with the outside world. I might even be able to telephone my family.

I said, 'But I am booked for the hospital too.'

'No. Only this doctor here. We are to take you to Kiri-kiri.'

'There must be some mistake. Better ask Mallam D. I am also to be taken to hospital and then to Kiri-kiri.'

'Mallam D. hasn't been in this morning,' said Akpan.

'He did say yesterday I would see the doctor today. You are taking this man to the teaching hospital not so?'

'Yes.'

'Well if you went to the hospital first I can also see a doctor.'

The inspector shrugged. 'Let's go.' I prayed that Mallam D. would not pick that moment to come in.

We were about to enter the car when I saw The Gorilla dismount from his own car and move towards the entrance. I plunged into the car and sank in the corner of the seat as the inspector and his colleague sprang to attention. As we drove off after that potential check I asked,

'Who was the Big Shot?'

The junior officer answered: 'Who? You mean King Kong?'

'Is that what you call him?'

'Oh yes.'

'He must be very high up. Who is he?'

'Assistant Commissioner Yisa Adejo.' Then he added, 'I hope he is not in charge of your case.'

'No. Why?'

'We call him Commissioner of Torture. Or King Kong. In fact he has more titles than Gowon himself. Anyway they wouldn't put a man like that in charge of your case. He's illiterate.'

'Shut up!' snapped the Inspector. 'You and your loose talk. You'll get into trouble one of these days.'

'Oh come on Oga, you know say na true word I dey talk. He and that Ceulman, they come from the same mother.'

At the hospital I saw my own doctor, Koku Adadevoh. The Inspector stuck with us. I complained to Koku that I had seen symptoms of an old complaint. I knew the routine – he would take samples and require me to report to him again. This was all that mattered – to establish a link outside.

As I expected he ordered me to report at his clinic three days later. This time the Prison Authorities arranged the visit. And ten minutes after our own arrival the Security Branch descended on the clinic with perfect timing.

In the corridor when I looked up were Mallam D., another officer and the inspector. I glanced outside and there in the parking lot was a station wagon loaded with Security officers. I experienced real distress when the officials began to insist that Koku go with them. I already saw him keeping company with the terrified doctor from Moscow. It was an intolerable burden of guilt upon my shoulders.

They talked first to Koku in his office while I waited helplessly outside. Then the pair came out. They went into the lavatory next door to the clinic and searched it, looked through the windows around the building, returned to bully the prison officer for not actually staying in Koku's office with me. He answered them defiantly that he knew his job and it was no business of theirs how he performed it. (It was strange, this and other coincidences. The officer was the brother of a female member of my acting company, a non-Ibo Mid-Westerner.) I argued with Mallam D. about the unfairness of harassing the Doctor. I begged them to leave him alone. A waste of time. He was permitted to come in his car with a driver. The motorcade took off for 'E' Branch.

From that guilt feeling my mood changed to one of anger. It was no good regretting the fact that I had somehow brought Koku into it. Everything now focused itself on this intolerable harassment of an innocent man. And before we left the hospital Dr Adadevoh had been accompanied to his surgery and all my case notes, samples and slides seized. The laboratory report was not yet in but they took him to the laboratory, demanded and received the report, took them all along to 'E' Branch.

The moment that the lift doors opened and we stepped onto the fourth floor, we encountered a pacing violent reception committee in the form of The Gorilla. Straightaway he began barking orders at the top of his voice. The man was filled and brimming over with the sense and exercise of power. The plain clothes men rushed in a hundred directions to carry out orders which none of them could interpret judging from the number of times he cursed and shouted. The mildest expletive was 'Don't be damn stupid. Not in there!' They fell over one another to open doors only to shut them again. Mallam D. and his colleague fell in with the obsequious frenzy, charging in a hundred directions and expecting us to keep this heedless, mindless, disorientated pace with them. If I had not seen the frothing face of Yisa Adejo and the cowed expression on the faces of his men I would have believed that it was a set exercise for deliberately driving mad an incoming suspect. It was a bedlam ruled or misruled by a demented hulk of flesh. At some point the prison officer and I were shoved into an office only to have the door flung open a moment later and poor Okotie literally frogmarched out in a different direction. Hardly two seconds passed before my door was flung open and an officer came and said, 'You are to come with me.'

I rose as leisurely as I could and followed him at my own pace. It was next door, the library. Hardly had the door slammed shut than it opened again and an officer was catapulted into the room to stay with me. He found himself a chair facing the window and muttered darkly to himself. Before the door shut properly I heard the inimitable voice of King Kong, employing the same hysterical register which he had used on the Commissioner from Ibadan:

'You took bribe. I know you took bribe. If I have a gun here I will have shoot you dead. Yes I will shoot you dead without consequence.' I was sure that the victim of this barrage was the Inspector who had taken me on that first visit with the hospital.

The officer with me muttered 'Poor —.' He rose and went to the door and continued to listen.

Nearly fifteen minutes later the door opened and behold, The Beast himself! He repeated that long stare with which he had sought to consume me at our first encounter. This time I looked briefly back, then turned my back on him.

The building shook with his slamming of the door.

Hardly five minutes passed then Mallam D. entered the room – 'Come please.' I sighed and followed him. We went down the lift, out at the door, then, to my astonishment, continued through the gate to the world outside. He waited for the traffic to ease and then we walked across to the building opposite the police gates, the private hospital run by Dr — the physician who earned notoriety by turning state witness against Tarka, Enahoro, Awolowo, etc., in the 1963 Treason Trial. What on earth was the game now?

The good doctor was expecting us. He came out with his hand outstretched, apologized that he had to keep us waiting for a moment or two while he finished with the patient with him. I had never met him before and was astonished to hear him address me so familiarly. I looked at the face of the man, the face of an unctuous toad. My repulsion was immediate. While we waited outside I could not help reflecting how stubbornly all my encounters continued to be linked. Just before the war broke out I had found myself on the same plane as his brother, a very old acquaintance and a businessman. On the journey he had invited me to stay at his flat in Dolphin Square. During the Balewa régime certain very strange coincidences had made us suspect that he worked for the government either as a foreign spy or simply for the internal Security. Once I was even convinced that his presence in a certain country at a time when I was subjected to constant police surveillance had been no coincidence. I challenged him in the plane about his real occupation. He assured me that he was no spy but a businessman. I accepted his invitation and stayed a few days at his flat mostly out of curiosity. All his callers were businessmen trying to establish companies in Nigeria. It proved and disproved nothing. Still, if he was ever a spy, he was certainly a serious businessman also. And a hospitable one. I enjoyed my brief stay in Dolphin Square.

And now I found myself at his brother's clinic waiting – for what? I asked Mallam D. no questions but waited. Dr — came out and I was invited in.

'Well, Wole, what is it all about?'

I stared. What was this 'Wole' impertinence?

Undaunted, his smiles only grew broader, greasier, his face was one crease of grease. He waved flatfish hands that seemed without nerve or bone. 'All this. Why are the police molesting you this time?'

'You'd better ask them, hadn't you?'

'Well, what have you done?'

'Haven't they told you? Look, just tell me, what am I supposed to be doing in your clinic?'

'I don't know. They asked me to examine you that's all.'

'Examine me? What for? I have my own doctor.'

'Oh well you see, I sometimes do examinations for them . . .'

'Them. Who are them?'

'The police.'

'I see. One moment.' I stood up and went out. D. was still waiting by the door. 'I want to talk to you,' I said.

'Has he finished?'

'He has not started. Can we move down a bit?' He accompanied me, puzzled. 'I don't want to be examined by that man.'

'What is the matter? Do you know him?'

'I don't even want him to touch me. I don't want his hand on me at all, do you understand that?'

His manner changed at once. 'I am sorry but he is our doctor. You say you are ill, we have to have him examine you.'

'There must be other government doctors. If for some reason you are afraid of my doctor you can take me to a government hospital where I'll be examined.'

'Well it's not er . . . convenient. It has to be Dr —.'

'Then I do not cooperate. Listen D., I have cooperated very well so far. I have been quite amenable to your chains but I will not be examined by that man.'

Mallam D. turned quite ugly. 'Well that is too bad. If you don't agree to be examined you will make things very awkward.'

I laughed. 'For me? How do you propose to do that?'

'I have been nice enough to you. I have treated you quite well in fact. But if you start refusing to cooperate now you will make things very awkward.'

I repeated, 'I don't care what you do. I will not be examined by him.'

'Not just for you. You'll make things awkward for everybody.'

D. met my eyes briefly, then looked away repeating. 'You will make things awkward for *everybody*.'

His meaning was quite unmistakable but I wanted it in plain language.

'Are you referring to my doctor?'

'I only repeat what I said. You said at the hospital you did not want to get your doctor into trouble. Well you'd better cooperate.'

As if by deliberate timing, an officer arrived just then and handed to Mallam D. my hospital card and the laboratory reports. Mallam D. took them and waited for my decision. I turned and preceded him into the doctor's office, where the good man was waiting to welcome me with that unctuous, dribbly anticipation.

'Take off your clothes please.'

I took them off but my eyes never left him, never left his

hands and the instruments he picked up. While he padded all over my chest with his stethoscope I continued to watch what his other hand was up to. He decided that he had to take a sample of blood and I watched from where he picked up a pin for the job. After the jab I waited for any sensation of giddiness, my eye on the scalpel which I had marked down to slit his throat at the first sign of treachery. Bringing me to this man and the blackmail employed over my own doctor was breeding in me an increasing paranoia. But the examination ended without incident.

'Please put on your clothes.' Then, 'And now tell me, is there anything you want? You know, I'm their doctor, if an order comes from me they have to carry it out. Is there a special diet you will like me to recommend? Anything at all, I am here to help, you know.'

I looked at him, feeling I wanted to spit in his face. But I finally smiled.

'I don't need food. I fast half the time. I need clothes however. I have only these clothes and it gets quite cold some evenings.'

As if I had granted him a boon he muttered 'Good, good, good' and began to write furiously.

'Anything else? Are you sure you wouldn't like some special food?'

I stood up. Outside in the streets, I stopped and looked at D. 'I want you to know that I submitted to that on protest. For me it was a most humiliating experience. I was nauseated at having to submit to an examination by that man and I protest against such humiliation.'

'Humiliation? Why do you call it humiliation? He is a qualified doctor isn't he?'

'At the moment I am more interested in my doctor. Are you going to release him or not?'

'Don't worry about that. He'll be all right.'

'Will you now release him? Now.'

'Yes.'

In certain situations even more than the norm, touch becomes a personal, intimate, psychic, political, emotional and intellectual thing. To be touched by a stool-pigeon protected by a medical banner, and by an especially physically revolting specimen of that genre, to be touched, pawed, inspected by such an object was an exercise in degradation. My strong reaction to being touched by him must have received an equally forcible expression for the words to have stuck in the mind of Mallam D. or in the mind of his superior officers to whom he must have given a report. It could be no coincidence that it was a near exact phrasing which was later used in the famous tale of escape.

Predictably the police (and the government) panicked after the public episode at the hospital. They rushed to press the following day with a release which said, 'He sleeps well, eats well, is allowed to see his own doctor . . .'

8

I SETTLED down into the monotony of Kiri-kiri which had itself settled down to a routine of read-stroll-read-eat-read-sleep. There would be no more interrogation – that much I had learnt. Books? Mainly cheap novels on a little shelf in the Superintendent's office. There was no proper library. I asked if books could be obtained for me from the main city library but the incident of the hospital had in the end only caused tighter strictures on the detainees in our prison. Primitive, inhuman directives were issued in the name of Security by the Gestapo to hold detainees in closer confine, to reduce their contact with the outside world to absolute zero. This included even the older detainees, those who, like the 'stalwarts' had been held since the Ironsi régime. The Superintendent after his bold stand on my kidnapping from hospital had knuckled under, recalled to the fact that he belonged to a suspect tribe. The only exceptions were the two soldiers accused of murdering the Ibo photographer. They alone continued to receive letters, newspapers, visitors, to leave the prison in the morning and return in the evening any time their officers could spare time and vehicle to take them away for 'investigations'. It was a regular act to see them leap up, grab some clothes and dash out, half-dressed for the outing, shouting 'Sure, sure' to the requests of other detainees for cigarettes and other contraband.

And so one day, inevitably, the order came for their release. The other detainees jumped to clap them on the back and shout 'congratulations'. The prisoners were silent, expressionless. A detainee asked the Sergeant, 'I bet you have earned some promotion' and Jack Palance, his cleaning operations suspended, added energetically, 'Sure, they must promote him. Imagine, all that time he had spent here.' Stunned, I remained in my cell while all these cries of felicitation went on around me, unable to believe that I had heard aright. The remaining prisoners who inhabited the back cell for various infringements sat and stared. When the noise had subsided and the gates clanged shut on their departure I went outside to look at the faces of those merry-makers. I was curious to find out the level of sincerity. Could it be that the release of one person triggered off hope in their own breasts for eventual liberty? I found them all seated around the yard with blank faces. The emotion had been cut off as artificially as it had been aroused. One hissed, 'Murdering swine' and went back to his cell. Some others shook their heads as if they could not quite believe it. Then why? Why the false approbation? It could only mean one thing – that these two murderers had exuded such power in their detention, their perverse, unjust, unnatural release had endowed them with such authority that each detainee in that block instinctively felt that they might, once outside, put in a good word for them. By shouting approval of the release, they were announcing to these genocidal instruments of government policies that they were good, loyal citizens to that government.

Three days later, unable to accept any longer the dispensation of prison walls I began the letter to my political colleagues. I use this term in preference to the other, 'political comrades', to distinguish attitudes to situations of conflict, to distinguish those who on the one hand believe that prison – to quote this immediate situation – is some kind of hallowed ground in which an inmate must not only obey the laws of the administration but desist from any other involvement in the struggle that placed him there, conducting himself always in such a manner as would effect his early release. On the other, as comrades, those who acknowledge that prison is only a new stage from which the struggle must be waged, that prison, especially political prison is an artificial erection in more senses than one whose bluff must be called and whose impotence must be demonstrated. And it is not merely the injustice within the prison that should be tackled, it is not only the fascist continuum of outside power within the prison that must be defeated though this, naturally, forms the bulk of an inmate's struggles. Where necessary, where his social conscience is called upon, a commitment to absolute ideals cannot plead the excuse of immobilization to turn his back on the fight for an equitable society.

While my colleagues dithered over the demands of this renewed call for justice, knowledge of the existence of the letter came to one of the hundred government stooges among the academic staff in Ibadan. He contrived to obtain the letter, made a photostat and dutifully passed it on to his military bosses.

Before the letter, a decision had been taken on my release. Following the report both of Mallam D. and one Chinkafe, not only had the order for my release been made – I was not yet formally detained – but the information had been prematurely leaked by the police press office. A journal actually carried the news.

The tragedy of young eager functionaries of the system such as Mallam D. is that they imagine that they are thoroughly in the know of the various motivations of power, for they see themselves as part of that power. They think when they permit themselves to be used for sordid ends that their actions are in fact acts of self-preservation since the victim has directed his actions against their own existence within power. They think, in short, that they are in the most secretive, the innermost condition of power, that they know *everything*. My decision to refer to Mallam D. only by his initial even though I now have proof of his collaboration in the plot is due only to the fact of his youth and naiveté and the possibility that individuals like him may yet be salvaged. The rest, Yisa Adejo, Kem Salem, Femi Okunnu, Remi Ilori, the doctor, etc., are irredeemable species, varying only in degrees of animality or time-serving.

With the betrayal of the letter to a member of the Supreme Military Council, my affairs entered a completely new phase. More than ever, it became quite simply a matter of life and death. Normally all the false information which went to the police on my activities were transmitted to me even in gaol; they were easily available because, among other reasons, they had first to be concocted, then debated, then formally submitted for sifting, vetting and evaluating by Propaganda and Intelligence. And the sense of power, of participation in historic events opened many mouths to a hardly creditable degree. This lethal document however went straight into the hands of the uppermost hierarchy. Suddenly the police, even the Security, became aware that other forces were at work other than they.

The rest, like Mallam D. and Tony Enahoro, were poor ignorant tools, tools today as they will always be in the hands of unscrupulous power.

One morning Security officers arrived at the prison, I was taken into an office and, to my astonishment, fingerprinted. For a stupid moment I actually hoped I was about to be formally charged and served papers for a forthcoming trial. But they only packed up their ink-roller and departed with my prints. Next, later that afternoon, I received a visitor, my wife. We talked for about an hour, not privately but in the presence of Mallam D. and three prison officials. The meeting took place in the Superintendent's office.

The following day a press release was made by Tony Enahoro.

The *Sunday Post* 29 October 1967 reported that:

'A famous Nigerian playright, Head of Drama and Lecturer in English of the Lagos University, Mr Wole Soyinka, has been detained under the emergency regulations.

'Mr Soyinka has been omniously connected with espionage activities for the rebel leader Odumegwu-Ojukwu against the Federal Military Government.

'Chief Enahoro emphasized that he was authorized to make the following disclosures by the Federal Military Government.

'The Commissioner then said the Police investigations have shown that Soyinka was in Enugu on August 6 with arch-rebel Odumegwu-Ojukwu. Mr Soyinka was also said to have admitted in a statement that he came to an arrangement with Mr Ojukwu to assist in the purchase of jet aircraft to be used by the rebel Air Force.

'In the same statement Mr Soyinka was said to have admitted he had since changed his mind on this.

'Also on August 9, Mr Soyinka was at Benin with Colonel Victor Banjo and agreed to help in the overthrow of the Government of Western Nigeria. Soyinka further agreed to the consequent overthrow of the Federal Military Government, the Commissioner told the Press.'

It was neat, beautifully compact. The unexpected bonus of a domestic reunion insinuated the following picture in a reader's mind: in return for his 'confession' the repentant traitor has been allowed a visit from his wife. He is happy, contented and relaxed, glad to have got the whole thing off his chest. The Military machine had some highly efficient experts on public psychology working on my affairs.

9

ALL was secrecy within the prison walls. The Gestapo had ordered a total black-out on the outside world for me and all inmates of the back cell before Enahoro's press conference. Not only would a rebuttal be embarrassing, it would prove dangerous, render suspect any official account of the execution of the final act. On the day of the conference not one single newspaper was floating in the block. The routine for serving a detention order was never even carried out; normally a paper is served on the detainee, usually by a senior police officer, accompanied by the superintendent. The captive signs a receipt for the order and keeps one copy: perhaps I have never really been detained since my signature even on this document is still missing! The flimsy shroud of ignorance in which they sought to envelop me could never in any case have held. Apart from my own private communication links the prison grapevine had long tentacles. By noon not only had I learnt the news but I held the press cutting in my hands. I pondered the enormity of the situation.

My private link was operated through two faithfuls who had taken up residence at the army post by the prison. They used the names 'Dan' and 'Sojo'. At most hours of the day they were to be found at the palm-wine shack where they caroused with the soldiers and met with prison warders on or off-duty. They communicated easily with prisoners who worked outside the prison walls, mowing the gardens or painting the walls of the senior prison officials.

Each day one or the other met a mutual friend, an army officer of strange, indefinable duties. We called him G. I owe my life to the vigil of this trio.

On the afternoon of the publicized confession I received this note from Dan:

They are moving you tonight. Plane expected on airstrip just before dark. Official destination is Jos, but confidentially no destination. Understand? G. says he can handle it but he needs time. Safety margin too narrow at moment. Can you create eruption, any eruption? If possible full-scale riot. Try pl. anything to gain time. By the way who is Peter? He is their inside man – don't let him near you.

Peter? If he indeed then they had chosen well. Peter and I beamed and smiled daily upon each other but I knew him well. The warders spoke often of him, so did the prisoners; but the warders especially, stung by his overbearing manner, his meteoric rise and 'connections'. Standard Six Elementary. He began as a carpenter employed by the prisons, was singled out for no especial merit for training in England in prison occupational craft. On his return he had been promoted straight to a cadet and then in rapid spurts to the rank of Assistant Superintendent. The warders spoke bitterly of the tribal nepotism of his rise. I had made two observations only of the man. Slyness and an incredible capacity for sadism. I had watched him in operation once against prisoners brought for questioning in an adjoining cell. The prisoners called him Fat-face. Both they and the detainees claimed that, ambitious for the post, he had organized the unofficial death hunt for his boss by renegade soldiers, Yoruba and Northern residents of Agbomalu at the time of the Mid-West invasion. When the Superintendent took to the bush for three days he ran the prison. A taste of his brief régime had united both warders and prisoners against the prospect of his substantive succession. They were glad to have back the Asaba fugitive.

My first instinct was to ask to see the Superintendent. I asked the warder to go for him and to emphasize the urgency. He left. I thought of what I would say to him to make him act at once on my proposed request for immediate transfer from that block. The guard was away ten minutes, returning with a Senior Warder. No, I insisted, this was something I could only discuss with the Chief Superintendent. What about the Assistant Superintendent? No, emphatically no. I did not wish to see Peter. The man promised to find the Superintendent at his house. In the meantime I wrote a quick note denying the stupid forgery, handed it over to a fellow detainee for the next 'mail collection'.

Half-past six and still no Superintendent. It was now only half-hour to lock-up. I began to think next of the character of the Superintendent. Was he likely to accept the fact that my life was in danger? Background – a Mid-West Ibo. I considered if that placed him on my side or not. The answer was No. The most vulnerable Nigerians at that time were the Mid-West Ibos, especially ever since the Mid-West invasion. They had been hounded, hunted and killed since that event and were considered greater security risks than even the real Ibos themselves. On the day after the invasion both the Chief Warder and the Superintendent had spent over three days in the woods surrounding the prison, waiting for the blood-lust to die down. Asaba Ibos required ten positive acts of loyalty to one of the rest of the nation to prove themselves human beings. To remain self-effacing, commuting between home and place of work, quietly, avoiding notice, carrying out orders implicitly and without question – this was the only way to retain a livelihood and to remain at liberty or alive.

At quarter to seven I knew he would not come. And was equally certain that if ordered to stay at home and to sign the order for all required keys he would have no option. And in any case there was Peter. How does one protect himself against one's keepers at a moment's notice?

I ran through a brainstorm of ideas, then summoned two

inmates whom I had occasionally proselytized in those few weeks together.

'I need a riot,' I said, 'I must keep the entire prison awake until I am out of danger.'

I read them the note and explained my predicament. They agreed to cooperate and, with only ten minutes to go, we set in motion a chain-reaction of events. They had their own dependable forces in gaol – I had observed their seemingly unlinked clandestine operations, even long after lock-up.

The Superintendent arrived with nearly two dozen prison staff, forced from his bed at last after ignoring my summons for that entire afternoon. I attacked him at once, gaining time with a long speech in which I accused the prison of collaborating in the plot by the government to liquidate me. I looked at Peter directly, losing all doubt in the legible frustration on his hate-suffused face. The Superintendent I had acquitted of pre-knowledge or collaboration. I announced my decision to commence a fast to the death or until the government withdrew the forgery of a confession.

I continued to speak, improvising, listening, waiting for a sign of the second phase of my plans which should have begun from the entry of the staff, triggered off by the other collaborator. He however lay in bed in a sudden paralysis of fear. He had had, as he confessed the following morning when he came to 'beg my forgiveness', a sudden vision of himself against a wall in Dodan Barracks facing an execution squad for his part in the night's work. His limbs had simply refused to obey him.

The strange exhilaration which I had felt in confronting Peter that night, of identifying to my satisfaction one face in the whole army of anonymous butchers and initiating a first positive act against the System; the end of a long period of passivity, of merely waiting and leaving initiative to the other side, the stymying (temporary, at least) of a crude and vicious challenge on my life, this entire fund of euphoria began to dwindle as I spoke and waited for those other sounds that refused to come. Slowly I grew numbed and stupefied.

Outside, however, Dan and Sojo had arrived with help. The plane which had begun to warm up on the airstrip cut its propellers and lay in the dark. For the moment little more can be said of the events which took place on the airstrip and the crisis which it caused in the top hierarchy of assassins. The rationale of the exact liquidation programme as revealed by G. had been based, during discussion 'in committee' on the fact that I once stood trial for holding up a radio station. They argued that the public would believe their prepared story which was: while being flown to Jos I pulled out a gun, tried to take over the plane and was shot in the attempt. A violent man meets a violent end; the dramatist over-dramatizes himself once too often.

Inside, the failure of the other inmate was a disaster of unpredictable proportions. After a great deal of confusion, rage and terrified suspicion of the level at which my SOS had been answered and coordinated, the assassins entered an ugly, unscrupulously destructive frenzy in which only the most sordid tools* would be used. The first dose of it came in the fantasy which was spun around the events of the night. I was moved into the Maximum Security Prison, caged twenty-four hours a day. But all this I had anticipated and could ignore. What I had not indeed thought possible was yet another forgery. I had been caught, the press release

*A typical move was the assignment of a known hack, one Remi Ilori, to the columns of the *Daily Express*, voice of the Committee of Ten, from which position much 'inside information' could be fed to the public. This scurrilous midget with gargantuan complexes later graduated to an outright police informer where the gratification of his fantasies spelt the fate of bewildered innocents.

stated, 'skulking along the wall'; there was a 'dummy' in my bed; and finally and most successfully demoralizing of all, I had, in denying an attempt to escape, claimed that I was merely 'protesting against *government humiliation*'!

In the period of mental devastation which followed that blow to my unsuspected heights of self-esteem, I did not even remember that the phrase had been lifted from my protest to Mallam D., the expression of my disgust at being subjected to their doctor's examination.

10

'CONFESSION – foiled escape – wail of humiliation.' A trilogy aimed at the most cynical or blindly loyal mind. A beautiful logic all its own. A masterpiece of credible fantasy calculated to shatter any lingering resistance to the omnipotence of the régime. If *he* could break and break so abjectly then anyone can break. This army is a force that can break anyone. And will. The sequence was loaded with whispers, furtive betrayals soon to be followed by purges.

In a moment of enforced calm I moved out of the echoes of voices in the streets, of voices in the markets, out of whispers in corridors, glances in gatherings, out of the rain of spittle and contempt, moved out from the target of pointed fingers, the giggle in the dark, out from the wise nods of geriatric consciences, out of the mockery, the assuaged envy and jubilation of the self-deluded. Slowly, tortuously, I commenced an exploration into the mind of the enemy and the future dangers. What are they doing now? Toasting each other in champagne, yes. What else? Back-slapping one another for the masterstroke, heaving sighs of relief. Yes, yes, but what else? Place yourself in their position, what would you do now? This moment! What would be the next step?

Press the advantage. No rest. No quarter for the dissidents. Make a clean sweep of every particle of opposition. Arrest. Purge! A little mysterious announcement, a little hint that, thanks to other revelations made by that new-converted pillar of the régime, it is now possible to cleanse the nation once and for all of all fifth columnists. Settle all the old scores! As for you . . .

Yes, come on. After all you are the writer, the student of human nature. Let us have some creative identification.

What is the worst thing you would do to the last possible danger, the sole witness to the foundation of falsehood laid for the superstructure of violent repression?

For this danger remains, even when I have filled the gaols to overflowing and built new concentration camps to house other 'confessed' saboteurs, the danger of a leak in the bubble remains with you living. When the secret graves have been filled up and the agonies of the tortured have sated even the public lust for vengeance, what would I do? What can I do to destroy you thoroughly, leaving no loopholes?

The answer came with paralysing clarity: Set you free. Yes. In the one gesture that cannot but be interpreted as fulfilment of a despicable bargain, open the gates and set you free. Your teeth are pulled, your claws pared, your voice broken. Simply by opening the gates and releasing you out to public gaze.

Tell me, what would you say? Denials? My friend, your comrades are dead, locked up, cowed and broken. Even if they are no comrades, even if you never set eyes on them or of their existence, the truth, yes, truth – recognize the malleable word? – truth, the truth is *that* truth of their arrest following upon hints of your generous confession. That is the Truth. We have re-created truth and truth is now defined in our image. Each man who loses liberty or life is added to the score of your betrayal. What will you say? How will you say it? Who will believe you? Who, above all, will dare believe you? Who will *want* to believe you? Who will *think* of believing? Truth, my dear friend, is the thousands who have vanished since we fixed your interfering little mind!

In an animal cage, in the spiritual isolation of the first few days the prospect became real and horrifying. It began as an exercise to arm myself against the worst, it plunged into horrors of the imagination. I had begun to lose sane distinction between the supposition and the reality. Even long after I had re-established contact with the outside world, had been assured that the truth was known where it mattered most, it took only a little trigger of recollecion to plunge back into that cauldron of racing pulses and nervous stress. Yet there was the strange fact, contradicting all logical expectation – my mind continued to function. If anything it had developed a sharp reckless cunning. Transferred to the Maximum Security Prison with lines of contact abruptly cut, realizing and near-panicking from the thought that I was more than ever at the mercy of the state propaganda machine, I became obsessed with finding a means of renewing that contact. I could think only of a scribbled denial of the fabrication handed in advance to that very inmate whose nerve had given at the critical moment. By now I realized he had probably chewed and swallowed it before the search which would inevitably follow.

It was a wild, all-consuming ambition – to get out a statement at all costs, to foil the plan of other denunciations which was surely building up on the cornerstone of cumulative forgery. The dual condition of my mind, the duality of its numbed despair and the weird instinctive cunning of those days struck me only long afterwards.

I watched, waited and schemed. My mind revolved a hundred schemes, scanned each warder, anatomized the trusty who came to feed the animal, delved into the soul of each inmate looking for that flash of collaborative recognition. A prisoner knows at once just who will aid him and who will not. And I was ready to take chances, there being nothing left to lose. My mind was racing when the chance finally came, a mere tantalizing flash of opportunity. I managed to arrest that flash and make it serve.

It was a chance in a thousand, a coincidence such as nearly makes one a convert to Providence, a combination of circumstances that came about ironically by virtue of the iron ring in which I was surrounded. Too much of the same precaution, one cancelled out another – my message was waiting.

I knew even in the headlong rush that I must phrase my statement to make it appear that it came from the other prison. It placed intolerable restraint on me but it was better than to be moved at once from this imagined insulation which I had breached. A breach is worth all in confinement. My note took wings and flew into hope-famished hands. A newspaper or two inside the country found the courage to print my words; a vicious witch-hunt was begun in the wrong prison.

That small victory had to console me in the abysmal existence of the following days. The horror of the picture I had conjured up had become a haunting reality. While I waited for confirming news I knew the corrosion of anxiety. It ate into areas of the invisible being, in corners where I could not reach.

They were blank days, days of impenetrable darkness and pulses that ran out of all control. There were tranquillizers, sleeping pills, visits from the prison doctor. A faint rally from sources of will cautioned against reliance on pills, warned me to reject all artificial help. After two days I forced myself to throw them in the lavatory bucket. Two days later I asked the doctor again for their replacement, admitting what I had done with the first supply. I kept the pills on the box which served for a table, invented a drill of picking them up during bad spells, counting them carefully, patterning them and putting them back again. I lay flat, sat cross-legged, stood on my head, underwent a repertory of practised and improvised positions in the battle to rule my pulse, quiet noises in the head. I begged me to permit one pill, one pill only this once and never again, moved quickly to take them again in my hands, count, then make patterns on the box with them. The taste of food or water vanished entirely. Cigarettes merely created dizziness.

Response to my surroundings came slowly, the recognition of passing inmates as human beings, as individuals with unique features. That crisis was over. If it returned I would find the strength to rule it. Knowing at last that my refutation had escaped the iron ring, and had even been published, helped. Even more uplifting was the confirmation of my fears, when Dan and Sojo finally made contact, that a programme of purges had been planned but was now forcibly abandoned. Or postponed. They would wreak vengeance on those who lay within their power but that source of pleasure could not now be expanded nor could it be based on a fantasy of betrayal.

11

DREAMS. More strictly, variations on one dream. I would be on the scaffolding of a building in construction, high up. Cold. Mists. The mist barely reveals the outlines of my co-workers on other parts of the building. They are shadowy forms in blurred contours. A relay of hands pass the bricks on to me from the ground. When the last brick is set in place I signal and a new brick flies through the mists, invisible until the last yard or two. But the aim each time is perfect. I catch it with barely a glance, literally by stretching my hand out for the brick to fall into. I place the brick in position, fill the gaps with mortar and slice off the excess. It is hardly work; every moment is leisurely, slowed-down motion, ritualistic. The mists swirl all about us; from time to time a face passes close, balancing on the narrow catwalk, trundling a barrow to another part of the edifice.

It is a long while before I know that everyone else is gone. I did not hear the lunch gong. I could not have suspected it had rung since the bricks continue to drop into my outstretched hands. It is the silence that strikes me first and slowly I realize that work has ceased. The work has proceeded till now in virtual silence but now that silence has grown even deeper. I lean over to ask my own relay if they wish to stop or to continue until that line of the wall is completed. Only seven bricks left I say; the figure is always seven. There is no response from them and I notice now that they are also gone. A brick comes flying slowly through the mist though there is no one below. I hold out my hand for it. It slips, I lunge for it and fall over. I am a long time falling in the void.

Later I recognize the physical landscape. It is one of the

threads that have gone into the weaving of that metaphysical web which holds men dead in their tracks with the frightening certainty of having returned to a point in a cycle. The landscape of Shaki conjured up long-buried images of the Dutch lowlands where years ago, as a student, I once joined in building new houses for victims of a flood disaster. I recall the pure uncomplicated giving and camaraderie and I know what gave birth to the earlier nostalgic sadness. The rest is horror, the long fall in the abyss, night after night, the awful silence . . .

12

THROUGH the bars I could see across the rooftops of other buildings in the yard. Acres of desolation between the buildings, huge swathes of space inside the walls. These man-made hives seemed feeble pock-marks on the authentic face of emptiness. The clumps of ferns, the potholes and the swamps spoke of recent reclamation from a sea that still promised a fight for re-possession. I could, I imagined, hear its soft near-stagnant wash over the crowded palm crowns just visible over the walls. Voices of the idling, gossiping, hoping prisoners drifted up towards me like echoes from another world. From some dim region of memory I was nudged by a voice, a touch, a thread of cobweb from the dark. It was that harrowing moment of reach, touch, slip, reach again but utterly fail to grasp. I was not capable even of the effort to reach my mind, a woolly receptacle floating in ether while this drop of dew from distant past settled gently on its rim and turned again to vapour in a fever that had just begun.

Time vanished. I turned to stone. The world retreated into fumes of swampland.

I have been here before. I have passed through this present point again and again. My head is filled with the smells and senses of that other time and with recognition comes the added pain of a repeated leave-taking. I try hard to stay the moment, to come to terms with it and if possible, mark it in a place, a time. Desolation increases with my acute certainty that the sensation is deeper than the mere located place or event. It is closer to a phase of being. A self taken for granted in terms of humanity, faith, honour, justice, ideals. It resolves itself, in so far as anything has resolved itself today, lightly on the rims of consciousness. A knowledge of where I have been till this moment, knowing it for a phase to which I will never return, yet aware also that this ritual of transition is a perpetual one and that the acquisition of experience in fording the pass does not lessen its overwhelming sadness.

Again and again I recognize this territory of existence. I know that I have come to this point of the cycle more than once, and now the memories are so acute that I wonder if it has not been truly in a mere prophetic expectation of it all, in the waiting upon it in captive attendance, wondering merely, when? What meaning then shall I attach to it, what name, what definition give to the monstrosity of this birth? I try to feed some muscularity into the marshmallow of sensations.

A private quest? Stuff for the tragic stage and the ritual rounds of Passion? A brave quest that diverges from, with never a backward glance at history's tramp of feet along the communal road? Is this then the long-threatened moment for jettisoning, for instance, notions of individual responsibility and the struggle it imposes? Must I now reject Kant? Karl Jaspers? 'However minute a quantity the individual may be in the factors that make up history, he is a factor.' Must I now say to him, yes, a dead factor? About as effective as flotsam on ocean currents. Hang instead on to the ambiguity of the other face of fulfilment? – 'Man can only grasp his authentic being through confrontation with the vicissitudes of life.' I have quarrelled too often even with the egocentred interpretations to which the existentialist self gives rise. Any faith that places the *conscious* quest for the inner self as goal, for which the context of forces are mere battle aids is ultimately destructive of the social potential of that self. Except as source of strength and vision keep inner self out of all expectation, let it remain unconscious beneficiary from experience. Suspect all conscious search for the self's authentic being; this is favourite fodder for the enervating tragic Muse. *I do not seek; I find.* Let actions alone be the manifestations of the authentic being in defence of its authentic visions. History is too full of failed prometheans bathing their wounded spirits in the tragic stream.

Destroy the tragic lure! Tragedy is possible solely because of the limitations of the human spirit. There are levels of despair from which, it rightly seems, the human spirit should not recover. To plunge to such a level is to be overwhelmed by the debris of all those anti-human barriers which are erected by jealous gods. The power of recovery is close to acquisition of superhuman energies, and the stagnation-loving human society must for self-preserving interest divert these colossal energies into relatively quiescent channels, for they constitute a force which, used as part of an individual's equipment in the normal human struggle cannot be resisted by the normal human weapons. Thus the historic conspiracy, the literal brain-washing that elevates tragedy far and above a regenerative continuance of the promethean struggle.

To survive, but to survive in a transmitted form, full of nebulous wisdoms, corrupted and seduced by sagehood homage, carefully insulated from intimacy with the affairs of men, that kind of bribery which Oedipus at first snatched at, blinding himself physically to eradicate in entirety the route to socially redemptive action – this is the preference of all establishment. Against all questioning and change, against concrete redress of the causative factors of any crisis, society protects itself by this diversion of regenerative energies into spiritual in-locked egotism. To ensure that there is no reassertion of will the poetic snare of tragic loftiness is spread before him – what greater sublimity than the blind oracular figure, what greater end to the quest for self than graceful acceptance, quiescence and senescence!

Do I or do I not recognize the trap? I summon history to my aid, but more than history, kindred knowledge, kindred findings, kindred rebellions against the lure of tragi-existentialism; for rage is no longer enough to combat the temptations to subside into unproductive, will-sapping wisdoms. I seek only the combative voices and I hunt them down from remotest antiquity to the latest incidental re-encounters on casual forums. 'Tragedy is merely a way of retrieving human unhappiness, of subsuming it and thus of justifying it in the form of necessity, wisdom or purification. The rejection of this process and the search for the technical means of avoiding the insidious trap it lays is a necessary undertaking today.' When? Where? I neither remember nor care. I recall only that I once made a note of it to use in what a student called my special anti-literature seminars. But the words hammer strident opposition to the waves of negations that engulf me, to the mob hatred that I distinctly hear even in this barred wilderness. It nerves me to mutter – Brainwashed, gullible fools, many-headed multitudes, why should your voices raised in ignorance affect my peace?

But they do. I cannot deny it.

From this pit of anguish, dug by human hands, from this cauldron stoked by human hands, from this deafening clamour of human hate the being that emerges is literally an 'anjonnu'. He will return neither understanding nor tolerating as before. He will no longer weigh or measure in mundane terms. Reality for him is for ever tinged in the flames of a terrible passage, his thoughts can no longer be contained by experiences. You, outside of these walls, whose hysteria I confess penetrates my proud defences, I know you sense this menace of a future revenge and must, in self-defence redouble your efforts of annihilation – spiritual, psychic, physical and symbolic. And this is why I must dig into my being and understand why at this moment you have the power to affect me. Why, even when I have rationally rejected the tragic snare, I am still overcome by depressive fumes in my capsule of individualist totality.

Said Hermias of Aternias, with his body broken and in a breath that barely held, 'Tell my friends and companions that I have done nothing unworthy of philosophy.' That longing in all human beings that will sooner expend last breath on words of affirmation than conserve it on behalf of life, believing that life is justified if only at the moment of quitting it, the remnant spittle of a parched tongue is launched against the enemy in one defiant gesture of contempt, supplying a final action of hope, of encouragement for the living, validating one's entire being in that last gesture or in a word of affirmation. Overcoming pain, physical degradation and even defeat of ideals to sum up, to send a reprise of faith to the comrades one leaves behind, and make even dying a triumph, an ultimate affirmation.

I know why you reach me, you mindless mob. I see myself consigned to a living death, denied that affirmation. And worse, not merely denied it but with my living corpse displayed to the world in the rank embalming fluid of its antithesis: recantation! Issuing as if from my catatonic body, the ventriloquist propaganda of frightened, desperate yet powerful criminals devoid of the vaguest notions of decency, justice or fair play! I race through catalogues of totalitarian situations where such 'self-vilifications' have issued forth even long after real or living deaths from victims of power insanity, but find there little consolation. I caution in vain against the acceptance of power morality by listing the lies and holding them up to fundamental lights. I grind them in the crucible of permanent truths, demanding as a start: Let us assume you did try to escape, just whose ethics are affronted except those whom you have proved morally debased? Must this charade, the sudden 'moral' awakening of millions whose moral sense lay heavily dead over the mass murder which has created your individual persecution – must this comedy be reckoned sane or wholesome? *That* moral sense? That putrid cadaver of abdicated will that resurrects only at the scent of a voiceless, powerless victim, and is activated by the kick of booted power?

And yet it is not enough. Not even the procession of past and living wraiths who float into vision in parallel trials, reinforcing a faith of individual decisions. From within my lifetime absorption in the fate of the individual in confrontation with bigotry and repression they emerge: Abraham Fischer; Nicodemus Frischlin (earliest recorded instance of the formula 'killed while trying to escape?'); Cardinal Mindszenty (who chose his own prison); a bullet crippled figure in a wheelchair, Dr Arias, fleeing the Dominican dictator; John Wilkes moving just within and out of parliamentary immunity, even the Apostle Paul, with the repetitive aid of the 'miraculous'...

With St Paul I am brought to a sudden halt. An effort at self-mockery creates a hurtful grimace, yet it unwinds a little the self-strangulating knot that has formed within my guts. Ah, yes, you fancied yourself quite an Epistolatian didn't you? Epistle of St You-know-whom from Kiri-kiri to the Ibadanians ... be of good cheer, the Lord is with you, but beware of those wolves in sheep's clothing who roam among you, rooting up the corpse of the yester-year...

The effort at humour salvages yet another ghost, this time from the local pages of irony: Tony Enahoro, megaphone of official falsehood. The irony is one of those belly jokes that history plays on men. When he fled from the scene after the abortive coup and was obligingly held by the British government on behalf of their feudal favourites, I flew to London, urged by a simple conviction. It was the conviction also of a small, unpartisan and largely anonymous group which alone of the many movements has preserved an undeviating vision of future society. Our belief was: the repatriation of Enahoro would be too great a loss in the thinning ranks of the radicals. Perhaps Enahoro's friends had already begun private pressures to prevent his return; I know only that the public campaign did not begin until after my work in London. I enlisted the aid of the only two politicians I knew, Tom Driberg and Wayland Young (Lord Kennet), and recruited the more politically aware students into an active lobbying programme.

Prison projects scenes of vivid, total recall. Wayland's face I can almost touch, saying: 'I don't really know much of your political situation – is he a good man this Enahoro?'

I replied, 'We need him, and in circulation.' I had not then ever met Enahoro face to face.

At home the 'intellectuals' said, Coward, let him return home and face the music. To which there was and remains only one reply: the soul of the revolutionary dance is in the hands of the flutist.

What was his name, that other Wurtenburg Professor, a compatriot of Frischlin, perhaps also his contemporary? The worthy doctor who in spite of his conviction of the superstitious, untenable injustice of witch trials nevertheless prepared over two hundred successful prosecutions of witches who were duly roasted at the stake. A dichotomy of conviction and responsibility justified by seeking, in the meantime, ways and means of weaning his medieval society from its barbaric ways? So now the role of the intellectual is reduced to simply that! What exactly is the evaluation we must place on your doctorate dissertations you boneless craniums whose tomes shall undoubtedly assail us titled with variations of 'the Social Anomy of 1966, its roots and consequences in the Nigerian Civil War, etc., etc., with special reference to the role of the imperialist commercial interest, etc., etc'. Two hundred witches? Two thousand? Two hundred thousand? Two million? Twenty? In presentation volumes bound in silence?

In my private realm of thoughts I seek keystones to shore my being against formless assaults that come in the wake of bouts of aggressive certainty. It is strange how that creative revelation of Picasso's has taken to haunting me: *I do not seek; I find.* It is like an incantation sneaked in the mind under hypnosis. I ask it finally, what is it? What are you saying to me? What are you trying to suggest that I did not know before? Some new twist to fit this situation, to reconcile me to this circle? For instance that, passive or provoking, protagonist or acquiescing, I was fated for this passage? That a visionary's course is one which, even with closed eyes and folded arms, finds? For example: every situation creates its own response? Antithetically, to vary the emphasis a little for that daily truism of abdications: eyes have they, but they *will not* see? It is strange and I do not really resolve it. The phrase beats time on my chest like an ambiguous talisman. Not in the least ambiguous however is another, a loud assertive chime and I cannot even recall if the words are Jasper's or Kant's: *it is always our responsibility to decide critically whether or not it is immoral to obey a command of authority.* Yes, I allow only for this sole factor of decision; the physical power of choice.

Dreyfus. Dimitrov versus Goering. How much longer will it go on, this pattern of power-initiated crime and the political scapegoat? A hideous image looms from those Nazi mists, the blood-thirst of a bestiality of power, a rabid snarl and slavering model for the Yisa Adejos of the world, animalistic regressions which evoke a shudder even from the reconciled heart of carnage. Now in hindsight I wonder if it had been such a wise action to transmit from gaol a letter containing evidence of their guilt while I lay in the power of such men. (The liberal conscience even of Dimitrov's time knew better than to rest easy with the idea of those Bulgarian fall-guys in the personal charge of Goering.) I fault myself now, accepting implicitly that Kantian imperative, recognizing that since I had settled within myself all doubts about the bankruptcy of Gowon's moral order from that moment of his release of the two murderers, it was not enough to send word to a band of emasculated intellectuals. I should have done then what I now stand accused of doing – escaped. For there existed then, and exists even now in spite of its reverses a truly national, moral *and* revolutionary alternative – Victor Banjo's Third Force. Morality, and therefore actions which come from a moral inspiration create the only 'auth-ntic being', they constitute the continuing personality of the individual and cannot be substituted by absolving palliatives. The gap in my guts, the hurtful hiatus that threatens to suck my egoist essence into its own void is the evasion of hat moral imperative; the despair comes from a knowledge hat I cannot now carry out this sole affirmation nor can I nvisage, in this barren encirclement, the possibility of a ational substitution. As for that wounded ego whose epredations on my peace of mind have been and will (I susect) continue to be my worst enemy and friend in this place pick on the words which have evoked in me the worst phyical nausea. I force down the bilge that has welled even vith their mere consideration and remind myself of the evil otency of the framers of those words and their knowledge f mass psychology. It is a cruel exercise but there is no help or it. I force the words through my lips and listen to the quelch – 'he claimed he was protesting against government umiliation.' I chew the phrasing as ratsbane and drink it own as hemlock – 'he claimed he was protesting against overnment humiliation.'

You criminals, you have imbued your cause with unlimied power. Your contemptuous insight into the minds of a hysteria-manipulated mob has rendered you immune to further confrontation – this is your purpose and I acknowledge its present success. If doubts are created, even in one solitary example, if an acknowledged absolutist voice is polluted, if affirmation is turned into recantation in the mind of the mob then you have established your race of serfs whose docility will be justified for ever by 'if he could break, then who are we to struggle?' For the few who are and have always been rulers in their own self-sufficiency there will be a grain of self-doubt implanted by the recollected instance.

I ought truly to have a contempt for this world of zombies. I shall, but you have yet to create them. I think that finally, you cannot. True, the voices which I hear are not the voices that I seek to hear. They are not testimonies of that quasi-mystic bond which, even allowing for self-delusion, exists between the loneliest of all combatants and the people whose cause he ultimately espouses. I have not heard for instance the long-waited cry of justice which demands, Bring him out for judgement, not – Crucify him! Let us be witnesses at the unmasking. Instead I see hands thrown up in horror. I see furtive slinks of shame in the streets, in dark corners of homes. I smell hate, evil, fright and capitulation But it is your smell, the smell of irredeemable corruption tha travels with you and clings to all over whom your breath o lies has blown. And I hear a fresh wind coming up from beyond the boundaries of expediency.

Listen to what Adolfe Joffe wrote to Trotsky before hi death by suicide. 'Human life has meaning only to that de gree and as long as it is lived in the service of humanity. Fo me humanity is infinite.'

For me, justice is the first condition of humanity.

13

SHAKI. August and November 67. Twice I have invaded the Maximum Security. This block is special, it is loaded with rotting, decaying humanity. In my solitary splendour I thought often of them, recalled their suffering and their courage. And sought to triumph over my own conditions no worse than they had done.

They stank.

The Prison Block was two floors. Above us, a floor to which I would return after the plot had been hatched and the goose thoroughly cooked, on that floor dwelt the rich thieves of the old NNDP government, lords of the prison, gourmets of kitchen delicacies, the sartorially privileged. Each floor contained two rows of cells with an intervening passage which was nearly as wide as the cells. At the end of the passage was the entry from the yard, two iron gates; at the other, the dead end – bathrooms, toilets and sinks, and a huge space which served as a lounging place of sorts. The block itself was part of a compound which encased its own recreation grounds. There was a tennis table and space which served for tenniquoit and badminton. Army and civilian detainees used the grounds. Even prisoners. But not the Ibo detainees.

They were let into the corridor and bathrooms twice a day for an hour at a time. They occupied one entire line of cells on the lower floor. Opposite them was the other line, empty except for beddings stacked high against the walls – reaching sometimes to the ceiling. Only one cell on this side was occupied – by Yon da Kolo, a businessman. We had shared that cell at first, before my abrupt removal to the Medium Security Prison, Kiri-kiri. We had mosquito nets. We had a cupboard and a rough table. We were free to move up and down that echoing corridor and use the vast space which remained a mocking, tantalizing waste to the Ibos most of the day. But at that time, August, they could even move around, move from cell to cell. They slept on the bare floor, they had a clear view across the passage of blankets and beds, at the empty cells these beddings occupied. Some of them had no blankets and some cells were occupied by up to eight people. The cells were designed for only one man apiece, at the most two.

There were petty traders among them, students, doctors, senior and junior civil servants, crooks also since they were all human beings. There was an old man with an all-white head of hair. I found Agu Norris among them, a famous trumpeter. His jokes were incessant and morale-uplifting for the others. This was the first visit, August. I did not think their conditions could be 'improved' upon until my return there in November.

Now they were locked in permanently. The cells were opened – for the entire lot, a total of nearly sixty men – for precisely thirty minutes each day. And that half-hour was not for airing in the open air. The main gate of that floor was kept locked. Because they could not wash their clothes, because they had to defecate in pails in their cells even in daytime, because, in those few minutes – thirty minutes for nearly sixty men in crowded space – that the doors were opened, the taps were often dry and because sometimes for the whole day, for the flimsiest of reasons their cells were not opened at all, they stank. For da Kolo and me even in those 'milder' days of August, the walk to the bathroom was a moral ordeal. Our condition in the midst of theirs was a visible oasis to men paralysed by sun-stroke.

Now the cells were not even opened for them to receive food. The bowls – shallow aluminium objects – were slid to them under the iron doors, sometimes tilted through the vertical bars if the food was one of some hard consistency. They took turns to obtain fresh air from the little window. Seeing them, smelling them, passing them in daytime as they sat on the floor was bad enough in August. Now even to go along the walls outside, past their windows, stopping to talk to them in defiance of the stool-pigeons was to be assailed by the smell of rotting flesh that wafted from within those cells.

During that first stay I said to Yon, someone must speak, someone must protest this criminality. He said, little guessing how prophetic it would prove – 'Take it easy, you don't even know yet what you are in for.' The stool-pigeon was always about, an NNDP convict from upstairs who dutifully reported the conversation. Two days later the Head of Lagos Prisons visited us in person. In the kindest solicitous manner, he said, 'Oh I don't think you two should be forced to share a cell.' The logical step, one would expect, was that one of the empty cells on that side would be opened. But no. That same afternoon I was transferred to the sister prison, Kiri-kiri.

Only to be returned to the same block in November. Upstairs and under lock and key. When that iron phase passed I went into the courtyard for exercises and spoke to them through the windows. Cigarettes I could offer them, but what they really needed was fresh air. Out in the open, not corridor air.

Unexpectedly, one morning, they had a full half-hour of it, to the accompaniment of the most comical episode I ever witnessed in my whole stay in prison. That morning I understood also why many prisoners survive – their gaolers give themselves away. Those torturers reassure the victims time and time again that they the victims have not attained their persecutors' low, that they therefore contain a spark of human essence worth preserving. It does not matter how this comes about, whether as a result of the animality of the gaolers or by a sudden display of mindlessness, or by revealing such a ludicrous aspect of themselves, presenting the prisoner suddenly with a grotesquerie of the supposed *homo dignis* – the prisoner suddenly says to himself, This creature cannot really touch me. He cannot save me therefore he cannot destroy me. This creature is irrelevant, he is not real. I represent reality.

Watching the governor's performance on this day, I could not even honestly charge him with inhumanity. Some (albeit warped) logic is involved in acts of inhumanity. This governor was beyond rhyme or reason. I nearly swore that he was a Biafran agent secretly employed to entertain the detainees.

The raid began at dawn that morning. The previous day – it was in fact a long time coming – the Ibos had decided to reject their food for the day. But the stool-pigeon on our floor had eavesdropped. Adebanjo and I observed him led out after normal lock-up at his own request for an urgent interview with the Superintendent. It was bound to be some tale-carrying but we had no knowledge of the crisis on the lower floor. (Sometimes I suspected that that man employed an inverted listening periscope.)

And so, early the following morning, before the normal opening of cells, the raid commenced. The governor believed in shock tactics. He had brought with him a whole battalion of warders all armed with their special riot batons, formidable three-foot cudgels. They took positions at the double in all sorts of 'strategic' positions, lined the little courtyard of the block two deep and manned the head of the stairs in a menacing stance. As a military operation designed against a possible outbreak of dangerous and violent criminals, it was impressive. We wondered what new defiant prisoners-of-war had earned this distinguished reception drill. No sane man could have imagined for a moment that it was designed for the human refuse who occupied one side of the lower floor in Block X.

The generalissimo, when the stage had been set, swaggered into the corridor: 'Open the cells and bring them out. At the double!'

As the doors were unlocked one after the other: 'Outside! Everybody outside! on the Double – One-Two, One-Two, One-Two, One-Two . . .'

But the prisoners were all civilians. They saw no reason why they should march to military orders. They shuffled out sullenly, defiantly. The governor flailed his swagger-stick to impel some movement in them and jabbed the nearest in the shoulder. It was his luck as always to pick on the wrong one. This was Joe who had in Dodan Barracks spat at the soldiers who were indulging in their sadistic pastimes with him. He was about six foot three, his height and a curious curvature of his neck gave him the appearance of a chimpanzee at the crouch. He turned and gave the governor a long cool stare. The frightened man backed away from the warning in those eyes and stumbled into the other detainees just emerging from their cells. He sensed at once that he had made himself ridiculous so he squared up and jabbed him again – in the chest, shouting to keep up his courage:

'Move. At the double. March outside or I deal you. With you properly.'

That always happened to him also. Ideas and words fused into unintelligible bluster whenever the governor was aroused or was trying too hard to impress. There would be more of that before the morning was over.

Joe turned away and moved slowly forward. An obsequious warder came to the governor's aid by giving Joe a shove. Soon they were all in the courtyard.

'Form two lines. Quickly. Two straight lines at the double.'

It was a wretched sight. They looked beaten, dispirited, despite the slow motion of defiance which they had adopted for the confrontation. There is something shabby about all unequal conflicts. Their effort at a concerted defiance was bound to end like others, the scapegoats would be carted off to the back cells where they would be chained to the wall and the cell flooded. They would be scientifically beaten. One thing they could not fear to lose was privilege. They literally had nothing to lose but their stench. It would take some effort to think up some new group punishment for them but the governor could be trusted to try. I read the weariness of it all on some half-dozen faces while they watched the Superintendent go through his act. He could not even wait for that prolonged, deliberately stretched manoeuvre of the formation of lines to end on its own. He pranced in and out of them, shoving here, pulling a coverlet there, seemingly oblivious of the smell which even in that open air floated upwards to us watchers as, for the first time, all the differing staleness of several cells were brought together into a foul chemical fusion.

He was satisfied at last. He surveyed the parade and seemed to compose himself for the address. This he did by walking up and down, giving them the benefit of his omnipotence. At last:

'Now! I want you all to pay attention. Yes, I am going. To talk seriously to you. That, you must listen and make sure. That, it does not go in at one ear and come out! At other ear. Yes you think that you have come here to make trouble. For me! I am telling you now. That, I will. Also make trouble for you. I am a soldier. You know. I fought in Sudan and in Egypt. I am one. Of the first Nigerians to be promoted a Provost sergeant...'*

Unbelieving, I reached for a pencil from its hiding place

*Since the following monologue will not be believed, I must name the following witnesses of its veracity – S.G. Ikoku, Yon de Kolo, Olu Adebanjo, Agu Norris.

and tore off some toilet paper. This was a scene for Shaky-Shaky.*

'Yes, the first Nigerian. You can ask the late Ironsi himself. He was with me. I senior him. He will tell you. That if I want to remain. In the army I will senior. Him. And the late Ademulegun and all. The others. They are all my junior.

'I study archaeology. I am not just. A prison governor you know I study in Khartoum. Archaeology. And if I am in university today I can tell you. That, I will also lecture in human ecology. Yes. You are enemies. Of the state. Sabotagists! That is why you are here. You are. Sabotagists. And therefore we keep you here. As such. And treat you. So how dare you come here again and make. Conspiracy. You are trying to conspire. You hold meeting yesterday! I know. Against me that, you hold meeting. You will refuse your chop today, that is the meeting you hold. Do you know me? (striking himself on the chest) I maintain discipline. I can treat you like. Gentlemen but if you behave like a hooligans then I will show you that I am a great. Hooligans than yourself. Oh yes, do you know me? I can be a rascal. I can joke laugh and be merry. But if you want to show me that. You are tough I will show you ...'

The service ribbons which he had put on specially for the occasion swelled until they threatened to burst their moorings. He flattened them back on his chest with another huge thump but the chest remained distended. '... that, I am tough. Put your complaints properly if you have. But I will not tolerate infringe. Ment. I am a psychologist. I know. Psychology. I study archaeology. I am not just. A prison. Governor march them back!'

As they trooped back into their cells they were immedi-

*A radio comedy series put out by the Nigerian Broadcasting Service. The comedy is based on two characters, lorry drivers, and the colourful murder of language by their tycoon-boss.

ately followed by the food servers with the morning's bowls of weevils.

'And serve them food!'

Each bean in that mess looked, even from upstairs, as if it had been machine-gunned to death.

'That man!' He pointed to Joe; he had selected his scapegoat. 'Take him to one side. He think he is tough and he is a ring. Leader. We will give him some days. In the back cell and to learn sense.'

We learnt later that Joe had turned round at the entrance, looked him in the face and spat.

'And for the others' – he followed them into the block and his voice shrilled down the passage – 'you will see that they remain lock up for two days. Don't open them. At all. This rebellion must. Be nimp in the bond.'

The doors were locked on them. They pushed their food out of the cells untouched. In the afternoon the beans were taken away and replaced by a soggy dough of farina and a lifeless incurable disease that went by the name of stew. This also remained untouched. Nor did those detainees touch their supper.

In the afternoon occurred one of those scattered acts that remind one continuously that the mindless ones are neither the total sum nor the true face of humanity. The warder for the afternoon duty, a Benin man, came in swinging his keys and opened up the Ibos. 'I hear you are not to be opened out but I have not been officially informed.' He let them loose for an hour.

I used that humane opportunity to go down and talk to them, taking them also that sole prison commodity of consolation, cigarettes. In Agu's cell was a young student from the University of Nsukka. He had been arrested on a passenger lorry at the Maryland (Ikeja) check point with other Ibo passengers in the lorry and taken to Dodan Barracks. Like hundreds of others, an unregistered captive in the cells of Dodan Barracks since March. Biafra seceded in April. The war began in June. His parents lived in Lagos and he was on his way to stay with them for the Easter holidays.

Agu Norris said: 'That governor, we must thank God for him. If we leave here sane na because of that comedian.'

The student said: 'Tell me, what is the difference between half-hour and nothing at all?'

'None,' Agu replied.

'He is a fool. Don't open them at all he says. As if that bothers any of us here. Does he know how many weeks we went without seeing daylight in the Black Hole of Dodan?'

I asked him for explanation. Agu said, 'We are all from there. One day they simply decided to transfer us here. But we all graduate from Dodan.'

'But were you charged? Were you accused of anything?'

'I was,' Agu admitted. 'I couldn't make head or tail out of anything. They asked, have you been to the East recently? I said Yes. They asked why? I said, my home is there. I went to see my people. We never really got beyond that ABC.'

I turned to the student. 'And you? Any interrogation?'

'No. The only interrogation we had was to be taken out by the soldiers for the Dodan roulette. That was the name I gave it. The soldiers would take you out and line you against the wall to be shot. It could be a live bullet or a blank. It depended on your luck.'

'Show him your back,' Agu said suddenly.

'You were flogged?' It was my first thought, knowing that Army pastime only too well.

'No, I was lucky. Just the roulette.' He began to take off his shirt. 'I got something else though.'

It was not merely his back. Some kind of fungus covered all his skin, a green and yellow fungus which spread like a contagious plague all over the body. 'It is better now,' he said. 'At least I think so. I caught it in that dark hole. I think it grows faster in darkness.'

'Na disease from outer space,' Agu said. 'You wan' see the disease from human space? Go to cell No. 3 and say I tell the man to show you his back.'

'Which one?'

'My friend, any back there is worth seeing but the particular one I mean will know himself. All the creeks wey dey for Niger Delta, dey done draw am for in back. By the way, you know wetin save me from that blala?* They take me there for treatment when one of the soldiers recognized me. He say Ah-ah, dis na Agu Norris, na musician. I done hear am for night-club before and I like in music. Na dat save me. But they no take me back so I see the flogging wit' my own eyes and I tank God say I dey play music. They tie them to posts for ground, flat on den belle. Sometime twenty-four strokes, sometime thirty-six. If you no cry they no go leave you. That man wey I say get Niger Delta for in back, they gi' am twenty-four everyday. Everyday. When 'e faint na in de lef'am. And no treatment for the wound. When he come here na in 'e begin get treatment. Go look am. Tell them I say make the lizard show you in back.'

'The Lizard?'

'Yah. You know the proverb – all lizards na in dey lie down belly-face but we know which one get belly-ache. Well, we know wetin dis one get.'

I went and looked at a back of purulent sores. There was no skin. None at all. It was a mass of sores which no longer had definition as each weal had merged into another.

I returned and asked them for details of the Black Hole. Between them they settled the length and width. It was nearly completely square. Eleven people shared it of which

*Slang for Koboko, a cow-hide whip.

only three could stretch out at a time. A little hole set high in the wall was all the window. To obtain fresh air from it they took turns standing on the latrine bucket. This little hole of a window was set right against the roof so that very little light came down into the cell. For five months they had lived in perpetual twilight and dark. They grew accustomed to sleeping where they sat, in a foetus crouch. The great treat was to go out to empty the latrine bucket. This meant air and exercise. And there was the occasional kind-hearted guard who would extend that treat for the lucky man, let him hang outside for a while and even give him a cigarette to smoke. On a weekend when his superiors were not too much about, one let them empty the bucket eleven times.

Once, when there was a confusion in the bucket roster, they even came to blows. Fresh air and exercise were that precious.

My mind returned to the back I had seen, the still suppurating furrows, dark raised permanent swellings, the pot-holes where the tip of the whip must have dug more than once. A few scabs that seemed an inch thick. And his neck, even to the base of the head, covered in weals.

'They were flogged in the open, you said.'

'Yes.'

'And they screamed?'

Agu laughed. 'My friend, you must invent new word. You are an English specialist not so? Invent new word.'

'But Gowon lives in those barracks. He must have heard the screams.'

Agu said, 'Frankly I don't think he knew. He lived far away from the guardroom.'

'Those screams must have penetrated concrete,' I insisted.

Agu persisted. 'I don't think he knew. I don't think even some top officers knew. Oh, there were bastards among them, but, for instance, take that guard who used to let us empty the bucket eleven times in one shift. So there were also decent ones.'

The student looked at Agu for some time. 'We've had this out before. Agu really believes in this er ... what does he call himself again – ah yes, God's Chosen Implement.' He turned to me, 'In that dungeon I kept thinking for a long time about what character he reminded me of. I hit it finally. It was when the screams of the tortured men reached me in the cell that I remembered. You must know Flecker.'

'Flecker's *Hassan*?'

Agu looked puzzled. 'Hassan had even less to do with it. He never came there.'

'Not the Brigadier,' I explained, '*Hassan* is the title of a play.'

'Your own?'

The student continued: 'That was the picture that came to my mind. The picture of a quiet sadist who dined and wined and lulled himself to sleep with the sounds of the tortured.'

Agu gave up. 'I no longer know what you two acadas are talking about.'

After a while the student said, 'The hunger strike was my idea.'

'It was a good one,' I said. 'The question is, how long you all can keep it up.'

'The whole day for everybody. Those who can't will scrounge something off prisoners some way or the other. It does not matter. Do you know what brought things to a head in my mind? It wasn't so much the conditions, even though that's bad enough. We are not after all animals, to be cooped up like this. No, it's the army detainees and prisoners that caused it. They are in that block opposite. One has got six years for stealing army beddings and furniture. Another was given two for forging petrol vouchers and selling the stuff. Several sentences like that for petty infringements and so on. Then two weeks ago a corporal was brought in – he wasn't yet tried or court-martialled mind you. He was sent by his field-officer to Lagos to be made an example of. He had shot thirteen detainees in Asaba including some prisoners-of-war. In cold blood. They were kept together in a stockade and he was on guard. A young man, a Yoruba, quite a nice boy. They all come here to use the table tennis with the V.I. Prisoners. He admitted shooting them in panic, said they were talking in Ibo and he asked them to speak only English. They ignored him. He decided that they were plotting something so he turned his machine-gun on them and killed them.

'He was released two days ago, re-assigned to a new division. He was right outside here when the order for his release came. They were all discussing it, his fellow soldiers I mean. Even they didn't think much of that system of justice.'

'Did they say who signed the order?'

'Only that it came from the office of the Chief of Staff. The boy was the most surprised of the lot. Expecting a court-martial and at least several years in gaol. Ah well, I supposed one day apiece for a murdered Ibo is quite sufficient.'

'It is war,' shrugged one of his cell-mates.

'I thought of that. Then I asked myself, if it is war why are those petrol forgers in gaol? No, it is only part of the same slow extermination process. It's been bred into them. A free-for-all epidemic. That young man had done his bit, he is set free. The silly prison governor is also doing his bit, that is why he dehumanizes us. I needed to do something in protest no matter how vague or irrelevant.'

I assured him it was not irrelevant.

'I am afraid you know. I am very much afraid for the Mid-West. Even after the whole place is completely retaken and there is no more shooting. The Northern atrocities will be child's play to it.'

There was silence in the cell. Each occupant within it had his own memory of that massacre and became occupied with in. The food staled under their doors neglected. The student's voiçe could not have carried yet it was easy to feel that that indelible trauma had communicated itself to the rest of the detainees, so quickly did a hush of depression spread through the other cells. The student stood against the window looking beyond me. I became conscious of my superfluity and walked quietly away. The cells as I came past them seemed peopled by corpses, propped against the walls.

Evening and the Superintendent came accompanied by the food detail. But he was no longer comic with his blustering and threatening which he yet managed to combine with the beginning of pleading and promises; he was merely obscene. Again and again came the whine in his voice, 'But what exactly is your complaint? Just tell me, what is your complaint?' No one heeded him or spoke. He ordered the doors opened and the food placed in the cells. The doors clanged to again but the prisoners did not move. When his footsteps had receded, we heard the sounds of aluminium bowls scraping on the ground. Soon the corridor was lined with bowls of untouched meals.

Night. The monstrous, aggressive, yet mournful stridencies of gates falling to, and bolts themselves imprisoned in airtight holes. Each prison has its quota of lunatics; before long the cry of one from a distant block began to pour out the dark secrets of his soul. A clank of his restraining chains accompanied it; at night these sounds came clearly over the air of Shaki. It was near full moon, his howl was part of the motion of that leprous intrusive eye.

Towards midnight it had begun to fade from consciousness, merging simply into the silence of dreams.

When the new sound came, a short while before midnight

it did not appear to belong to our world, nor to that world that faded daily outside these walls. An alien sound, it began as a soothing flow, welling into a dark flood, coiling in and out of the night. It touched and wrapped itself around the skin, gentle as sleep, yet too strange to be part of what we were, what we daily felt, what assailed or sustained us. I knew it came from somewhere deep down in earth, from crushed soil, I knew the fragile tentacles of pain and triumph.

That brutalized humanity beneath us were singing, and the listening bodies of inmates became a tangible, communal thing. I felt that every soul in that block was wide awake, listening, hardly daring to breathe or move. Nobody could remember for how long they sang. No one shouted, no one complained that his sleep was disturbed. It lasted between two or three hours, perhaps, each song flowing into the next with hardly a break. A song ended, a new voice commenced another and almost with its first notes it sounded as if it was a continuation of the last. A mood of anguish and strength pervaded it all. Nothing but the sound of hymns at morning and evening prayers had been heard ever before from those people. Now suddenly in the dead of night the darkness in their hearts had called up sounds from hearth and shrine. It involved us all, strangers to their homes, in one common humanity.

And this was confirmed the following morning. Even the stool-pigeon had been moved, and perhaps even secretly shamed. With the ascent of those night voices we had heard the loosening not merely of their bonds, but ours, felt the roof eased off to unveil a common sky. They wound their voices round our innermost guts and made each man partake of the brotherhood sacrament of blood and guilt and pain.

Almost simultaneously as the cell gates were opened the following morning came the question from everyone's lips, 'Did you hear them? Did you hear them last night?' And the accompanying response, 'I couldn't sleep. Even after they stopped I couldn't sleep.' Gnarled blooded criminals and even the most rabid of the NNDP convicts whose entire political faith was Ibophobia stopped on their way to the bathroom at the cells of their arch political enemies. I heard them say, 'Did you hear them? Did you hear them singing?' It was the first time that they had ever acknowledged the existence of Ikoku and Adebanjo but they had to share the experience and these two they felt were the most sensitive creatures close at hand. Each sought an explanation without demanding it, each sought a significance that was not easily definable. Each grew afraid of the response that had been elicited within himself and its interpretations and demands. Above all, there was the consciousness in them, for the first time perhaps, that physical bonds and anguish had been transcended if only for a few hours, by these, the lowest vermin by official grading, of the prison community.

Yon da Kolo, alone still in his privileged oasis among the waste, was the most visibly agitated. I went down to talk to him wondering how it had affected him on the same floor. I found him pacing angrily up and down his cell, giving voice to incoherent thoughts, angry at something he could not grasp, but mostly at himself. As soon as he saw me he exploded!

'Out of that filth? Out of that muck? Do you know, sometimes I have found myself nearly despising them simply for being treated as they are. It is easy you know. If you see misery long enough you grow to despise it. So what was that about? What was it that came out of them? You don't know, you weren't within this sound chamber with them. The whole thing . . . it was like being tortured. It was hurting me and yet it was . . . I don't know. You people are the writers. If you can't . . . Strength, that was it. Strength. It had such strength you know. It gave me strength, even while it hurt me. I have never been through a night like that, never in my life.'

He passed my cell upstairs about an hour later, clutching his soap and towel and stopped to explain. 'I gave up. I have been trying to screw up courage to walk past their cells to the bathroom but I couldn't do it. It's as if I am scared I will find something in their faces which is not human. I tell you, I can't forget this night.'

Adebanjo said, 'I wish the human ecologist could have heard them.'

Footnote to the Red Cross

When you visited the prisons in December 1967, I watched from my window as you inspected the lines of Ibo detainees in the courtyard outside the block. The day before your arrival their cells had been opened, for over two hours for the first time in more than a month. The prison governor, the clown whom I call Generalissimo, had issued orders himself, only a month before, that they were to be issued no more soap. Not only that, he ordered the warders to remove *all* unfinished scraps of soap from the cells. The reason was that the detainees had complained that they were not receiving their normal entitlement of soap. And this was true. Soap which should come to them was being short-rationed by a complicity of the trusties and some warders. So for a month until yesterday they have had no soap.

Yesterday however, the magic day, their cells were opened, they were given soap and made to wash their clothes and blankets. They were aired and sunned, barbers were even provided for those who wanted a hair-cut. That line of clean-smelling detainees whom you saw was not therefore the mass of refuse who had lain unwashed, in unhygienic conditions for months. They had to be brought out in the open of course so that you would not see the evidence of overcrowding. Did you connect the space in that lower block with the number of detainees outside?

Finally, it is elementary that you insist on speaking privately to prisoners. Your standard questioning of prisoners surrounded by their keepers, about their conditions, was a painful farce to watch. The prospect of reprisals for giving a wrong answer is surely not unknown to you. If you cannot 'investigate' thoroughly, don't visit political prisons at all; it feeds the inmates nothing but false hopes.

14

THEY came in the middle of the night, a senior officer accompanied by three warders. The latter were swathed in their black night capes, the former adopted a manner and tone that was brusque and final. As they fumbled with the lock my mind leapt instinctively to the former attempt on my life at the Medium Security.

'Pack your things!'

It was barked like an order to a dog, yet so distant was my mind at this point from their immediate presence, so wrapped up in the shadowy walk I was about to take that I obeyed him like an automaton. And the other corner of my mind, instinct with all prison survival needs, had begun to plot how I could distract him sufficiently to unearth my scraps of paper, the pencil stub, the notes I had prepared for the next access to my outside contacts...

I was relieved to find that some other detainees were awake and had gathered near the entrance to my cell – their cell doors were never locked at night. Adebanjo in particular, had drawn close to one of the warders and I could hear his stage whisper above the noise I continued to make with latrine box and bucket – 'Where are they taking him?' With a corner of the eye I saw the warder shrug.

How had they failed to warn me this time? I thought of G. and my two comrades. Had their Intelligence finally broken down?

As I stepped outside my cell, Ikoku asked me if there was anything I needed and forced me to take some of his cigarettes. Adebanjo pressed his towel on me. I accepted them, thinking, I may need nothing where I am going.

The officer stepped aside and I led the way. At the end of

the corridor, with the pressure of that narrow passage increasing my fears and the heavy menace of those warders behind me I stopped and turned round, shouted at the top of my voice:

'I want you all to know that I shall make no effort to escape. If anything happens to me take note of that!'

As we went down the stairs I heard Olu Adebanjo's voice ringing up and down the corridor telling all the inmates to take note, reminding them that I was leaving that block in the middle of the night, hale and sound for an unknown destination. We walked through the desert stretch of the prison grounds, my bundle under the armpit of a warder. At the office the three guards departed, leaving me alone with the officer and an elderly type on duty. The former retained his scowling but finally took his depressing existence somewhere else. Before he returned the old man looked at me for a while then burst out suddenly:

'Why don't they leave you alone? Where are they taking you this time?'

I turned up my palms to indicate my helplessness in such matters. Suddenly the Generalissimo erupted on the scene, in mufti. He was full of beans as if he was engaged in some uplifting operation on behalf of humanity. At that hour of the night this incredible being appeared newly scrubbed, oiled and groomed, bubbling with a mysterious happiness through his magnificent agbada.

'Got everything? Oh, that's right. Have you been given your book?'

'What book?'

'Haven't they given you your book? The book you wrote.'

He dashed off, returning with a copy of *Idanre*. I had not seen one till then. I turned it over in my hand. There was this huge print of my name on the front. Miraculously, I felt a surge of upliftment at this new-minted tangible slice of my inner being between my hands. I turned it over, saw the photo on the back, I opened the pages. It fell open at the poem to my daughter.

I asked the man, 'Why are you only giving me this now?'

He fluttered his hands. 'Oh, someone forgot to hand it to you before, that's all.'

'Where am I being taken?'

He stammered for an eternity. By the time he had got round to lying to the limits of inaudibility I had turned away and was reading my published poems.

And now the long wait began. An hour. Two hours. Then three. After two hours the restless Superintendent had given up and gone home, leaving me in charge of the Great Scowl. A telephone rang just before dawn, the officer answered it, turned round and announced.

'We are going back to the cell.'

That same afternoon G.'s belated note arrived. It was written to Dan and it said simply, 'Tell your friend not to panic if they come again.'

15

A Digression on the theme of ATROCITIES and COMMISSIONS and the LACUNAE in the mind of POWER

DIRECTLY after the liberation of the Mid-West from the grip of rebel vandals by the gallant Federal soldiers, the government of Gowon-Ogbemudia in the Mid-West immediately set up a Commission known as the ATROCITIES commission. The war was still on of course. If anything it was hotter, fiercer, more total than ever. The words were TOTAL WAR, TOTAL MOBILIZATION, CRUSHING BLOW, etc. Yet, in the midst of this summation of war-will, something was left over in both time and energy to enable the functioning of a Commission – the witnesses, the armed guards. the bureaucracy, and the expense. This was as it should be. It is necessary to record these things. The invasion in terms of this particular war and in terms of the – let us concede it – majority of the people of the Mid-West, was a crime. All crimes must be investigated, peace-time or war-time.

For me it was particularly welcome. I had, for a long time, begun to fear that this word ATROCITIES had gone out of fashion in our vocabulary and in meaning. After all the word does signify something. It identifies a phenomenon, defines a finished event or one in the making. It is indeed a most active word. Sometimes of course a word no longer serves, at least not by itself. Its reality must be validated by a response, by a positive acceptance or a counter-action. The Federal Mid-West government in setting up the Commission demonstrated to me that the word ATROCITIES evokes the latter response. It went further and demonstrated the precise form this counter-action should take. In my cell in Kiri-kiri, I was happy that this word had been rescued from desuetude.

The government of Ironsi seemed in its time to be no less alive to the responsibilities of this word, a responsibility which as shown above, was also given concrete form in November of 1967 by Yakubu Gowon. In May 1966 Ironsi appointed a Commission (same form of action) to inquire into ATROCITIES, known generally as the Minor Massacres in the North. This Commission was still at its work when Gowon seized (or was eased into?) power in June of that year. Publicly he declared that the work of the Commission would continue unhindered – this was one of his earliest statements to the nation. Privately he rendered the Commission defunct. The nation heard no more of this Ironsi-initiated Gowon-inherited Commission into the May ATROCITIES. It was, by the way, peace-time.

In September/October 1966 Gowon had an opportunity on a grand scale to launch a big commission of his own. He had every right *not* to believe in the value of Commissions into ATROCITIES. The silencing of the earlier (May) Commission indicated that this might be so. This was his privilege. A man, especially one with so much work to do, has the right to consider Commissions irrelevant in themselves. The following fact is therefore stated merely as a matter of record: in September/October 1966, another ATROCITIES did take place all over Nigeria including Lagos, the seat of Yakubu's government. But where it really manifested itself in grand style was in the North. The ATROCITIES were so public even in the South (Lagos) that delegates to a Constitutional Conference which had been launched by Yakubu Gowon were physically man-handled by Gowon's Army right in view of the House of Assembly buildings where these constitutional talks did take place. Man-hunts, publicized by machine-gun stutters, took place around Ikoyi where Gowon lived, and the executions and torture games that went on in his official residence, Dodan Barracks, on civilians who were simply arrested on the public road — Ikorodu checkpoint was the favourite kidnap point – were common daylight occurrences known to Yakubu Gowon. As for the events in the north – let us simply sum it up and say that ATROCITIES did take place on a scale so vast and so thorough, and so well-organized that it was variously referred to as the Major Massacres (as distinct from the May rehearsals), genocide, and sometimes only as disturbances and – this gem is by Ukpabi Asika – a state of anomy! Yakubu Gowon himself went far enough to put it under the broad sphere of ATROCITIES in his *appeal*. The word itself, appeal, is significant. It tells much about Mr Gowon. The italics are mine:

Fellow Northerners,

Today I want to direct this appeal specifically to you all.

I had very much wanted to visit you personally because I know that there are many of you who have never met me before, but this visit has not been possible owing to pressure of work.

You all know that since the end of July, God, in his power, has entrusted the responsibility of this great country of ours, Nigeria, to the hands of another Northerner . . .

This important point (important to Gowon) he reiterates, for it is clearly the Northerners who need to be appeased, not the victims. The effect of such appeasement language on the maimed and mangled victims is, of course, unimportant. So again he re-emphasizes the point:

Here I would like to repeat what I have said earlier. The responsibility for the well-being of Nigeria is today in *our* hands and this is a responsibility which cannot be treated lightly.

Light treatment of responsibilities should not, of course, be defined to embrace the sectional provocation of this statement, nor can any but the most rabid anarchist suggest that one way *not* to take responsibilities lightly is to avoid a tone of *appeasement* in face of ATROCITIES. However, let us continue:

Since January this year, when some soldiers put our country into confusion by killing our leaders, both political and military, the country has not recovered fully from that confusion.
The sadness caused in people's minds by the January event has led to troubles by civilians in the North in May, causing loss of lives.
I receive complaints daily that up to now, Easterners living in the North are being killed and molested, their property looted. *I am very unhappy about this.* We should put a stop to these. *It appears that it is going beyond reason* to the point of recklessness and irresponsibility ...

I think I am going beyond reason!

Notes added some days later:

I have just remembered what I set out to say: Now that the ATROCITIES Commission lacuna in the tabloid of power mentality has been filled up in the October 1967 (Mid-West) awakening I wonder if, having cleared the Mid-West of the last remaining intruders and, fully secured and carapaced in the shining armour of an ATROCITIES-free nation, an ATROCITIES Commission will now be set up to inquire into butchery and torture of the Mid-West Ibo civilians by Federal troops and their civilian aides. In Shaki before my transfer I received eye-witness accounts from a Federal soldier, a young school-leaver who saw his ideals shattered by the wanton execution of civilians. He protested, then, feeling that his life was in danger, deserted and fled to Lagos. He was arrested and incarcerated a week later. The daily executions and torture were still in progress when he left. He saw entire families wiped out in cold blood. ATROCITIES? Or simply – war?

Kaduna 68

16

THE procession begins from the Superintendent's office. Safari-file, a row of porters share a misery of possessions, hardly a burden for a five-year-old, and we begin the journey through animal cages. Interlocking cages, they appear to the uninitiated as mazes designed by mad scientists for testing the intelligence of mice. Who will test your intelligence, slaves, yours and these animals whose snarls you obey? For diabolical occupations, oh yes, that kind of cunning needs no testing. I shall be your evidence, your scientific witness. From mice to men is one easy intelligent step, cages and mazes to disorientate the mind. Called testing. Or conditioning. And perhaps it is useful to begin there, novitiate, that these cages are part of the whole business for assessing something. And the assessors? The worse for them that they know not what they do. Dismiss them then for inconsequences? Tools? Mere functionaries of the process? Contemptible errand-boys for a reality which alone is *you*? No self-deception now, you know they have the power to hurt. True, but so has a slimy, poisonous snake, striking blind.

Cages. Cages of concrete and a mere wicker-gate of corrugated iron for passage. A stolid form guards such loopholes and the gate itself is a barrier of heavy bolts, unspeakable padlocks. A hand is inserted through a hole in the gate, an eye peeps through, a key is turned and a bolt drawn. We pass through. Again journey's end not yet in sight. A disembodied hand wrestles free bolts that thunder in each yard of echoes, always that square-cut hole in the gate, a torturer's hand and the gate opening inwards, pulled to hide face and body of the door-keeper. Are you afraid of me? Or ashamed, that you cover yourself with a shield? Or come to that, why does it take eight men to lead me to my cell? Four before and four behind. Is the mere presence of a uniform no longer sufficient talisman?

A question in every eye of the inmates exercising in their yards: who is he? Who is this new victim? The pace is fast through the catacombs. But for certain 'technical' hitches I know of, you would have brought me in the night, sneaked me in to avoid the questioning eyes and their inspired suspicions. Nothing escapes a prisoner, least of all the details of a new inmate. Within a few hours they will work it out bit by bit, comparing deductions until truth is attained. Yet another cage. And the same hand reaching through the square-cut hole ... suddenly I touch, then embrace a conviction – we will never reach destination. There is none to reach. We shall go walking down these passages for an eternity. I shall go down eternal passages with a squelch of boots before and behind me on arid gravel, I and those rags of my human possession borne before me like a publication of felony. We will walk down the unending passage and the procession will fall off one by one, one before and one behind and with them even these dubious proofs of my human landmark.

Except for Polyphemus. Polyphemus – the name springs effortless, naturally to the mind – Polyphemus is unriddable. Unriddable of? Certainly unreadable. (You are pleasant, novitiate, you still have the capacity for these little pleasantries? Polyphemus will force pleasantries from the other side of your mouth, you wait.) He brings up the rear does Polyphemus but I cannot rid my mind of him, of that early presence in the office as my items were checked and his eyes sized me up waiting for that moment when the official aspect is over and he is alone with his dinner: me. Black enough to puzzle the loudest black purist for new black definitions, Polyphemus is eight feet tall, a thickly cicatriced tower of menace who grunts, looks quickly away when I plumb his vacant depths with a glance, then furtively commences his inspection of a strange morsel which might try his digestion. If there are racks at the end, thumbscrews, rubber truncheons and wet towels I know Polyphemus will be the priest of the rites of submission. Not cigarette burns mind you, not electrodes on nerve organs or any such refinements. Polyphemus belongs to the heave and hurl, slap and spatter treatment. When marrow is visibly on the walls he might pause, puzzled.

I know at once when we reach destination. The walls are higher and the crown of broken bottles, tunnels of barbed wire even more forbidding than before. And now the fore file pause and make way for Polyphemus to come up to the gate. A key emerges from the folds of his flesh, an enormous form slouches over the lock. Huge as the padlock is, it vanishes in his palm. I use the few moments of waiting to sweep round this cage and encounter the incredible stare of a monkey. Crouched as if on the verge of leaping he metamorphoses after all into recognizable humanity albeit irredeemably mad. So thin that he is nearly fleshless, his skin is of a dirty ash with cinders of jutting bone and a fixed grinny stare on his face. My guards nudge each other and point at him. The madman is a friendly joke. Quickly my eyes race through other faces. Another inmate further off stares with a face full of compassion. Damn you ! Damn you and all like you ! Offer nothing but hatred. Hate. The pure burning flame of hate to warm you through the damp and hone your spirit to a fine weapon for survival. Not pity for the victims fool but simply, no more victims ! Else simply lay down and die.

A ragged, comic sight my pieces of possession. Comb, an off-white vest shrunken from wash and usage, a spare pair of trousers glossy from usage, a hand-towel, toothbrush and paste – the aspirins and the thalazole have been seized pending doctor's inspection; the following day he does release them – and three books from my last abode, piecemeal from over-usage and from rains that came suddenly one night flooding everything in the cell. Later even these disappear one morning, no warning, no reasons given. Pens, pencil, all scraps of paper swept away, even to the empty cigarette carton whose linings provided precious writing material.

It happens just a few days after. To a set, clearly much-practised drill, a search squad burst into the yard and break off in every direction. They search all crannies, poke in the ground, turn out the beds, and shake out the holes in the net. It is a small pocket yard so they fill it without effort, their boots tramp over my skin where I stand just outside and watch. Polyphemus gives the directions but the exercise takes place under the placid supervising eyes of a senior officer. Their mission however is not merely to take. The first stage over, my being disinfected of all corrupting and sustaining (and menacing!) presence of paper and print, the essentials of living are checked and where missing or inadequate, provided or substituted. And I stand thus equipped: Outside – a shower (without the shower); a latrine, a hole through a concrete base, squatting. Inside – Sleeping Cell; a water-bucket with lid; an aluminium cup and bowl; an iron bed; a mattress of unyielding matter; a blanket, a browned but clean-washed sheet, a hard, undigested lump that is the pillow; a box latrine with pail for night use; four raffia stalks on the bed corners propping up the filthiest mosquito net conceivable, a dust-trap unused and unshaken for, I soon discover, reasons of its obvious futility in barring entrance to any creature smaller than a crow. Blind. Flying full wing-span. In the other cell, the 'Daytime' Cell: a chair, a table, another latrine box but meant as a cupboard for food supplies. This latrine-box is made of brown wood and though washed, permanent discolourations on the wood mentally contaminate everything. The breaking-point comes one day when I reach behind it and a plague of mosquitoes rise from its dark crevices, fat as bluebottles (the real bluebottles are fatter than bees), their dark-laden bellies instantly suggestive not of the blood of prisoners from over the wall – all that blood cannot have come from ME! – but of filth and corrupting flesh and excrement. Crazed by the sight I attack them with a broom then toss out the latrine box and the food on it. The following day a cut-out kerosene tin is supplied.

The cells, non-adjoining, are the middle pair in a four-cell hut within the isolation yard. The others are permanently locked. Each cell measures four feet by eight. Normally this is the punishment block, the cries of the prisoner undergoing 'treatment' from here would reach no one at all except perhaps that last cage adjoining mine, and that is the hard-case cage reserved for lunatics, lifers and the violent ones. Most of those who come for a disciplinary spell in this yard would come from there anyway. But these are later discoveries. My present inventory of objects and their lives extend only to my high-ceilinged cells (to prevent suicide by hanging I suppose), the tiny windows set high in the walls, opening only to a horizon of bottle-traps and barbed wire, the exercise space round the hut within the yard, the hostile presence of the guard doomed – oh yes, doomed – to lock himself in the yard and make his eternal rounds until relieved. And the deep, leaden knowledge of a breachless isolation that comes from seeing oneself at the mercy of faceless, anonymous forces.

I recognize, and welcome the beginning of a withdrawal process, an accentuation of the imposed isolation by an instinctive self-isolation. I find first of all that my body rejects all objects, a process which did not take place during my four months in Lagos. The very contrary took place in Lagos.

My body adjusted to its surrounding, picked up a rhythm of the prison, accepted and absorbed the pulse, sounds, the touch of objects and the feel of food. It reacted only against things which would normally disgust me: filth and bad smells, treachery between the prisoners, callousness among the warders. I slipped into prison life as one dives into a stream, an unnatural element but one to which the body does adjust. The reverse has happened here. I reject everything, make no contact. One object after another is rejected by my skin. Lying down, even this involves no contact. Walking, I do not feel I touch the ground. The process accelerates towards total completion. Reality is killed and buried with memories of the past. Words play a part of it, hypnotizing the mind and desensitizing the body. For instance, as the last gate was opened I found I had set up an aimless cycle of words. Over and over it repeated itself, over and over until my conscious mind at long last took note of this incantation. A quotation from a long-forgotten book? Or simply the creative mind's originality-at-all-costs variant of that familiar theme: Abandon hope all who enter here? No matter, it goes thus and in an accent of bell chimes: In time of evil come I to this place of evil brought by evil hands and who knows but I may come to evil in this evil place ... Then it begins over again. Only now, weeks later do I recognize that I had embossed it over the archway of the last gate as Polyphemus palmed the huge padlock in his strangler's hands and the gate swung open into hell.

All sounds now beat against, not the spiked walls of the yard but against the cell walls. I have begun to close in. The process is helped by my most able tormentor, Ambrose. Other guards mostly choose for their beat the perimeter of the yard, walking leisurely inside the walls and casting dutiful glances at the cell as they pass the front of the hut. Not Ambrose. He walks right on the paved front of the hut, turns at the end, then marches back again. Literally pacing up and down. Bastard! Who is the prisoner, me or you? One thing I have not done, strictly avoiding doing, is pacing. As yet. Ambrose's hobnailed boots up and down the corridor – I refuse to look, to see or acknowledge him – his heavy military tramp, the mind-blowing monotony of his pacing forces me, consciously now, to accelerate the pace of my indrawing. There is no other protection. But it means also that the outer lines of defence are being abandoned. Even distant sounds now beat not as before on the walls of the yard, then of the cells, but directly on walls of the mind, losing direction and perspective. I decide it is a better choice. Let the world now centre on my person. Ambrose at his pacing again, and the capsule is not yet complete, not yet airtight, torment-resistant. A great rage engulfs me and I know I am close to violence or surrender. I can ask him nicely or order him angrily to move away. Both have an equal chance of success for one thing has become clear to me in this place – I don't know what the warders have been told or what views they hold in their knowledge of me but this fact is obvious: without exception they stand in a certain awe of me. That they would not hesitate to put an end to my life if ordered I am equally sure of. But they are full of deference. A factor that is stored away in my inventory, to be used when and as required and possibly reinforced.

Of Ambrose's pacing I decide finally – do nothing. Master it, banish the sounds, get used to it. Ask for nothing, reject nothing visible. Betray nothing, nothing of what affects you. Indicate neither pleasure nor pain, neither thrill nor disgust. Build up the self-protective capsule, smooth, leaving no handhold for them to seize on. Paint one unchanging grin on that capsule and let their probing minds be matched by its vacuity.

But still the past intrudes. And since I have successfully

killed the vulnerable past – love, ties, memories of genuine self-fulfilment – it is immediate events that crack the protective capsule, forcing futile rage and opening doors to self-recrimination. Such a mood can only turn up the soft under-belly towards the torturers. I set about the only choice, but with deliberation. I begin to relive the entire sequence of events even in time-span though not always quantitatively exact. In fact, hardly ever. Thoughts, even memory, flash through the mind with a regal contempt for the crucifying ache of planning, waiting, executing, waiting, concluding and recommencing in active time. Again and again I effect a brake: you have all the time in the world, fool. A few months reliving a few months past means a few months obliterated in an empty future. It will, I slowly acknowledge, become the pattern of existence. Only control it Kronos! Control the debris or memory in the waters of Lethe. A little at a time, making it in turn obliterate the concrete reality of the present. The pun amuses me though I shrink from the concrete floor.

Water is the only exception to this body rejection. As rain from the sky or even at its most frozen in the harmattan I go under the showerless pipe and beat my brains into place beneath the force of a fireman's hose. Cleansed, isolated, often in the afternoon with a rainbow hanging on the sprays. A solid turbo-roar as its jet pounds the concrete floor – *then* my feet do not shrink from the floor. But after, the slowing walk into a patient coffin . . .

17

Hraagrh hraagrh hraagrh . . . ptuh – splat!
Pig!
Hraaagrh hraaagrh hraaagrh . . . ptuh – splat!
Pig!
Hraaaaaagrrrrh hraaaaaagrrrhaaarrh . . . ptuh – splat!
Vile heathen pig!

Not that there is edge to the anger. Nothing but a weary flaccid rage, a tired incredulity . . . do animals like you exist? Do you belong to the same species as lay claims to souls, to sensing and thinking? . . . The sordid threesome is over for now, my fingers unplug the ears – a futile effort in any case; this slough depth expectoration breaks all anti-sound barriers. Nothing resists the odious trough when it tunes itself for scouring. Average eighteen times in a single shift. His naming was easy – Hogroth. Slowly the stomach settles back and ceases to heave. Three months already and yet I have not learnt to live with it. I know I never will.

Sometimes he gives warning. I heard his scabby hand dip in the fire-bucket and soon after, a slosh of water doing the rounds of his cola-coated mouth. That is when my fingers fly to plug the ears. I know what will follow. Unfailingly, as if all the toads were one and that mighty fulsome toad was wedged in his throat – Hraaaargh! – and splat! – the gob of spittum hitting the wall.

This man, this thing has a family. He has wives, he has children, he has more than likely some other family hangers-on who defer to him and call him Baba. Certainly friends call on him and he calls on neighbours. He attends public places, stands among a crowd to stare at some bleak wonder, spends a day at some social occasion, an evening in a local pub, makes one with the vacuous presence of others at a hundred officious doings. Well then, do you make that porcine sound at all these occasions and in any sort of company? Yes you, pig, you with your concrete mixer throat, regurgitating mortar and slag and dung plaster? Do you?

Four yards away a gob of slime hits the grass verge of the gutter, the end of a blurred arc that begins on *ptuh*! and ends in *splat*! The churning in the throat is resumed, preparing the world for another goro*-gritty gob. Pacing, sitting, talking through the hole in the door to his fellow guard on the other side, even as he dozes off on an upturned bucket head fallen back against the wall, a mouth of many colours opened wide, a pock of carious teeth, green-yellow fungused, a thick cola-varnished roof vanishing through dark inlets into rancid vats, somewhere in the midst of his marshland wanderings a strand of cola tickles the treadmill lining of his throat and switches on the dread infliction, a threesome dredging follows and the reddened slime is ejaculated on the world. He does not wake. The accompanying snores are uninterrupted.

His neck is twin to the vulture's. Identical twin, loose skin scroungy, withered and blotchy. It would take little to put an end to the scourge except – how does one live after with the recollection and feel of contact with that flesh, however brief? I have no spare hands for the job. Still, left with no choice one could scrub the skin until it all comes off. Plenty of time to grow a new one while spending a whole life in gaol. If hanging then it makes no difference. If life, scrub the hands until they bleed and sit in the sun until all contact is burnt out. But never again would any guard, close-imprisoned with a solitary, dare inflict such revulsion on his charge. Hogroth dead. New glow in the universe. I hear the prison celebrating. The trouble is, how many of them does

*Local term for colanut.

one kill. For there are others. Each, with hardly any exception has developed his own brand of harassment. It works through sound because the crypt is an echoing chamber. On high and low register they come to the repository, to the maleficent magnifactory of sounds. From the neighbouring Slough of Despond we, the crypt and I, hear the cries of souls in torment, the wail of flagellants, wolverine howls in the dead of night, mumbled dialogue with unseen spirit visitors, the mad cackle of hyenas. On select aerial highways they pass into the Crypt, magnified a hundred times, re-echoed in mind chambers a thousandfold.

The Sow is another enemy. No, not the Sow so soon after Hogroth. Take Caliban, light relief.

Caliban, I have never seen. Visually he remains a mystery. But I know he has a leg and a half. Or three. Certainly one leg is twice the length (or the weight) of the other, their uneven thuds are unmistakable as he pounds his nightly round in the hollows of my head. Shuffle, then sledge-hammer. In the dead of night, to the shuffle-clump rhythm of his unequal strider of wraith of smells passes and re-passes. It is the reek of yeast in extreme fermentation, a passage of stink-bugs trapped in cheap oily scent – is he so liberal with scent because he must disguise the stench of alcohol? Caliban drinks a private potion unknown to man or beast and the combination of his exhalations and the scent fill the cell even from his brief passes.

And Caliban sings. In the dead of night, to a rhythm of the shuffle-clump Caliban breaks into a colloquy in the very idiom of his strides – alternate bars of a mystery dirge first into himself and then in a reckless challenge to the heavens. The sky is cowed by the potent breaths and wisely stays mute. From a remote corner of the yard comes a new sound, shattering the sky-soul monody of Caliban. It is the battle of his rain-cape tangled in the watering-can or caught in the throes of the lemon-bush. The battle lasts a long time. First, the silent struggle, transmitted wholly by the violent shakes of the bush or the howls of the watering can and Caliban's boots seeking firmer purchase on the treacherous gravel. Then curses intrude, forced from the tortured soul of Caliban. His long disrupted one-two tempo broadens now to equally uneven slithering steps and now the monster, keenly analytic in the depths of his inebriation, circles cape and obstacle for several minutes, then convinced finally that only a surprise attack will work, leaps again into the fray with a strong torrent of coercive curse.

Sleep drifts slowly back through the night's assault, but once again is forced to retreat. A violent snap rends the air, a sailcloth snapping taut in the wind. It is Caliban once again. His cape is freed and now he shakes it out and spreads it for his five o'clock prayers. His chanting is designed to reach by sheer physical thrust the waiting deity on the other side of cosmos. He tells his beads with the same power of sound, snaps the sailcloth at the end of prayers, kicks the bucket once or twice, deliberately, a triumphant kick I can only suppose, resumes his uneven prowl until the arrival of his relief. Caliban never sleeps. Nor do I when Caliban patrols the night.

18

I HAVE mastered Ambrose's treadbeat but I am faced now with a new menace of sound; it drills the capsule, threatens to shatter it altogether. How this sound has remained so long unnoticed is, I think now, either a tribute to the power of the Ambrosian torment, or to my earlier powers of exclusion. Earlier, because the sonic torment is now apparent which it was not before.

It comes from the Grand Overseer who, followed by some five or six officials including Polyphemus and a junior cadet, makes his morning inspection. They sweep into view, he against the barred frame, shutting out the light, the others out of focus in the background. I wake invariably just a few seconds before the actual apparition, triggered alive by the sound of boots scraping to attention and the bolt in the yard gate savaged from its hole.

Till now it has been peaceful. Unseeing, unbeing – yes I believe I have even annihilated my being as I have the environment – a vague floating sensation is all that remains space and timewash. If ever the mind can be blank, truly blank, I have achieved it. From necessity, from an instinctive knowledge of the means of survival. Food, a mere chore. I permit it no taste, no pleasure or disgust, no contact physical or sensual, neither intimacy with my body nor recognition by the mind. At some point I have registered the pattern of food, instructing my body – eat this, always eat this. Reject this, your body can do without it. The oranges I eat, mastering my dislike of oranges. I hate the sticky bloodless acid that squirts from the rind, I am bored with the taste of orange itself. Not like tangerines, thin wedges of the sun in the mouth. Or the grapefruit. Not like a dozen other fruits with character. Not even like the mango which because equally sticky I hardly ever bothered to eat, but a fruit whose distinctive flavour I acknowledged. But oranges are the regulation fruits and its mundane flesh alas contains an inordinate amount of Vitamin C. That much I recall, so eat your oranges! Again and again I remind myself, this is no place to be ill.

But infections of the mind continue to threaten from all directions, and of these the sonic variety is the worst. And to this new barrage, the sound of a stuck record, I wake one harmattan morning – *Good morning how's today kck good morning how's today kck good morning how's today kck . . .* I struggle awake, and I know now that this record has been playing for weeks. A thin shifty face on the other side of the bars, the Grand Overseer on his rounds, inspecting nothing, remedying nothing, potent in no cause but to set my teeth on edge – good morning how's today kck good morning how's today kck good morning how's today.

Like yesterday bastard, and the day before. Like tomorrow and the long days after you insensitive blot!

I take to getting up as soon as the door is unlocked, my cell door that is, adding to the stretch of time that extra hour which was formerly killed by lying still in bed, doing nothing, feeling nothing, letting the fumes of sleep disperse slowly in their own time, sometimes drifting off again and postponing the encounter with walls, guards, food, wind and even sunshine. Shortening the day. Drifting with increasing ease into those exercises of weightlessness which, when at liberty, I would perfunctorily practise for a few moments' relaxation. I take to rising earlier, walking off the tension of waiting for the predictable mindless greeting. In the open air I feel somehow less vulnerable.

A tactical error. In bed the scream was muffled in the cocoon of a relaxed body, the oath that accompanied my shrinking from the non-greeting when I would feel, literally, like climbing up the wall. Any noise which I made through the blankets he had been only too happy to receive as satisfactory response to his set inquiry. I varied it each day: from 'Growing into sunset' to 'Like your grandmother's cunt'. Muffled in blanket or pillow it sounded the same to him. I was a fool to abandon my prone advantage. Now with his thin face in three-dimension of the open air, no longer cardboard flat, pinched flat against the bars, with the returned tension of seeing him and waiting for the greeting I have to fight off the temptation to clap both hands against his cheeks at once. For I have this growing conviction, that if only I can bring off this assault, his face would flatten into a record between my hands. I would pick up the disc and smash it against the wall, silencing the silly trick for all time.

I flee back to the refuge of the bed. The persecution continues. It is harmattan and no man in his senses takes a cold shower before mid-day, but now only this defence remains. I gather sponge and soap, flee into the frozen sanctuary of the open bathroom. When I hear the imperious tap of his swagger-stick on the gate I turn on the tap. A shudder racks my body and an icy stream crushes my skull. But it is safety.

Back then to mending the capsule. The snail drawing in its horns, sealing the open end of the shell in hardened saliva. A porcupine rolling into a winter ball of amnesia. Leafdrop, sunmotes even hailstones I may ignore. But not *iska*. Not that lacerating harmattan wind of the North. Not in a cell with one wall which is mostly a door whose upper half is entirely open except for half-inch bars. Iska makes nonsense even of the lower half. Its wooden pieces leave gaps inches wide for the greedy penetration of the wind's malice and rage. For a harmattan windstorm the Crypt is the most perfect trap that was ever built. The wind hurls itself from wall to wall, batters at and shakes the hut, howling and wheezing alternately like an infernal machine poised between explosion and roaring into space. I hear it distinctly gather in the corridor just outside my cell, pause there and regroup, commence a new assault in simultaneous directions knifing my blood vessels, dehydrating bone and marrow. Then the cell becomes a new centre of the storm, the wind pours through every crevice, building up to an unbearable pressure of ice before it gradually releases itself through the open bars and the ceiling-high window. The cycle continues through the night. Sleep during its pauses is marked by one dream and one dream only. I am glazed in a block of ice during a magic show having foolishly volunteered to be sawn in two by a magician who loses his nerve and absconds. Screaming or, rather, gesturing with rolling eyes for help, some of the audience rush on stage and attack the glacier with hammers. I wake to the pounding of iska on my chest.

Good morning how's today kck good morning how's – Cold! I need an extra blanket. What? How many have you got? One. What! Only one? He turns to Polyphemus. Chief, do supply him an extra blanket from the store. Store? Yes, I think we get some. I supply him today.

It is the second time, I reflect, that I have broken my law of survival. The first was over the mosquito net. Genuinely alarmed by the daily river of blood on the bed sheet, by swarms of mosquitoes which rose when disturbed from dark corners in daytime, fat blood-bloated mosquitoes in their hundreds, I resolved to demand a usable net. It was an argument with myself which I was glad to win. Listen, the thesis went, in the other blocks there are hundreds of inmates and the mosquitoes share this blood supply among them, at the most each inmate would receive the attention of four mosquitoes. You, on the contrary, are alone in this yard with at least a hundred mosquitoes to yourself. To demand a net is not therefore a privilege but a necessity. If denied, it is injustice. It was not denied. I received a net which was not only clean but had only three holes, all reparable.

That small triumph and the knives of iska promote my resolve to demand a blanket. A week later and the blanket is still to come. I have reminded Polyphemus twice. Kept longer in his bed by iska, or perhaps for more sinister reasons the Grand O proves not so religiously committed to his morning inspection as I once believed. I no longer see him. His assistant keeps up the duty a while, turning up muffled to the eye in overcoats and scarves. Head bowed to the wind he races through the yard, dumb. Finally even he gives up the pretence. It is a peaceful time. All records are silenced. The warders are wrapped perpetually in their great capes; regulation permits them now to wear thick sweaters under their khaki shirts. Without exception their chests are lined also with woollen vests, mostly of the military issue of World War I. Ear-muffs abound. Even the trusty who brings my food now wears flannel underwear. The night patrols are wrapped like eskimos, thick leggings and extra-felty capes. Polyphemus uses the strangest apparel of them all – a heavy military overcoat which seems rubberized. For the third time in two weeks I remind him of my need for a blanket. And the last time also. I resolve never to ask it again. Iska must be met in shirtsleeves and one blanket.

I have no ointments. Nor shoes. Only slippers. My body is the thick dusty centre of a dry cold. The skin has turned to scales, lips, palm and soles have turned old leather. I watch huge crevices yawn on my heels and the sides of the feet. My body becomes of a new absorbing interest to me, a new occupation to while away the hours. I have not till now taken much notice of the physical fact of the body, only of its sensations. Now it has become a strange terrain where flakes come off every part merely by rubbing. There is an inch-thick callous on the heels where the cracks have begun.

I peel off slabs of dead flesh, my nails breaking crisply in the effort. The lips are painful and bleeding, their cracks begin to contribute to the harvest of flakes. I rub my hands together only lightly and their static magnetizes bits of toilet paper. The hair crackles insanely when I pass a comb through it. It breaks off like tiny twigs.

The eyes suffer most from cold and dust. They have turned perpetually rheumy and the right one I fear is even impaired. I become convinced that its sight is going and wonder, would a monocle be amusing if I am compelled to wear glasses? Not here though, fat chance of that. Requests to see the doctor were received with a casual nod of the head. Interpreted it said simply, 'Request noted'. Later they were received with open boredom. The nurse came once, threw up his hands and shrugged his shoulders.

The game with my body has palled. My body, now defined as the touch of grime from my shirt, has begun to disgust me yet I dare not give the shirt to be washed until the sun is out again. I have only one choice: continue to take that afternoon shower even in the phase of a weak, rheumy sun or wash the shirt and remain in bed all day. After the shower I have desperate need of warmth from every clothing. And I have only the shirt and a vest with holes the size of those in my rejected net. The latter I can risk to the wash, but the shirt serves for a wind-cheater; if it fails to dry in an afternoon I am at the mercy of the evening fury.

A strange sensation with my skin. It has now reached a state of dehydration which makes it fissure, painfully. The process takes place in the hidden hollow of the back. It means I must make no sudden gestures. Stretching must be slow, I may not hunch suddenly and I may not stoop at all. I must move to permit a slow even cracking. I learn the lesson slowly, with sharp jabbing reminders. The fingers have become alien outgrowths, stiff at the joints, they require coaxing to perform the most ordinary chores. A cup which failed to adjust quickly to the added weight of water in it slips from my fingers. I learn to sense my grip more surely through a barrier of callous on the hands.

A brainwave. Until now, being no lover of margarine I have always sent back my supply to the kitchen (often pretending not to notice a warder slip it into his pocket to augment his family diet). Desperate now for some kind of ointment before my skin turns alligator hide, I begin to experiment with the margarine. I start with the contracting earth crust in the hollow of my back, contorting to grease it yet avoid the sudden skin-split. Then the lips, even the soles of my feet and of course the finger joints. Nothing will save the feet until the harmattan is over but all other scales surrender to the ministrations of margarine. Fingers, lips and hollow of the back become once more supple and human. It must be, I suspect, like moulting. In another week I acquire a smooth enviable skin, a skin that merely awaits discovery by a talent scout – then – contracts galore for advertisements for the latest beauty cream ! This skin . . . also . . . stinks horribly.

19

THE cadet came in one morning with an armful of neatly sliced sheets of paper yet bearing the familiar untidiness of cyclostyled bureaucracy.

'Good morning Sir. We have some forms for you to fill.'

His smile was the smile of the bearer of good tidings. I waited for him to explain what drew such joy in his innocence. He handed over a sheet of paper and his grin grew toothier. 'At least you won't have to worry about your family. Nothing more terrible than for a man to be here worrying about family problems.'

I held the form at an instinctive length of suspicion from my body. Very simply it required me to fill in the name and address of a beneficiary for my salary, then sign the form. On the other side were dotted lines for the name and address of employers.

'Whose idea is this?' I wanted to know.

'It s government order. Gowon has passed a circular to all government departments and corporations that the salaries of detainees must be paid in full to their dependants. Up to private firms and business companies. Every detainee must get paid.'

'And the self-employed?'

'Pardon?'

'The self-employed, who pays their salaries? Who looks after their dependants?'

A prolonged stare of blankness. Finally he said: 'Well, we don't know about that. All we know is that the circular has been, sent round and these forms arrived for filling. Why worry about all those jobless people? Your family is the main thing; charity begins at home.'

'In Lagos,' I explained, 'I was in a cell-block with a self-employed electrician, some farmers, petty traders, lawyers, a band-leader, and a salesman, to name only a few. Will they and the thousand similar types in all prisons receive these forms?'

'Certainly,' he answered me. 'We must distribute the forms to every detainee. That is the directive from head-quarters.'

I turned the form to him and pointed to the section where the name and address of employer must be filled. What will such people fill in this section? Isn't it to the address on that blank that the form must be sent?'

'Yes.'

'So what are they to write on that section? Who looks after their dependants?'

He took off his cap the better to scratch his head. Finally: 'I don't know.'

I returned the form to him. His incredulity was touching.

'You won't fill it, Mr Soyinka?'

'Gowon and his advisers can't wish justice away with this childishly obvious bribery.'

'But your family Mr Soyinka! I beg, think of them. How are they going to manage without ...'

'Don't worry, they won't starve. We have friends and we are a large family. My wife has a job.'

'Even if she is Rockefeller, Sir, money is money.'

'Not always. Or at least there is something called blood money. Or hush-money. Have you ever heard that phrase? Hush-money. It means payment to keep you quiet. Or to make you feel good towards your persecutors.'

'I don't agree sir. This money is not their money. It is your own money. Your salary. It is what you would be earning if they did not put you here. After all you are not a criminal. As far as I can see this shows the difference between convict and detainee. If you were a convict you would be sacked from your job. But you are still head of department, therefore you must be paid. That is what the government is saying.'

'You are wrong. Even if the scheme were widened to include everyone there is still the fundamental fraud. What gives them the right to play charity with public money when the situation demands only justice?'

He remained angrily concerned on my behalf. 'Sir, if you don't sign the form now your family will suffer for nothing.'

I reassured him, standing strangely apart from an alien ego that was eased out of doubts, indulging my starved strength with a sudden angry confidence.

'Everyday I spend in this hole will be paid for by someone. My work, my suspended life, my deprivations. It is not possible to measure such debts in terms of cash.'*

*In 1970, because I wanted time to devote to my writing I resigned from my job at the University of Ibadan. I gave no reasons, leaving the door wide open to the fantasies of an idle academic community. One of the favourite stories went this: That Yakubu Gowon had sent special instructions to the university to pay my salary entitlements for the period spent in detention, that on receipt of this unexpected nest-egg I had decided to take up a Hollywood contract and spend the rest of my life in glamour and clover.

I learnt for the first time also that after my formal detention, the University Administration decided that I had not *technically* taken up my post as Director of the School of Drama, and so the university had no financial obligations towards me.

Just as well that I declined Mr Gowon's charity.

20

A WEAK sun through filmy air, there was a lull in the harmattan blowing when the Grand Overseer at last re-entered the Crypt preceded by a warder who carried two chairs. Polyphemus brought up the rear, then hovered in the background as the dialogue progressed.

I had requested this interview. I saw life in Kaduna falling into a definite pattern or non-pattern. I knew the working of the routine-conditioned mind; if the purely fortuitous beginning suited the time, the facilities, work-shyness, lethargy or officiousness of the prison and its officers, then that beginning became set and unchangeable. Any possible improvement must be won early or put away from the mind thereafter. So one morning I interrupted his 'Good morning how's today' with a notice that my day would acquire a tinge of rosiness if he would deign, at his leisure, to grant me an interview. Only when you have the time, I insisted, I need about an hour at least.

Nearly three weeks later he found the time. I had naively thought that I would be led out to his office; instead he had elected that I play host though he would contribute the furniture. We sat outside, under the tepid sun.

'I have a number of questions,' I began, 'and requests. But the questions first since the latter would depend on the answers. I know I am here for a very long time . . .'

He made reproving noises: 'No, no, don't say that. You'll see how soon the war will end and then . . .'

'Even if the war ends today I will not be released. You see, I know why I was framed, so I've prepared my mind for a long stay. I am concerned only with how to make the best of living in these conditions. I wish to know what facilities the prison can offer me. Books for instance. What is the situation about books?'

He persisted. 'I don't know why you believe you will be so long in here. If you are completely innocent . . .'

'No. In time of war, no man is completely innocent. But I am completely innocent of the charges against me. For a start I can tell you truthfully that I made no confessional statement.'

'Tell me, how did you come to get involved in this affair?'

'I have not just become involved. I have always been involved. In May last year for instance I was up here.'

'Yes, I know.' When he saw my astonishment he explained, 'Only by chance. I met someone who saw you in a night club the day before the riots.'

I asked if it was anyone I knew.

'You won't remember him. But he knew you from your newspaper photographs. He mentioned it when we read the news of your arrest. I think he said he came over to your table and shook hands with you.'

'It's possible. I met many people on that trip. You see, we knew there was going to be trouble . . .'

He demanded suddenly, 'What did you think of the January 15th coup?'

I recognized the standard defence. Since the massacres of 1966 it had become the defensive approach not merely of those who, being Northerners, were most directly blooded in guilt but even of those who were made accomplices by acquiescence. In turn I gave him my standard reply:

'A mismanaged affair. The idealists were there and the basic motivation was of genuine revolutionary zeal. But the group also contained those who were not so pure in their motives.'

'Aha! Exactly. I mean, everybody knows that Nzeogwu* was quite sincere . . .'

*Leader of the January 1966 Coup.

Nzeogwu. Does he turn in his grave misused so constantly as a standard, automatic concession? I have watched tongues slide smoothly and easily from the direct challenge of a choice to the ends of unctuousness which his name was made to serve.

I said. 'Yes, the whole world knows about Nzeogwu.'

'And the killings were so wicked. They were simply one-sided.'

'It was a pity that any killing took place at all, but it is the rare and lucky revolution which manages to avoid blood. However, some of us saw the likely consequences of what you have rightly called the one-sided killings, that was what brought me up to the North. I was involved in a movement which tried to minimize, if not completely avoid the consequences. I was caught in the rioting. It is a callous thing to admit because death is a very individual thing, one shouldn't really measure it by statistics, but I was relieved that the death-toll was lower than what we had feared. And after June we thought, surely that was more than enough.'

I waited, inviting him to comment. Since he merely nodded ambiguously I asked him in turn, 'What did you think of the September massacres?'

His answer was a surprising departure. 'They were warned,' he said. 'I personally warned several of them.'

'The politicians?'

'No, my Ibo friends. Most of them were to blame for their own suffering. They couldn't say they had no warning.'

It was the strangest addition yet to the formulas of self-vindications. And yet another inadvertent refutation of the 'spontaneous' theory of that genocide.

I recalled another, my first, one that took place before the event. The revelation was made in a European capital where I had been attending a month-long programme, mostly cultural, in for me the strange role of a government nominee. The third nominee, Onuara Nzekwu, an Ibo, knew that it was as much as his life was worth to attempt to board the plane at Ikeja. Even I was turned back at the airport in an atmosphere of tension, filled with ominous manoeuvres by the soldiers on duty and could not leave for a week.

That I persisted in risking a renewal of that airport encounter was due, not to the value I placed on the seminar but to the periodic need which suddenly overwhelms me for some insulated period of existence away from tensions within the country. A hyper-charged involvement of the entire year, seared with losses of friends and comrades, smeared in the naked humiliation of an entire populace by an arrogant, raping, murdering, terrorizing soldiery, weeks (after July 29th) of running a sensitive link in the 'underground railroad' rescuing Eastern soldiers – Ibo, Efik, Ogoja, Rivers – and even some Westerners (these were merely hidden), of whom not even the lowest was too mean for a remorseless hunt-down by their colleagues (half my wife's wardrobe went on their disguise), impotent to answer and alleviate the thousand pleas for help that came to me from helpless civilians (Westerners, Mid-Westerners as well as Easterners) whose relations or friends lay in the whimsical grip of soldiers, witnessing daily the emasculation of a whole people by a band of vicious, opportunist outgrowths of the mystique of power – by the middle of September 1966 I was in that state when I would have charged an armoured tank with my head simply to spend forty-eight hours outside the country.

I regained my passport and, insisting this time on a daylight flight, spent the waking moments at Ikeja Airport pretending not to notice that Airport commandant of infamous doings who had come in with some men and sat only a few tables away eyeing me warily like one would a vulnerable but possibly indigestible morsel.

Perhaps the fact that I was a government nominee fooled that diplomat* in — into thinking that I was now a government man, a supporter of the Gowon regime, or perhaps the loyalist example of his junior colleague, a tubby Yoruba, who was third at the lunch which he gave me in the swish diplomats' restaurant overlooking a river, the memorable event of the 3 weeks in — remains the plain statements by this official at that lunch. He said:

'The Ibos have not yet learnt their lesson. The full exaction has not yet been made for January 15th but don't worry. One of our people came over recently, our diplomatic courier, and even before that a former minister spent a day here and we had a long chat. It's only a matter of days and then, believe me, the Ibos won't trouble us any more.'

I asked him what he meant, despising the grin of approval on my face.

'Just wait and see. Haven't you noticed how they continue to create difficulties at the constitutional conference? That Ojukwu! They think they have something to complain about because of May and June. They haven't learnt their lesson. This time they are going to get something real to complain about.'

Three days later, the first news came to me of the Ibo pogrom. It needed no effort to recall that lunch and the dialogue. It is for ever branded on my mind.

*This embassy official is now full Ambassador in another European capital.

21

NEVER again be such a fool, never! Who did you think you were? Tell me, just where did you think you were? Did you really think these people *are*?

Three weeks of books, then nothing! I had been so pleased with myself, the meeting with the Grand Zero had yielded the all-important concession on books. Even so it took a full week for the first book to come. It arrived from the prison 'library', a ragged, mutilated volume with the barely decipherable title *Letters of Queen Victoria*. It took only one hour to read the remnant pages, nine days to finish the entire collection of books in the prison, the most bizarre assortment that ever gathered dust and cockroach eggs on dog-eared pages. Nor had I a choice in the order of reading. At first I railed that a list had not been brought to enable me to make a choice – it was obvious I would not be taken to the books to make my own selection. When on the ninth day the Cadet announced to me that I had just read the last, I understood. After the rapid disposal of Queen Victoria, the incredulous cadet began to bring them four or five at a time. I kept company with P. G. Wodehouse, Agatha Christie, the plants of West Africa and the piety of other lands.

There must be a public library in this town I said. Why does not an officer obtain books for me? The promise was made, a junior officer instructed. I said to the cadet, the subject is unimportant. Just find me the fattest books and bring them. The fatter the better. Charles Dickens made two successive calls, then that reprobate Boswell, and he was followed by a yet greater reprobate and the fattest volume of all, an over-fed toad in the illiterary person of the Director of Prisons, a bulging volume to end all volumes.

No words were needed to inform me of sudden changes in my regimen following his unexpected visit. The books stopped abruptly, and to this emptiness the guards came one day and nailed one blank slate.

The little square hole in the door is a peep-hole on the living. It sneaks into the yard of Purgatory, the house of lunatics, lifers, violent and violated nerves, cripples, tuberculars, victims of power sadism all safely hidden from questions. The guards thrust their fist through the hole and manipulate the bolt from either side. And I on my stroll through the yard casually oh so casually steal a quick look at the rare flash of a hand, a face, a gesture in that Purgatory. Alas, too often, all I see is a mere blur of khaki, the square planted rear of the guard on the other side.

Until this morning lying in bed I hear the noise of hammering. All morning the assault of blows is multiplied and magnified by the unique echoing powers of the crypt. (When it thunders my skull is the anvil of gods.) I step out to investigate and I find a squad of warders at the gate hacking and sawing and nailing until by noon, the breach is sealed. Only the sky is now open, a sky the size of a napkin trapped by tall spikes and broken bottles, but a sky. Vultures perch on a roof just visible from another yard. And crows. Egrets overfly the crypt and bats swarm at sunset. Albino bats, sickly pale, emitting radio pips to prowl the echo chamber. But the world is dead, suddenly. For an eternity after ceasing the hammers sustain their vehemence. Even the sky retracts, dead.

Buried alive? No. Only something men read of.

Days pass, weeks, months. Buoys and landmarks vanish. Slowly, remorselessly, reality dissolves and certitude betrays the mind.

I am alone with sounds. They acquire a fourth dimension

in a living crypt, a clarity which, as in the case of thunder becomes physically unbearable. Pips from the albino bats pock the babble of evensong – moslem and christian, pagan and unclassifiable. My crypt they turn into a cauldron, an inverted ball of faiths whose sonorities are gathered, stirred, skimmed, sieved in the warp and weft of sooty mildew on walls, of green velvet fungus woven by the rain's cunning fingers.

Buried alive? I must struggle free through the trapdoor of my mind. I must breathe, deeply.

Unnumbered days of sitting in the yard, staring into nothing. A creak of the chair brings the gaoler 'casually' strolling round, his tread too heavy on gravel to be absorbed into the cotton-wool mind, too sharp, too hostile, too fearful of being caught in some ingenious trap, too nervous and pleading, apologetic and uncertain for one to sink peacefully into an interior landscape of repose. Yet hours pass, and days, and weeks. When the harmattan rages I move inside and shut the door. He sits nervously outside, paces up and down wrapped in his heavy coat, distorting his eye-sockets to see over the frame. I lie still, staring at the holes in the mosquito-net. I wait, judging the moment when I can reach a tentative antenna out of the cocoon without the descent of a heavy tread on the probe.

22

Of the many ghosts that haunt me here, the most frequent and welcome are the ghosts of dead relations, grandfather especially, and the two ghosts of Christopher Okigbo, Adekunle Fajuyi ... Banjo, Alale also visit, but hardly as ghosts ...

My grandfather sits gnome-like, chuckling secretively, every chunk of his body pulsing with love and strength ... Where have you been, where are you going, when are you coming again, why do you never stay? Ungh. Don't tell me, it isn't I that need an answer. But they all come to me and ask me those silly questions. I tell them, don't ask me. Ask him when he comes. All I know is that he is hidden somewhere in that chattering box because that is where I hear his name. I turn on the box and it says you are doing something in Australia. But he was here only yesterday I say, only yesterday! Anyway if you don't complain at what you get neither will I. Bring out the wine gourd from behind that cupboard. It's gone stale but you gave me no notice as usual. And I suppose you can't stay till evening for the fresh supply ...

How fitting that knowledge of his death should reach me also over the air, as if in gnomic vengeance for leaving him so little of myself beyond a voice in the air. There I was in Stockholm waiting vainly for Chinua and others in the tense month of April '67 trying once again to build a common front from the rubble of '66. Like a ghost pursuing a miscreant the telegram that bore the news chased me from point to point of disillusion and desperation ... I wonder, will I ever again have truly private memories, unlinked, uncluttered by the stress and tensions of that immediate past?

Christopher rushing in his whirlwind manner into the office of an Adjutant in Enugu. I am sunk in a deep armchair behind the door where I had been placed by the Adjutant after my earlier summary roughing-up by Biafran Security, so Christopher does not immediately see me when he enters the office. Hot and breathless he delivers the instructions he has brought from the front. The war is three weeks old. The Adjutant takes rapid notes then says, Look behind you. Christopher's eyes pop out of his head, then he breaks into that singular Cherookee yell-and-jig which has raised squirms of unease among a host of self-conscious acquaintances in every corner of the globe. He calms down minutes later, makes room for me in the convertible by flinging his major's uniform in the back. As he drives towards the front:

'You know, I learnt to use a gun right in the field. I had never fired even an air-rifle in my life. I swear it, you know I'm not a violent man, I'm not like you. But this thing, I am going to stay with it till the end.'

Christopher sitting hours across the table from me while I awaited trial in a police cell in November '65, discussing poetry . . .

Fajuyi,* of all these ghosts, appears to have the most solid flesh. He paces in bafflement, chewing his lower lip, given to sudden movements.

'How did you do it?'

I look blankly at him, feigning ignorance. The light of mischief in his eyes is too plain not to understand his meaning, but I say, 'How did I do what?'

He throws up his hand in mock-despair, then roars: 'Hold up the radio station! You know damned well what you did.

*Lt. Col. Adekunle Fajuyi, first Military Governor of the West. Murdered by the June 29th coup-makers.

How did you do it? There were soldiers and policemen guarding the place. How did you slip in and out again after holding up everyone . . .'

I interrupt him with a reminder that I have stood trial and been acquitted.

'Ho ho ho ho that's a good one. Now you never mind what the court said. I want to know how you did it.'

'You don't believe in the integrity of the courts?'

He lets out a roar of laughter, then sobers suddenly, 'Well I do believe in the courage of *that* court, and of *that* judge. What about you? How do you find the Western courts of justice, generally.'

'Subverted. No one believes in the courts any more.'

He stops by a huge Victorian escritoire in a corner, relic of the ponderous tastes of former colonial governors, pulls up the bevelled lid and takes out a service revolver. He toys with the gun.

'You know, he was here, sitting just where you are, in that very chair. I sent for him. I was very anxious to meet the man who was responsible for all the chaos in the West. When people no longer believe that they can obtain justice in the courts then they must take the law in their hands. So, I take the view that the Chief Justice is personally responsible for all the death and destruction which took place here. The day he deliberately adjourned those election petitions then came back to announce that the cases had been overtaken by events, he became responsible for the mess. Murder, arson, rape, the whole lot. They say we soldiers are simple people; it's true. That is the way my simple mind sees it. Anyway I sent for him. When he came, I knew that my simple judgement was right. I said to him, tell me exactly what happened that day in court. I want you to give me your own version. You know, he began to tremble. He was shaking so much that I thought he was going to fall off the chair. I asked him, what's the matter? I said, are you afraid of me? I waited and waited, but the man couldn't speak.

'That was when I took out this gun. You know, we soldiers are really simple. I hadn't meant to frighten him at all, in fact I was trying to calm him down. I took the gun, opened the breech and showed him. I said, Look, this is the only gun in this room, it has no bullets. Just because I am a soldier is no reason to be scared of me. We are alone here, you and I. I opened the door, the windows. I assured him that there was no one hiding in the room to shoot him. All right, let's talk. Millions of people went to the polls to choose their government. You the Chief Justice of the region are supposed to be above politics, so I assume that whatever you did was in accordance to your training as a judge and in keeping with the higher ideals of justice. Now, all I want to know is what happened in court that day, from your own point of view. Tell me the story step by step.

'Our people are very funny. You know what he did? No, I'll tell you first what I expected of him. I thought he would either give me a good or even a foolish defence or else he would hand in his resignation on the spot. That's all. All right, so someone has failed in his duties. It is disgraceful and he must pay for it, but it isn't the end of the world. The honourable course is to resign! But do you know what the man did? He went on his knees, there, right there, an old man like that, a whole Chief Justice, he went down on his knees and began begging me. I was angry. I shouted at him to get up but he wouldn't. He kept saying, I beg you sir. So I walked out. When I felt he should have recovered himself I sent the guard to go and tell him to leave.'

Another long stretch of thoughtful silence. 'That is the whole trouble. People don't like to go. Perhaps I am looking at things too simply again, but that is the way I see it. Our people never admit it to themselves when their usefulness is over. The politicians want to stay on for ever so they plunge the country into chaos. A judge knows he has acted corruptly but he begs to stay on. He has been running around since I sent him on compulsory leave. His intermediaries are trying to get round Ironsi. Anyway that is the first decision I've taken for this region. He goes. And if he doesn't give me that resignation quickly I shall simply remove him.'

Then, abruptly: 'You ought to come back here. The region badly needs rebuilding.'

I say to him: 'Lagos University behaved well during my trial. I owe them some service at least.'

'They have plenty of people. They can do without you.' He laughs suddenly. 'I can decree you, you know. What would you do if I brought you back by decree?'

I pretend to think it over. 'Well, I don't really know. I am not very good at being commandeered. I might simply disappear.'

Again he roars with laughter, 'Like that mysterious intruder at the radio station.'

I reply, sternly, 'Sir, may I remind you that I was . . .'

'Acquitted and discharged. All right. But you must give it some thought. Our need is greater than theirs, remember that.'

'The truth is I am allergic to being in government employ. However, I'll work for you if you need me, only I won't be employed by you. I mean, if you have specific projects on which you need outside help, that kind of thing.'

His threats ring in my ears as he accompanies me to the door: 'I'll take you up on that sooner than you think!'

Rumours of the impending court-martial, even secret executions of the coup-leaders, Jan '66. We form pressure groups, sign petitions asking for their release from gaol.

It is an uneasy petition. The facts which have begun to emerge, the details of casualties and the inference to be drawn from them are enormous threats to national feeling. In spite of the failure of the initial action and its attenuation by an establishment figure like Ironsi there is the realization that a situation, any situation which is born of a destruction of the past remains always malleable in the hands of a committed few. A rejection or condemnation of the creators of that situation implies a victory for the forces which were overthrown. A decision to participate in, much less organize a movement for their vindication cannot therefore end with a mere signature on a petition. First of all the decision of each individual to sign that plea can only come about from a reasoned acceptance of the inherent imperfections of that situation, including acceptance of the culpable acts that brought it about. I rage at the stupidities and ill motivations of a part; recognize even the continuation of a fraudulent, base, partisan and petty-minded exploitation of the new situation by a few; I am faced with the unedifying spectacle where old comrades misunderstand the new situation in entirety, divest themselves of reason and integrity and plunge greedily into the immediate material and intellectual exploitation of the situation.

But there comes a moment when the committed must ask; do I accept the action – in this case the January 15th action – as the basis for the ultimate goal or do I reject it? To reject it means two courses of action; immediate and public denunciation of the executors of January 15th, and the demand for a restoration of the pre-January 15th position.

The other choice, acceptance of the January basis, was a demanding alternative nor could it be made without some deep resentment, at least for those who had been involved in the wider strategy of the Western uprising. The Army's intervention was accepted gratefully because it anticipated the other army intervention planned by the Mafia-feudalist alliance to take place two days later. I had spent the last few nights before January 15th in shifting hiding-places because I had warning of the scorched-earth programme for the West, a clean sweep of 'dissident intellectuals' and trade unionists and even a few judges that had failed to toe the political line. I passed the eve of the coup in my office at the University of Lagos, close to a 'fishing' canoe which lay in the lagoon behind the university. It had all been arranged by an Efik in the anti-smugglers squad at Obalende Headquarters, one of the many inside supporters of the movement.

I had not washed on the morning of January 15th when two foreign journalists, Walter Schwartz of the *Guardian* and Lloyd Garrison of the *New York Times*, crashed into my office, hot to test a hunch that I might know something of the coup. Instead I began to question them. I made them repeat details of what they had heard or seen until Lloyd Garrison commented, 'It strikes me that you are not at all surprised.'

I was not surprised but puzzled. In so far as an army event had taken place I was not surprised. But the details they now supplied me were most strange. This was not the form which I had expected the army intervention to take. It was asking too much to accept that Akintola, recently returned from his decisive meeting with Sardauna, had been shot dead, or that the diabolical schemes got up between the two of them, with Balewa's direct consent, had been forestalled by a 'pre-emptive strike'.

I could not, when the nature of the 15th January was finally digested, deny the rush of euphoria. I did and still wish that the revolt in the West had achieved victory as a people's uprising. Given a few more weeks this would have been realized. Every town and city had fallen except Ibadan. Government, as defined by the rejected men of NNDP, no longer even made the pretence of functioning in the West, where nearly all local councils were run by the caretakers of the insurrection. The next phase, the erasure of the authority of that government in the capital, Ibadan, had commenced and would have been completed in another fortnight. Akintola and Balewa and their NPC overlords read and understood the omens alright. They had also security reports of the police and army intelligence. In sections of Ibadan the night already belonged to anti-government forces. There was no choice except capitulation or military treachery. The NNA leaders chose the latter, met in Kaduna to organize the details. It was too late to quicken the process of the strangulation of Ibadan in time to forestall the planned cynical declaration of emergency and the ruthless extermination of all opposition to an obnoxious tyranny. Even if the rumoured plans to assassinate Akintola as he returned from Kaduna on the afternoon of January 14th had been carried out, it would not have deflected the steam-rolling preparations of the Mafia-feudalist reaction. There was nothing left to do but prepare for continuing underground resistance after the now inevitable blow.

With its lapses, self-betrayals, incompletion, and ultimate desecration, was January 15th acceptable or not as a basis for a national struggle? Violence and death are personal things, and finally there is left only this code by which responsibility is shed or assumed: knowing in advance what the results would be, given the choice of a role in advancing or participating in the course of action taken by those young officers, would I have accepted such a role? There were no qualifications to my affirmative answer.

After the long nightmare spell the luck of the West finally altered for the better. We watched Fajuyi from afar, probing his actions, his decisions. The first meeting had told me all I wanted to know, but I remained wearily familiar with the pattern of the gradual corruption of power. We met again.

I had decided to take him our plea on behalf of the coup-leaders in person.

Fajuyi said: 'They have to be sorted out. There are some bad eggs among them who had personal scores to settle. The young Chief of Staff, Gowon, has been assigned to carry out an investigation and will report back. I have myself interrogated some of them. I tell you, it's the devil and the deep blue sea. I don't envy any of us; after all we are all in the same soup. If we take the wrong decision – ! But we must take a decision. As soon as Gowon makes his report we'll do something, but God help us if it's the wrong thing.'

'Talking of decisions, what is happening to Awolowo and co.?'

'We all agreed to release them but Hassan keeps raising objections. Not that he is against it but he says we should wait or it will make his people accuse the government of being anti-North. He says they have already begun to complain that the coup was definitely anti-North. Anyway, he wants us to wait for the right moment.'

'The North is important,' I conceded, 'because it mostly happened there. But only the new North, not the old. There should be no concessions to the old North and something must be done quickly to make that new North a tangible force.'

'How does one do that?'

'I'll let you know because I think you can help. We know that most of the initiative will have to come from the West. We are not being held guilty for the deaths of 15th January so we have an advantage. A group of us are planning a tour of the North soon – I hope I can find time to go myself.'

Watching him closely, I came to a point I had promised myself to bring up with him. 'I saw you arriving at a function in a Rolls-Royce . . .'

He cut me short. 'Ah, I know what you are about to say,

and I'll admit that I didn't like it either. But there was nothing I could do at the time. We were nearly late and those Security men had already allocated the car for me. I was more or less pushed into it. But I agree with you entirely. It's disgraceful that we soldiers should take over the ostentation of those useless politicians. What do you think I should ride?'

I said, 'A jeep.'

He was taken aback. 'An open jeep?'

'Closed or open, a jeep.'

He shook his head. 'No, that's taking it too far. The Security men won't agree for a start. And I have to do a lot of touring, you know. I'm going to cover thousands of miles.'

'All right, for the tours, something a little more comfortable.'

'Like...?' Before I could speak he was going again. 'What's wrong with a Mercedes Benz? It's a common enough car in this country. Every tuppenny lawyer can afford one.'

I pretended to think over the idea, causing him to add quickly, 'I'll tell you what I could do. I'll pick one out from the garage – there is a whole fleet of them – and have it painted in military colours. That way it won't look so opulent if that's what bothers you.'

I laughed. 'All right! You win.'

'As for the rest of the cars I'll put them up for sale. The Cadillacs, the Rolls, all the submarines. The Government could use the revenue.'

May '66 a message from him to come and see him urgently. It was just after Decree No. 34, the Unification Decree. I was attacked almost as soon as I came in: 'You intellectuals are all the same. Why haven't you gone on that tour to the North?'

I excused myself. 'I haven't been able to get away. We are short-staffed in my department. But I have kept in touch with colleagues from the North. We are planning a congress for the end of the university session.'

'I told you to come to the West. I should have brought you by decree. When can you leave?'

'The university?'

'No. When can you make the tour? Come in the office. I want you to see the intelligence reports from the North. You really think matters can wait till your university goes on holiday?'

When I had read them I said: 'It is not merely the unification decree. That is only an excuse.'

'I know. That is why I would sooner have a non-police point of view.'

It was well inside the lecture term but I assured him I would leave within the next three days.

Birkin Ladi, about thirty miles from Jos, was where we encountered the riots. All the way North, travelling in company with Francis, a friend, director of a film company, the favourite topic was the unification decree which abolished the semi-autonomous regions and reduced them, as a first step, to groups of provinces. It was a bold revolutionary decision. There are several alternative ways of combating a corrupt and proliferating bureaucracy, of destroying tribalism and fomenting a single sense of nationhood. The unification decree was only one possible beginning among many, and it had the approbation of all except the feudalist monopolies in the North and the status-conscious functionaires of the nation who saw and dreaded the disappearance of grandiose and overpaid civil service positions. The acclaim for this drastic move however drowned the voices of dissent, some of which held genuine fears of motivations that were not idealistic, such as Ibo domination. On this atavistic distrust the Mafia of the North were already at work, aided by their Southern allies, many of whom had moved into the North loaded with money for the dirty work at hand. We were not after their vendable territory but after a supposedly different generation of enlightenment. I was not yet aware that between these two the distinction was more than blurred.

A bizarre encounter on the eve of holocaust, yet this comic fantasy in the tension of history accidentally confirmed the first evidence of disillusionment when it came. At the Hamdala Hotel, a fashion display formed the main event for the modern housewife of the North, sponsored naturally by the British Council. The innocent designer for this charade was Shadé, commissioned by the Council to give demonstration lectures to middle-class wives of the new Kaduna élite on cosmetics, make-up, fashion, deportment and allied female preoccupations. We went to a night-club with Shadé afterwards, accompanied also by a female journalist who had come to Kaduna to report the event for the women's page of the *Daily Times*.

I phoned our Northern colleague from the hotel. He agreed to join us at the club. He arrived under a barely suppressed tension and for a long time would say nothing beyond participating vaguely in the general talk. Over the phone I had sensed the first warnings of doubt but I dismissed them. The voice which answered me could hardly be described as one of welcome, yet this was a visit long urged on me by him and our Northern counterparts. At the club I waited for him to pick his own moment to brief me on the situation in Kaduna especially on the failure or success of his own educating mission. To my suggestion that we separate from the group he replied that he had an engagement and would have to return later. Finally he left as abruptly, as restlessly as he had remained at the table, promising to return under an hour. He did not once look me in the face. I have not seen him since.

Back at the hotel I drew blank trying to reach the other

names. As I had cadged a lift with Francis and was limited by his time-table there was nothing to do but leave notes saying when I would pass through Kaduna again. We were back much sooner than we planned.

A whiff of the violence was already in the air between Jos and Birkin Ladi. At Birkin Ladi it had expanded into a prospective scent of blood. The men were gathered in groups, milling round and round like sand spirals towards the vortex of violence. No effort was made to hide the swords and knives, the bows and iron-barbed arrows. No effort was made to disguise the long, calculating slit of death in the eyes which surveyed us, the strangers. Leaflets, cyclostyled, were circulated openly. I picked one up; it was written in Hausa so I put it aside for later translation.

Francis's uncle was a geologist with the tin mines, owned a gun and a licence. Driving to Kaura Falls we even did some hunting, little aware that we had driven barely ahead of a far more lethal hunt in the village we had just left. We returned late afternoon to a village of unearthly quiet and a feel of eyes behind shutters and doors. At the home of the geologist we learnt that rioting had occurred, with some fatalities. I remembered then the cyclostyled leaflet and asked the man, a fluent Hausa speaker, to translate it for me. It was an open, inflammatory call for a Jihad against the 'yaminrin'. It called teachers to keep their schools closed, parents to keep their children at home and all true natives of the soil to stay within doors until 'we have wreaked our will on the southern infidels'.

I said to Francis 'I must leave at once, by train. I don't know what my standing is with the Security bosses in Lagos but I can't afford to be where the riot is. Ironsi's men might take it into their head that I came here to foment it.'

Francis decided that he would also cancel the rest of his business tour and make for sanity.

We drove just ahead of the second wave of terror. The murder squads were just re-grouping. At our ears resounded the rallying cry – *Araba!**

On the outskirts of Kaduna we came to a local 'buka', a food shack where we had stopped on the outward journey for food. The atmosphere was peaceful enough, the riots did not appear to have spread yet to Kaduna. Someone suggested that we catch our breath and stop there again for a snack. As Francis drove off the road on to the rough grounds I was hit by a simultaneity of impressions: a door that hung by only one screw of its lowest hinges; charred wall of the shack's interior; silent figures, still and watchful in the neighbourhood. Even as I shouted to Francis to drive on he clutched my arm and pointed. Sticking through the bushes was a human leg.

On the wordless drive into Kaduna itself, taken at the maximum speed, I recalled that the shack had been run by an Ibo couple.

We were lucky to enter Kaduna. Some minutes later it was dark and the city was sealed. No cars could enter nor could any depart. Already the streets looked deserted, the roadside markets unpeopled. The city was sealed, and yet, strangely, no night curfew was imposed. One could move freely within the city.

Excepting us, no one did. Perhaps it was because in spite of anticipating, we had failed to arrest the event, failed to grasp the pace at which it rolled towards fulfilment; it became suddenly important to me to learn all there was to know about this prelude – for not once did I fool myself that it was the definitive act – it seemed that my belated trip would not be a total failure if I could learn something of the future pattern of unrest from the present signs. I said to Francis, I'll take the car and drive round the city. Bored with

*Separations, Secession.

the enforced confinement in the hotel they all decided to come with me. Even the dress designer refused to be left alone.

I drove to the club at Princess Hotel, owned by a Yoruba called Adejumo. I had a comrade who worked there as a barman, a former trade unionist betrayed and victimized since the Morgan Commission strike. I had not planned to see him as he had lost heart since the failure of that nationwide movement. Now there seemed to be no one else.

Nor was there a Princess Hotel. The walls still stood but there was little else. The rioters had left only an hour before we arrived; a lone waiter emerged from behind a rubble of chairs and broken tables. I asked him where I could find my friend but he didn't know. And the manager? He began to hedge but we reassured him. We were Adejumo's friends from Ibadan; if we didn't see him how would we reassure his people at home?

Following his semi-coherent instructions we tracked down Adejumo's home in the heart of Kaduna. The door opened a fraction when I knocked. Unseen eyes peered from invisible crevices in neighbouring houses. Standing on the pavement before his house I felt suddenly vulnerable; the evening's excursion became an inexcusable exercise in recklessness and stupidity. For a long time the hotel manager would not even acknowledge the knocks. Finally we heard a sound, a terrified voice scrupulously established my identity before a far window opened a fraction, a cautious head gave first the others in the car, then me a long inspection before other hands opened the door and the manager ushered us in.

I contented myself with listening only to the story of the devastation of the club, the attack on non-Northern patrons and prostitutes, before abandoning my search. I had become very itchy to regain the safety of the hotel. Ours was the only vehicle again on Kaduna streets on the return journey. On the way back we came to the police station, heavily guarded. I made one more stop and spoke to the officer on duty.

As we drove back it occurred to me to ask Shadé if she ever ran into my colleague during the period of the riots. She said 'No,' then added, 'I suppose he was in the midst of it. He had a long sword under his gown, that night at the club. The sleeves fell off once and I saw it before he could hide it away.'

From comrade to renegade. There was no longer a question in my mind that we had witnessed the mere prelude to a wider anarchic terror.

In Ibadan Fajuyi pored over the leaflets I had brought back, asking finally. 'What is the next step?'

It was not yet completely hopeless. I said I would make a tour of the East as soon as possible.

He sighed. 'I wish I could talk to Ironsi. Unfortunately he no longer trusts me. Do you know how he addresses me these days? – "Hallo Radical". Ever since I put my foot down over the affair of the Chief Justice. He would have bowed to the pressures you know, he prefers not to antagonize people with names. If I spoke to him about this whole development he would be immediately suspicious of my motives. The people who surround him ...' He shrugged. 'Do you still intend to go ahead with the Congress?'

'That has become even more crucial. I shall give you a date after my tour of the East.'

He could not rid himself of a nagging regret caused by Ironsi's distrust. 'He used to phone me every evening ... but I've told you all about that. Do you know, the first I knew of his decision to rotate governors was over the radio. Can you imagine that? I am all for it of course ...'

'I am not.'

'Why not? It's all right in principle.'

'Of course, it's fine in principle. But not yet. We have had a long run of ill-luck in leadership and now we have you for a change. Who is going to come here? That ceremonial fop in the East or the polo-playing drunk from the North? And I don't care much for your Mid-West man either.'

'To tell you the truth I am not too happy about it. I would like to finish what we've begun, I mean, we've hardly started! Still, I always remind myself of what I criticize in others – nobody ever wants to leave. I am beginning to fear that the Army itself may not know when it is time to go. If the people once suspect that...!'

The visit East restored optimism, my return shattered it. In the East there was control, a dampening down of resentment and thoughts of vengeance, there was even a beginning of self-reassessment, not much but more than sufficient to create the public confrontation that alone would give birth to a national front. Dissatisfaction had begun with the élitist smugness of Ojukwu's administration. The hurt of the Northern events had turned the radicalism of the East inwards. A curious, unexpected phenomenon, its potential seemed unlimited.

A folder of ominous gleanings thrust in my hand on the night of my return from the East ended the brief buoyancy. The report centred on the activities of the Mafia among the soldiers, of huge sums openly shared among some officers both in some Northern and Western barracks, of the wives of the ex-NNA ministers in the role of couriers between the army and politicians. Fajuyi appeared to be expecting my call. We sat in the lounge of the State House and compared notes.

I was struck suddenly by the silence and the emptiness. Perhaps the empty feeling in me had dulled my outer sensibility towards my surroundings. It was at least two hours and closing in to nightfall before I asked, 'Where is everybody by the way?'

He waved his hand in irritation. 'I dismissed them. Each

time I cut down some ceremonial nonsense somebody thought up a new one. Especially those security men.'

I said, 'You can't ignore those entirely.'

'They are a nuisance. A few weeks ago I looked around and there were all these guards. I thought to myself what the hell, if someone wants to shoot me he won't do it here. He will wait until I am out in the open' – he gave a chuckle – 'in one of your open jeeps.'

It was nightfall. He fell into periods of silence oftener than usual. It is tempting to think that he had premonitions of imminent death. I see again his composure, the long stretches of thoughtful inertness. I drank but he did not. He had, in a characteristic gesture of will, given up alcohol – too many functions he complained, too many official receptions, and he was a hard drinker. He solved it by simply not drinking at all. And he had cut the ceremonials of State House to nothing.

He repeated his conviction that I speak to Ironsi. 'He knows you are not partisan so he'll listen to you.'

'I don't think he'll listen and in any case I don't believe he is capable of understanding a thing. He doesn't even sense things. Any leader, and especially a military leader who lets his wife go to the hairdresser with outriders and sirens blaring...'

The quiet of the empty house was shattered by his laughter. 'You people don't miss much.'

'It is not the fact that is important. It is what is indicated by such symptoms that is frightening. The man is heading for suicide but the way he's chosen will take the nation down with him.'

'Speak to him anyway. He's bound to pay attention to you.' Again he grew sad. 'He doesn't really trust me much you know. It's a pity. Oh – I never told you – at one of our meetings I tried to introduce some of those ideas, you know, about cars and houses and so on. And land. You know the way our top officers have began to acquire Crown Lands. I said we ought to lead by example.' He chuckled. 'You should have been there. I quickly gave it up. Once people start looking at you as if to say, he's trying on a holier-than-thou game it's better to give up. Anyway' – he waved his arms round the emptiness – 'I've tried to put my own house in order.'

'It's as good a place as any to make a start.'

'If we have time.' He shook off the unexpected ominousness of what had seemed an involuntary comment, became his sudden energetic self again. 'Will you talk to Ironsi?'

I shrugged. 'All right.'

'Damn! I've just remembered he's in the North at the moment. But you can phone his office and make an appointment.' He stopped abruptly. 'Ogundipe! Why not him? He's Chief of Staff, he's next in command. In fact . . . yes, that's it. He will understand a lot better. Speak to Ogundipe.'

We parted on the steps of the State House. It was around seven in the evening, 26th of July. I drove to Lagos the following day. From Francis's office I telephoned Ogundipe at the Supreme Headquarters. I asked him for an appointment, stressing the urgency. At the end of fifteen minutes I was forced to replace the phone and commence the struggle back from a haze of unreality. Francis asked me what the matter was. Even the words sounded hardly credible as they trickled from my tongue:

'He insists I first write him a memo.'*

Less than thirty-six hours later he was seeking refuge on a Navy vessel. And Fajuyi was dead.

*May '72 – A chance encounter with a man with whom Ogundipe first sought refuge has now revealed that he was not alone when he took my call and could not speak freely. The action had already commenced.

23

AND Victor Banjo . . .

If ever a revolution was lost to history, not now in one of those famous *moments* but by days! One full span of twenty-four hours, then two, then a third. Even after four days there was still hope for this movement. After the fifth the chance had begun to slip away. By the end of a week it was gone for ever. Another lost cause.

What kept him? What kept him in Benin while the naked underbelly of Lagos lay helpless in its gross inert corruption, waiting only to be pierced? I can guess at the answer, but that is no consolation. Waiting for a first sign of the active support assured him by those who were not however driven by an equal idealism, Banjo forgot that his was a nation of fence-sitters, that in crisis, established power begins by an advantage which exerts a psychological paralysis on all but the most uncompromising few. Because he had publicly declared his invading force against the Eastern secession, Banjo imagined that this was sufficient answer to the dilemma of the waverers. And so – speeches over the radio, long meetings with civil leaders of the Mid-West, long telephone conversations with supposed comrades-in-arms in other parts of the country. The revolutionary base, supposed to be 'consolidated' by his continued presence in the Mid-West began to crumble away.

He paid with his life. And with him Alale, Ifeajuna, Agbam . . .

Even when it is conceded that a nation is not merely what it is at a given moment but in its entire potential, a danger remains for all who sometimes wonder, as I often do, if the nation they know is not simply one of their imagining. For this consoling potential of the future is also double-edged, being both a potential for good or evil, for retrogression or progress, for reactionary consolidation or radical re-creativeness. History proves continuously that there is no certainty which will emerge as the ultimate direction, even from identical sets of circumstances.

Partly because the human factor is the most demonstrable determinant, I caution myself and try substituting peoples for nations. It is better to believe in people than in nations. In moments of grave doubts it is essential to cling to the reality of peoples; these cannot vanish, they have no questionable *a priori* – they exist. For the truly independent thinker it is always easy – and often relevant – to recall the artificiality, the cavalier arrogance, the exploitive motivations which went into the disposal of African peoples into nationalities. One overcomes the sense of humiliation which accompanies the recollection of such a genesis by establishing his essential identity as that which goes into creating the entity of a people. I cannot see that essence as part of the entity of boundaries. Judgement can only be applied to peoples, judgement that is, in its basic ethical sense can be applied only to peoples; loyalty, sacrifice, idealism, even ideologies are virtues which are nurtured and exercised on behalf of peoples. And any exercise of self-decimation *solely* in defence of the inviolability of temporal demarcations called nations is a mindless travesty of idealism. Peoples are *not* temporal because they can be defined by infinite ideas. Boundaries cannot.

The makeshift ambulances, 'kia-kia' passenger trucks, drove past the window of the apartment in Enugu where we sat discussing the war, bearing the wounded from Nsukka front. How soon would such a vehicle bear remnants of Christopher Okigbo from whom I had parted only a few hours before, he towards the sound of the guns, I – in what direction precisely? Towards what livable-with future full of accusing abdications?

'What is the message from the West?' Banjo demanded, for at least the fifth time. 'I mean, what are they saying? What do they really say about this war?'

'I only know what we all feel about the secession.'

He snapped back: 'Yes, and on that we are all agreed. Why could they not have been equally positive on the pogrom! The Ibos were not a danger to anyone. The May and July murders had sapped their capacity to make any serious trouble. What explanations did you people have to keep you so silent in the face of those damnable days of September and October?'

'The essence of this confrontation,' Alale said, 'is the rejection or entrenchment of the profit motive of genocide. Or of tribal chauvinism.'

Genocide *was* the chosen cure for assets probes. In Lagos, in so far as the former Federal Ministers, corporation chairmen etc. were concerned, they never even commenced. The hoarded millions of the Northern politicians remained intact, untouched by the government in spite of the vociferous cries of the Southern newspapers, and the new generation of the North. Examples were numerous:— a Northern Emir who was also chairman of a corporation had six million unaccountable pounds in his private account. Abruptly the inquiry was called off. Apart from suspension from his post there were no other consequences. Strange statements began to flow from the military governor Hassan, such as the need to concentrate more on repairing the cracks in national unity than waste time on former ills. Lagos continued strangely immune; the beneficiaries of the ousted civilian apparatus of private appropriation swaggered through the country, unscathed and seemingly invulnerable. Only the West remained scrupulously committed to the revolutionary ideals. There, full restitution was made. Publicly, and without compromise.

But the voices of dissent would not be silenced. Trade unionists, intellectuals and newspaper columnists denounced the treachery, demanded that the government carry out the aims of 15 January especially as these had been publicly subscribed to by the new government of the June counter-coup. At long last the civilian and politician profiteers admitted the danger to themselves. There had to be a distraction, and it had to take place on such a level as to completely obscure all other goals of society. The Northern Mafia got together with the Lagos counterparts and contributed the necessary investment for self-preservation. Cold-bloodedly the pogrom was planned, every stage plotted, and the money for operations distributed to the various centres of mayhem. The Ibos, twice victims, were again the most obvious, the most logical victims of this new profit-motivated massacre. But so that the lesson would be complete, so that no danger remained of a return to the old inter-regional interference in the affairs of this base for all reactionary conspiracies, the 'trouble-making' southerners no matter from what region were included in the massive sweep. But it was the Ibos who were the unqualified victims.

'When the East seceded.' I said, 'they left us the Mafia and the Military in an unbreakable alliance of mutual, lucrative guilt. And with a successful philosophy of genocide. Because if the East goes then there was no crime in the new entity still known as Nigeria. And the nation would be too busy mending its fences to bother with the – by then – monotonous demand for a complete moral purge. As for further hopes of building anything approaching a socialist state . . .'

Alale broke out again, 'You agree that is the only chance for Nigeria?'

'There is no alternative. The army must be returned to its status as part of the proletariat. The politician-patrician mentality is already destroyed but it has begun a new life by its anonymous infiltration of a naive, purely instinctive Army. We need a Third Force which thinks in terms of a common denominator for the people. If the East will pause, ask for a cease-fire and give the Third Force time to proliferate through all the key places . . . well, the time is right. I did not come all this way to ask the East to surrender. But the secession must be called off.'

Banjo shook his head. 'Ojukwu will never agree. In fairness to him I would say that there was little else he could have done. I saw the demonstrations. If he hadn't given in he would have been physically toppled.'

'He told me all about that. Wild emotional scenes in the streets and before the State House. I am willing to concede that his hand was forced; even so I think he is clever enough to have found a way out. If he really wanted to.'

'Of course! That is the whole point. He *didn't* want to find a way out and I'll tell you why. Because he is a born reactionary. He knows what I think of him. I've told him so to his face.'

And yet another reminder of the mortal realities of a war which was being fought only some twenty miles from us was brought by a young officer who entered the apartment and handed Banjo a scrap of paper. Banjo read it and passed the paper to Alale then turned to me.

'Do you know Joe Akhahan?'

'Yes.'

'He's dead. Helicopter crash. That was an intercepted Federal signal.'

The young officer had remained. He said. 'I was his batman during the Tiv campaign.'

Banjo remarked. 'Well we won't have to worry now which side he'll be on.'

The young officer said flatly. 'I don't believe it was an accident.'

The dialogue, like much of the dialogue on that Enugu visit, must remain part of the larger enigma of the war. As our own presence in that apartment, Banjo's living quarters, which also served him as office. For none of us there was Ibo. Victor Banjo, like me, a Yoruba. Alale, an Ijaw from the Mid-West, a Moscow-trained Marxist who had been with Nkrumah's CPP until, growing too embarrassing with his call for a reduction in the personality cult and the growing separation of the party élite from the masses, he had even earned himself a spell in preventive detention. Alale, lithe and restless, took the room in long elastic strides, burst out from time to time to demand:

'How do these Gowon types think they can build a nation on a successful genocide? Or Ojukwu on the emotional reaction to genocide? What of all these intellectuals we hear so much about with all their pseudo-socialist jargon? We used to laugh at those phonies when I was with Nkrumah. So what happens when something anti-social happens and threatens to break up the nation? Why do we never hear them at the time of the event?'

'You won't ever hear them,' I said. 'They are enjoying the anguish of having to decide between two evils.'

Banjo said, 'The nation is not faced even with a choice of two evils. Whichever way this sort of war goes, the only results will be the entrenchment of the worst of both evils.

'The Soviets fought their Civil War gun in hand and political ideology in their heads. That was a whole half-century ago. But we thrust soldiers today into the field with just the slogan Kill-Yanmirin or Kill-Hausa. And for whose benefit? The damned bourgeois capitalists who have already begun to lap up the profits of a rising war industry. How do we get rid of the alliance of the capitalist adventurer and a bourgeois military after the war? Don't all these intellectuals know their history? Have they never heard of Spain?'

'And the longer the war lasts ...' Banjo began. I interrupted to ask if he thought the Ibos would fight to the last ditch, a remark of George Orwell having floated across my thoughts:

> Whether it was right ... to encourage the Spaniards to go on fighting when they could not win is a question hard to answer. I myself think it was right, because I believe that it is better even from the point of survival to fight and be conquered than to surrender without fighting.

From what I had seen and heard, the Ibos were not likely to give in.

Banjo sighed. 'Who can ever tell what the Ibos will do? The whole thing was mad from the start, but who wouldn't be mad after what happened?' Again and again, like Alale, he reverted to the same core of failure, the nagging frustration from an unbelievable moral dereliction of which the nation had been so guilty. 'But what happened to all you people in the West? Otegbeye and all those people who are never off the pages of the newspapers. Not a word of condemnation from anyone. No protest to Gowon, not even a student demonstration, not one act of solidarity with the victims. How did the rest of the country expect them not to feel cut off?'

'Perhaps they wanted them cut off,' I said. 'There are mutual grounds for that on both sides for those with vested interests.'

'Entrepreneurs!' Alale spat out the word with disgust. 'You'll find them in business and in civil service. In fact the latter are worse. At least you know your business man. The civil service type is more dangerous. He pretends he only has the interest of the state at heart.' He slashed the air in neat karate chops, left, right and fore of his body. 'It is not the nation that needs fragmenting. It's the mentality of the people as a whole. Taken to pieces and put together again.'

What God (white man) has put together, let no black man put asunder. The complications of neo-colonial politics of interference compel one to accept such a damnable catechism for now, as a pragmatic necessity. Later perhaps, the black nations will themselves sit down together, and, by agreement, set compass and square rule to paper and reformulate the life-expending, stultifying, constrictive imposition of this divine authority. What is clear, miserably, humiliatingly clear is that a war is being fought without a simultaneous programme of reform and redefinition of social purpose. A war of solidity; for solidity is a far more accurate word than unity to employ in describing a war which can only consolidate the very values that gave rise to the war in the first place, for nowhere and at no time have those values been examined. Nowhere has there appeared a programme designed to ensure the eradication of the fundamental iniquities which gave rise to the initial conflicts.

There will be victors of course, but not the sacrificing masses of Biafra or the rest of the nation. Being glutted and satiated with the expected bonus of war, the elitist pyramid will elide in the natural mechanism of satiation, the fart, will suck in new élitist sectors, creating a self-consolidating, regurgitive, lumpen Mafiadom of the military, the old politicians and business enterprise. After all, a people's combative will is not limitless. The war will have put it to such an intolerable strain that little of it will be left over to challenge the war (power) profiteers when they begin to ride the nation to death. As they will, puffed with the wind of victory, incontestable rulers, the only beneficiaries of the stench of death. By priority the combative strength of a people belongs to the crucial task of internal revolution. To strain or expend it needlessly is to place the people at the mercy of the more far-sighted opportunists of flux and chaos.

Militarist entrepreneurs and multiple dictatorships: this is bound to be the legacy of a war which is conducted on the present terms. The vacuum in the ethical base – for national boundary is neither an ethical nor an ideological base for any conflict – this vacuum will be filled by a new military ethic – coercion. And the élitist formulation of the army, the entire colonial hangover which is sustained by the lack of national revaluation will itself maintain and promote the class heritage of society. The ramifications of the alliance of a corrupt militarism and a rapacious Mafia in society are endless and are nearly incurable. The war means a consolidation of crime, an acceptance of the scale of values that created the conflict, indeed an allegiance and enshrinement of that scale of values because it is now intimately bound to the sense of national identity.

Everything identifies when that slogan, national identity, is blared forth. Everything unites in the amorphous embrace of national unity. The thinking (I can find no other word, but the process is largely irrational) the thinking is that the values which are present when victory is achieved are the values which create victory. In the distorting mists of national euphoria the moral dereliction and ideological barrenness which led to the conflict are no longer seen as such, nor are they seen as continuing in the identity of the nation since that identity is not changed, has undergone no revolutionary purge either in its guts or at the head. A war, with its attendant human suffering, must, when that evil is unavoidable, be made to fragment more than buildings: it must shatter the foundations of thought and re-create. Only in this way does every individual share in the cataclysm and understand the purpose of the sacrifice.

I think, after all, there is only one common definition for a people and a nation – a unit of humanity bound together by a common ideology. It must be this identity or loss of it that I experience in moments of pessimism when the lines of Platen hover in my mind :

> And those who hate evil in the depth of their heart
> Will be driven from homeland, when evil
> Comes to be worshipped by a nation of slaves
> Far wiser to renounce such a country
> Than support the yoke of blind mob hatred
> In the infantile regression of a people.

Or in the more euphoric moments when, confidently, I recall Castro's lines :

> Esta tierra
> Este aire
> Este cielo
> Son los nuestros
> Defenderemos*

In defence of that earth, that air and sky which formed our vision beyond lines drawn by masters from a colonial past or re-drawn by the instinctive rage of the violated we set out, each to a different destiny.

*This earth is ours
And the air
And the sky
We will defend them

24

THE vulnerable moments are the moments before full awakening, those moments between surfacing to the top layer of awareness and the actuality of climbing ashore. I think of the perilous mornings in terms as this: perhaps too many other consciousnesses hover on a common surface in that hour, too many piles of clothing on the shore and drugged minds drifting in and out without self-markings. If a man in such a state were to pick the wrong clothing, or drift around for ever finding none, all mysteriously vanished . . .

Each day it takes longer to find my clothes. Odd items stare me in the face, a stained shirt, long underpants, odd sandals. Then I make mistakes and receive odd stares, sometimes a mocking laugh. How long does it last? A flash, as in dreams? Or an eternity? How long has the search taken? How much longer each long day? Whose are the faces dimly recognized? How does a mere metaphor take such real roots? It is not possible to have the same dream dawn after dawn. Perhaps the thought has bred terror and the mind leaps instinctively to the buried fear, timed by approaching wakefulness.

I day-dream back to that lake, returning again and again to my haunted search among alien faces, feet dragging in increasing fear, a fear of error, a fear of waking stranger to myself.

I know the cause. I know the event of some days back whose definition I evade. Plainly it is panic. But the immediate cause? The gate. The nailing in. I diagnose this unprecedented experience: claustrophobia.

Blind, crushing, an overspill of long repressions, a violent uprush of poison fumes in trapped sediments of my insulating capsule . . . suddenly in the dead of night I was forced up from sleep as if my self-capsule had become a mere bubble in the lake of consciousness. The capsule held, refused to burst. I clawed at the smooth surface and begged to let in air. It was a chilly awakening, harmattan night.

The cold intensified the bubble's isolation, panic came in stabs of icy pressure. Why? Why the sudden clogging of my lungs? A wild indiscipline commenced in my pulse, I heard it hammer at my head and my clenched fists became a living thing, a frantic bird pressuring at closure in the palm. It was pulse, sheer pulse. I felt my heart about to burst, the capsule disintegrate. A herd of stallions thudded at my temples.

May this be borne I asked? My skull is about to burst.

The placid lake erupted suddenly and I was lifted clean, plastic cage glass bubble tinsel capsule trapped pinned insect, lifted clean by the eruption and tossed from crest to crest of massive wave ripples. A long arm of the wave caught it in a vicious crook and drew it down again to silt-bed, we slithered from one slimy peak to another. No light, no direction. The lake is an underground cavern, sealed from end to end. There is no handhold within, only a roar in the ears of the vault, a naked earth-core dementia, shrapnels of water making for pulse centres creating disruption.

But you know it for what it is! PANIC! you know it for that alone! IT MAKES NO SENSE!

I heard my own shout and woke. Leapt ashore from the lake surface and made unerringly for my clothes.

But the capsule was sucked in again. And now I had struggled up in bed and sat cross-legged. This is what you want to do I warned: leap up, grab those bars and shake them like a frenzied ape. And scream! For there was this thing, this iron constriction below the heart and breathing had become a torment. And the body was rearing to buck, to leap in flight smash into the wall and tear it wide open, sweeping down all objects with that inhuman strength which had come upon me. I felt the titanic strength. It was there! A palpable force. If I let it rule my body even to shifting lightly from that mild restriction of my legs crossed under me, a force was let loose in self-destruction.

WHY? BUT WHY? Are you not master of this environment? Have I not crowned you king of solitude?

—Control. Control. Breathe in. Out. Don't let another sound escape you. Hold on to the two parallel bars on the door, your equation marks for those esoteric sciences that keep you busy. Two bars, one equation. Now balance sky to earth, earth to sky. Grip them hard but silently. Touch iron and ram it in your soul. Keep it there.

But when did you arrive at the door?

Earth. Earth. Sit on the floor. Blanket. If only it were not freezing. Pillow then, sit on the pillow to protect your ankles, wrap the blanket around you. Breathe. Itemize all objects beginning with the toothbrush on the ledge. What is it for? And soap? Count the bars one by one leaving out the equation marks. No, through the nose, breathe only through the nose. All the air you need can come through the nose. Don't pant, you have not been running, hardly room in here for that. Don't let the demons in. Now empty your mind. Anchor.

In this cold harmattan night I am covered in pools of sweat. Perhaps after all, it is better to remain in bed, flat. A larger surface is earthed. Arms flat down, heels dug into lumps of kapok, I await the careless moment of this assault, marshalling strength in lucid moments. How describe it? It settles down to a pattern, an acceptable rhythm of ebb and tide, misrule and clarity. A savaging by wolf packs then a brief refuge under an overhang. Fingers on a precipice weakening sickeningly. A long drop in void, a bewildered stillness in the centre of suction. Once I lay flat against a sheer vertical cliff face, held there by nothing but the force which first lifted me onto it. When? I could not tell. A limpet held by the most evenly sinister distribution of force, nothing would prise it loose, there was no gap for the insertion of a wedge of rationality. After each tidewash depth and dimension diminished. Patiently it is washed, eroded to a flat sensory plate. Is this my X-ray on the shale?

> Fragments
> We cannot hold, linger
> Parings of intuition
> Footsteps
> Passing and re-passing the door of recognition.

My memory at least proves tenacious. That 'mantra' will serve. Utter words, order moods if thoughts will not hold. Again.

And again. And again. Roll the words in the mouth. Taste wine-grace, pollen flavour, spirit dust. Travel beyond now, let the words prepare their passage, then journey through the passage spreading incense on the way. Dilate the nostrils. Greedily. But greedily! Swallow beyond repletion.

Victory? No, ebb and tide. But one may also be the moon and hold sway over danger, aloft though tossed and ravaged in murky depths. Somehow separate essential self from the twin reflection and make all harrowing phases more sensory sympathy. My shadow is trapped but not my essence. Repeat. My shadow is trapped but not my essence. Now cast a new spell in case of renewed assault:

> Old moons
> Set your crescent eyes
> On bridges of my hands

Comb out
Manes of sea-wind on my tide-swept sands.

My liver is mended. I await the vultures for there are no eagles here.

25

AMBROSE arrived on duty, late. Unless I am quick to stop or freeze him with hostility he always offers explanation if he is a minute late, or did not come at all on a former shift. The real purpose – to see if there are any leavings before the cleaner gets them.

Morning sah! with a salute. 'You no see me yesterday – I go court.' 'Ebening sah, you see I late small – we get small palava for office.' This morning it was, 'Morning sah, all we warder go take injection, thas why I late. Meningitis dey for town. Many people done die.' I betrayed a slight reaction and he seized his chance: 'Yes, I tink say meningitis na de name. Na dat ting wey dey turn man head backwards. Everybody inside prison must get injection today, all prisoner and detainee. So make you get ready your arm, sah. De ting pain small.'

Any event is welcome in prison, even the threat of cerebro-spinal meningitis and unpleasant needle jabs. There are the hours of awaiting the intrusion, the moments of the event, then the rest of the day when the concreteness of that event knocks holes in the miasma of a purposeless existence. I did not need Ambrose to tell me when they came to the yard of lunatics. There was the familiar authoritative rap on the door, the entry of the medical squad, the barked orders, the laughter which followed each yelp of pain. Ambrose rushed over and announced superfluously, 'They done come!' and rushed back to his post.

An hour passed. I heard the gate open and the team depart the way they had come. Ambrose, unbelieving, opened his gate a little to see what was happening, shut it again and came back. 'I no sabbe,' he said, 'I tink they forget say you dey here. Or perhaps they do your own tomorrow.'

Every inmate, including those in the death cell, has been inoculated against cerebro-spinal meningitis.

I try to recall what I know of this disease. Chiefly, that it is highly infectious, and not even by contact The germs are carried about in the air. Strolling in the crypt I find myself casting involuntary eyes over the wall, as if I might detect and dodge spores of this latest menace riding smoothly through the barbed wire to fulfil the hopes of those who ordered that I must not be inoculated.

For I know that it was no oversight. It is one more 'natural' possibility of the Ultimate Solution.

26

I HAVE never picked a pocket in my life – now, wait a minute, perhaps I have. One plays all sorts of games at school. A spy thriller, a detective novel, a private-eye film, any of these were sufficient to set us testing if our fingers or reflexes were not much more refined than theirs. Plus our new acquired knowledge of chemistry or physics. Now that my mind is on the subject I do remember now that I have picked locks, and not merely in play. A lost key-wallet, etc., not to mention the number of times the back-door key was manipulated and pushed on to a newspaper carefully pushed under the door – another useful tip from schoolday experience. But actually to pick a pocket, no, not that I remember. At the most simply a part of the general high-larking in school.

Yet, a few weeks ago – this, in fact, should have been the first recording with this pen – as smoothly efficient as any of Fagin's prize pupils, I did pick a pocket. And not just any pocket, not the rear pocket of his trousers or the pocket of a flapping overcoat but the breast pocket of this doctor's shirt. That the feat did not seem to me exceptional at the time strikes me even more strangely. It is further proof of how daily, no, how instantly fox-like one becomes on being locked away from normal civilized existence. What called the episode to mind is that the pen – a cheap Biro – has begun the first signs of giving out, and I found that quite subconsciously I began to wish the doctor's return. Puzzling why, I recalled for the first time the graphic instant of my first act as a pickpocket.

He came at last, the doctor. It was a routine tour of the cells, only, in my case not so routine. Among the prisoners the doctor goes unwatched, accompanied only by the nurse and a prison orderly, usually a junior warder. That, plus the trusty attached to the dispensary makes up the entire medical inspection team. Again, on entering a prison a new inmate has to see the medical officer of that prison almost at once, certainly he does so within the first forty-eight hours. For one thing it is he who must prescribe the diet, decide what tasks he is fitted to do after a thorough inspection, etc. In spite of requests, I did not see a doctor for months. On taking up residence the superintendent himself had prescribed my diet. He came in the morning and asked me what I was accustomed to eating. I had only got as far as two items when he indicated satisfaction. From that day, until the arrival of the new Superintendent I ate yam in the afternoon, rice in the evening. There came also milk, sugar, margarine and eggs in the morning most of which merely added weight on the cleaner and my guards, Ambrose most conspicuously.

And now, for no reason which I could fathom, the doctor appeared, accompanied by the Superintendent, two cadet officers, the chief warder, a senior warder and a squad of junior warders. The nurse waited outside. I submitted to the examination, answered his questions then asked one in turn.

'I have been here months. Alone. I have no books, no occupation whatever. Do you think this is good for my health?'

He thumped my chest and chuckled. 'Ho, ho. You look very healthy to me.'

'But do you think it is right? Do you think it's human? Because if you don't you ought to do something about it. I am accustomed to using and feeding my mind. Is it right I should be subjected to such a prolonged starvation?'

He turned blank. Never had I loathed the Asian accent as much as I did at that moment. As he spoke I recalled the entire history of the Indo-Pakistani incursion into the Nigerian Civil Service, two departments mainly – the Railways and the Medical Services. The dead Sardauna of Sokoto was mostly responsible for the mediocre talent brought into the country from Asia. One scandalous case among thousands involved a mere hospital orderly, the nephew of his Muslim host during one of his Islamic missions to Pakistan. In one of his many moments of expansiveness at the expense of the nation, the Sardauna guaranteed this orderly a top job in Northern Nigeria if he chose to return with him. He did and was created Medical Officer. He practised surgery with predictable results. Finally, in 1963, alarmed at the phenomenal rate of deaths under the surgeon's knife, an inquiry was ordered and the minion's antecedents were uncovered. Even so the final decision was merely: Forbidden further surgery. This butcher retained his post as Senior Medical Officer and held regular clinics.

I saw and heard the prison doctor, with his accent too caricatured to be true, simply as one of the lasting dregs of the Sardauna's importation. At first I thought that it was merely a joke in bad taste when he persisted in interpreting my plaint of mental starvation in purely physical terms, then suddenly realized that he was in dead earnest.

'My eyes,' I complained. 'The Harmattan or something has played havoc with them. I need to have them tested.'

In a trice his index finger had depressed the lower lids of my eye, rapidly, one after the other. 'Yes, yes,' flashing his optic pencil into each eye in turn. 'Yes, what about the eye? It all looks very normal.'

'I have spots before them.' I looked him full in the eye, willing him to understand and exert his authority. 'It must be lack of reading.' I felt foolish.

'No, no.' He kept bustling around, inspecting each eyeball with dead seriousness. 'Perhaps you've read too much in the past. Good thing to rest the eyes.'

I caught him at a moment when he had turned right round. He was now between me and the prison staff. I held his torch-hand and spaced out each word: 'They need to read.'

'Yes, yes ... sorry, did that irritate?' gently disengaging his wrist. 'Now I hear you have not been eating very well. You must eat you know.'

It was I think, at that moment, in the certain knowledge that I would obtain nothing from this visit, from this man, that my mind fastened on the ball-pen in his breast pocket. To write! To be able to set down thoughts on paper, perhaps to begin a new play, a novel, a short story, an accounting to myself ... it was all of that, but most importantly, it was occupation. A pen and I would be *doing* something. Time would be largely or minutely eroded.

'Spots,' I repeated. 'Like now, up there.' I pointed at the ceiling, but somewhat behind him, over his right shoulder. The pocket was to the left. Behind me I was hideously conscious of the prison staff watching but trying not to watch, listening but not listening, pretending that they have left an inmate in private consultation with his doctor. The Asian turned in the direction of my finger and I leant forward into him, plucked out the pen as his left breast turned past me. I palmed it, then placed my palm flat on the table, the pen ensconced inside it.

'Of course you wouldn't see it,' I said.

'It comes of your irregular eating.' He had begun to pack his instruments. I fastened my eyes on his in case he had noticed, daring him to damn himself utterly as a supposed member of a humanist profession by betraying me. But he had noticed nothing. Certainly there was no reaction from him. 'You should eat properly' was all he said, 'then you wouldn't have spots before your eyes.'

Thinking back, I think I wished that he had known of the

robbery. It would have meant the existence of a human conscience at hand, a lessening of the reality of isolation. Perhaps it was this which prevented me taking pride in the neatness of that brief, unpremeditated operation. I was too much concerned with following each moment from the view of his reactions, hoping against hope that he knew, that he realized my need and might even be moved to act on them. Why else would I now, with the Biro ink running dry, wish that he might call again? Knowing him as indeed he is, he is unlikely to return with a Biro sticking out of his pocket. If he does, would it be because he knew, and has returned deliberately to be robbed again?

The ink dries. It should be possible to calculate the arithmetical (or is it geometrical?) progression of ink drying up in a Biro. Or more pertinently, the psychological degression (any such word?) of inmates under the ministrations of a Sardauna doctor.

27

THE groans of anguish began just after supper-time. They came from the direction of that wall which faces the entrance to my cell. The wall has two flood-holes in it, both covered by iron grilles. The mesh is large enough to permit a cat to pass through. From bits of fur which are left clinging to it I know always when he has used the passage in the night. Then he darts across the intervening space so bare and full of danger, vanishes behind the hut, looking for scrap. A gutter runs through my domain just behind the hut. It links the yard of lunatics across the Crypt to the compound for women. The gutter is the subterranean link of all the catacombs of Hades.

Now there is a smell of death in the air. I cannot mistake it. So I must think only of living things, shut out the stench in my nose, the supplication of skeletal hands on my impotence.

We had a birth here some weeks ago. I heard a baby's cries and wondered how this could be. A baby in this hell? And it was evening, nearly the same time as the present intrusive groans began. It could hardly be a wife visiting her prisoner husband with a new-born child.

Is it not strange? I had heard the women's voices before but thought that they were children's. Several months passed before I knew that my crypt was placed between the yard of lunatics and that of women! Their voices are so thin, as if piped through a crevice in a distant cavern. They play childish games in the evenings – from the sound and the giggle they must be the kind of games children play. And those tunes which I had imagined came from without the prison? On a very quiet evening I even made out some words:

Brother Johnny
Brother Johnny
Do you sleep
Do you sleep
Wedding bells are ringing
Wedding bells are ringing
Ding dong ding

They sang in that listless, unmeaningful tone in which our schoolchildren sing foreign songs – *The Bluebells of Scotland, Ash Grove, The Lass with her Delicate Air* – which are forced upon the curriculum by unimaginative missionaries. The words are delivered flat even when such songs are accompanied by games. The words hold no meaning for them, the territory and sentiments are strange, and so this anaemic rendering is all that the misguided music mistress can obtain from them. It must be this remembered quality which made me imagine for so long that the voices which I heard at song and play came from children playing in the outer world under the mango trees. That world lies beyond Amber Wall; the sun rises just behind it.

A road runs along Amber Wall, not a busy one by the sounds. Or perhaps it is simply that it runs so far from the wall that the sound of vehicles seems muted. A certain amount of distortion does take place especially in direction. What is certain is that there is a wide swathe between the wall and the road and this space is occupied by a grove of mangoes whose tops are visible. I watch the buds appear, the efflorescence and the first green eardrops on the branches. Fat swarms of bluebottles follow human marauders at the first sign of ripening as all objects in the broad catalogue of missiles hurtle towards the fruits. They land often in the Crypt and I hear the guard swear and throw some back. I do not mind. Even the danger of being brained by a chance missile in the mango season becomes a spice of ecstatic possibility that livens up the tedium. A painful crack on the head is a token of life, of vitality. No, I do not think I would have minded at all.

I look up one morning – my early morning stroll just after opening hour – and there, right on the topmost branch, a territory hardly capable, I had always thought, of supporting more than the weight of the fruits, perched a little boy reaching for the topmost mangoes. His head was higher than the crown of the tree itself; he swayed gently with the motion of the branch. I was certain that there was just that last bunch of mangoes on the tree. Often the crown of the tree would move, violently shaken by one or more marauders on the lower branches but no one had dared climb this far before. His hand was on the goal when he looked down and encountered my gaze. He paused. We stared at each other. I smiled but his response was one of complete bewilderment. Then he took his gaze away and looked over to the other side. I saw his alert mind racing and questioning for he was now looking over into the teeming compound next to mine. The sun rose slowly behind him, too brilliant for me to sustain my gaze. I continued my stroll round the hut. When I came back he was back to staring into the Crypt. When I came round again he was gone, and the mangoes with him.

When I heard treble voices later that evening, I imagined him among others of his age, playing games in the moonlight. For the first time it conjured up, try as I would to repress them, childhood memories, a parsonage filled with children. I made a final effort and I shut down that scene, violently. In its place came the smell of flowers, a sunrise, the trill of a guitar, the wistful pagan ending of Cocteau's *Orphée Nègre*, the dance of spring by the two children, heirs to the evocative magic of sunrise, of seed awakening in the soil beneath their tread of innocence...

For unto us a child is born ... It was the cry of a newborn, that child's. It contained the distressing urgency that made up all its new world, a single-minded thrust of all the intensity of its tiny body. I heard a mother's crooning and I was certain. Another female voice, querulous and petulant joined in and the scene became almost human – the voice of the common mother in all our women offering anxious advice, taking the side of the child. But the voices remained muffled, the women unreal. They were not beings of the sun, not like the throbbing mangoes up against the sunrise. Ghosts, sheer weightless ghosts drifting in caverns of mists. Within their nether world the child is a full-throated freak, a changeling. I reflect now, somewhat sadly that the birth has come in the wrong season – it ought to be Spring. Still, if it is a girl we can ignore the timing and name her Persephone.

Still no solace at the Wailing Wall and close to midnight. I shut my mind to the other sounds that began some two hours ago, sounds that were soon bullied into silence. The other inmates, companions to the groaning man had set up a cry for help. I heard hysterical voices screaming Warder! WARDER!!! It went unheeded for nearly thirty minutes. Then it was augmented by banging – doors, windows, buckets. At least thirty voices were now screaming for help. And steadily below it all, in an unchanging tone and pace as if his pain had sublimated itself into this last automated sound, the groan persisted. I heard the sound of running boots, several. Heard the clang of iron as gates were swung open, heard the threats, the shouts. Heard the determined response of demands. Accusation. Heard these shouted down. One long tread of authority approaching the bed of the ailing man. I heard him bend down and make an examination that told him nothing. Heard the steps return. A babble of excited voices meant that he was leaving without saying what would be done. If anything would be done. I think I made out the repeated word – Doctor. He shouted it down flatly, angrily. The doors clanged to, the locks snapped their finality, the boots walked away. The murmurs of retreating guards were the protests of wronged men, of men whose leisure had been needlessly broken.

The groans do not cease nor do they diminish. The bloodless inhuman steadiness of this sound of human suffering is the most unnerving aspect of it all. It does not come from volition but from the weak inertia of a muted pulse. As if the man has merely left his mouth open and the sound emerges with his breathing out.

It is close to dawn when the sound stops. Abruptly. No weakening ever, neither faltering nor a rallying intensity. I know it is over.

My body is straining for the lightest sounds. One man has got up, he is gone near the silence to enquire. Others sit up in their beds, a few join the first by the bed. A minute later I hear the murmuring of prayers. The prayers continue until the doors are open. A warder steps in, pauses, shouts for his superior.

Soon it is that hour when 'all the dead awake'. As the key turns in my lock I ask the warder what became of the suffering man.

'The man died,' he said.

28

I HAVE named all four walls. The Wailing Wall, that from over which a babble of faiths wafts three times a day, and on some nights, the dismal groans of the sick or dying, this wall flanks some rarely used passage. Below the wall are two small holes for the escape of rain water. At their most revealing I have seen through it the flash of bare ankles of a prisoner, or the guards' familiar thick shoes. Sometimes the sleeker shoes of a cadet or other senior officer. My hallucinations also began here.

A trick of the light, the leaves of a creeper across the iron grill plus physical weakness on the sixth day of an absolute fast and I saw, clearly framed within the hole, unmistakable and complete with forelock and toothbrush moustache, the face of Adolf Hitler.

For minutes I sat unmoving, allowing the phenomenon to develop as it wished. There was no change except that the dark eye pools grew in intensity. I shut mine, turned my face to the wall, breathed slowly and carefully and turned again to look. Confronting me was the same cold face with its unchanged expression. I know that a scream escaped me and I leapt into the cell – I had been seated in the corridor, early evening. I stood in the darkness until the guard came to lock up, then went to bed. I closed my mind, refusing questions. It was hours before I slept, without dreams surprisingly.

The following evening, carefully gauging the time, I was back in that same position. This time it was the face of Albert Schweitzer. By shifting position I found I could have a large repertoire of faces. I got up and walked slowly towards the grill, watched the shadows dissolve, saw the creeper slowly delineate its contours and sanity recover brief ascendancy. The following day I reduced the totality of the fast, accepting groundnuts and oranges. Later, disturbed by a continued certainty that the faces turned, receded and loomed in what seemed a constantly adjusting telescope of ether, receding sometimes so far that they floated in sheer infinity without legs and body, moved, spoke and gestured with increasing insistence, I watched for an opportune moment in the day and cut off the creeper. From then the hole returned to what it was, a mere flood-hole. Finally it even ceased to exist. It was however, planning a resurrection of more deliberate insanity. It had cleansed itself of shadows merely for a sordid shadow-play.

A procession this morning on the other side of the flood-hole. It has no precedent. I question it long and solemnly, ankle after ankle, chain by chain. The sound of chains is real. It is also daylight. Slowly across the grill a degradation of human limbs – shuffle, clink, shuffle, clink, shuffle shuffle, clink . . . Bare feet, the chains are all visible, and the ankles. They are the same kind as were fixed on my ankles during my interrogation in Lagos, ponderous restraints of chain and buckle which bite into the bone at every motion. Shuffling is the only motion, an unhurried placement of right foot over left, left after right. No lifting of feet or the skin over the ankles becomes raw and then even shuffling becomes agony. A warder's glossy boots in contrast trying clumsily to match the prisoners' flattened *danse macabre* but how can they? They lack that metallic mastery, the 'even-rust' pace. Eleven prisoners and two guards in all have revived the flood-hole picture frame, replacing death-masks of the earlier dusks with a new pageant whose mystery I have yet to unravel.

Hard cases? Chronic escapees or homicidal maniacs? It seems strange that the guards should talk to them. The warders' voices have a light, studied casualness, an ease which seems forced. I hear no words, only voices. I suspect a story is being recounted, something quite funny. I am certain that the voices which laugh are the warders' but I sense no cruelty. With that arbitrary intuition that fleshes out the barest clues and sensations in confinement I even deduce that the story is one at the expense of officialdom, perhaps even against the storyteller himself. After the laughter, silence; a familiar strain in the pause before the voices resume.

Why then this effort to be kind? The charitable intent transmits through the barrier of walls, even through the facelessness of the actors. I know the bullying sounds of warders, the threatening, blackmailing, sadistic noises. Also the jocose, appeasing tones, I have heard the sounds of these dowsing their own authority; I know them all. The evening sounds after the senior officers have departed when, barring the surprise checks of the Grand O or senior aides, the bounds of gaoler and gaoled are erased and a mutually comforting humanity begins. Underpaid men with gargantuan problems of love, responsibilities and survival. I have separated the unctuous Judas voices also as they comfort the prisoner they have themselves betrayed. The rules of gaoler-prisoner confidences are carefully observed and only where necessary is the prisoner ever confronted with his betrayer – I know the Judas voice that welcomes him back from purgatory, the voice of the hypocrite which chides him for being too trustful of his fellow prisoners. The warders' voices on this walk are flecked in shades of the Judas tone but filled also with a shy sincerity. It is also the mutual night-comfort voice but strained, as if the sneak visit is expected but through a far more sinister unsuspected entry.

But still I do not understand. Hours later the procession shuffles back again, its distinctive pulse building in sound until the first toes drag into the picture frame, settling squarely in the centre to be slowly overtaken by the other foot, a chapped heel resting just within frame and a world-weary weight shifting onto it. This time I hear a response or two from the prisoners. The guards also have grown more normal, amiable; a relaxed exercise of the bond between the sufferer and those whom duty absolves from the crime of inflicting suffering.

It is a week before the procession is repeated. The pattern is the same as before, the mechanism just as precise. Heavy, tired, flat. Pasteboard shapes across the light. I have glued my eyes, nerved my ears to that flood-hold since the first passage, but again there is a break of some days. Three, I think.

This time there is a chain of three processional days in succession. And today's, the third and the *last* – for now I understand! – begins most strangely, and early. What blockages I must have erected even on my intuitions to have missed till now the goal of these processions! To have remained so faithful, so attentive to the passage means, I now admit, an awareness of some uncompleted act, a sense of the charade which was indeed no more than cruel prelude. I wake miraculously at my usual time, miraculous because sounds which should provoke my waking are all missing. It seems at first that I have woken late but the sun's inclination refutes this. I am conscious of waking into a dead silence. Missing are all the sounds of breakfast details passing through the prison, the cleaners, the early gang, the warders' parade and shouted orders. It is Ambrose's shift this week but when I go into the yard I encounter a young man I have never seen before. Even at this point I have not fully defined the strangeness of the morning as silence, only as some change in the day's tonality which I will ponder at leisure. (One learns how to hoard for later digesting experiences which the intuition does not label as immediately menacing.) I banish the unusual quiet, lengthen out my shower, then take a mindless stroll round the yard. On this early stroll nothing is permitted to intrude except the motion of ants, flies, butterflies and other incidents of insect or winged life – the day does not begin to drag until an hour or two after noon, and to that trial the hoardings of each day are left. Surely this conditioning alone must have caused my failure to interpret the death silence of that dawn, the charged footsteps of warders and officers, the latter most especially, the presence of at least a dozen alien footsteps among them, all equally charged and grim, and finally even, in retrospect, my own subconscious fearful excitement at the enactment of some unnameable ritual.

The chained feet when they pass offer no warning. Not even the fact that they are fewer by five. Today only six pairs of manacled feet drag across the frame. And this time the warders' voices are louder, laced with a nervous harshness. Their cheerfulness is markedly false and intolerable. Nervous in turn I take another walk round the hut. Facing the wall of the flood-holes – the Wailing Wall – is the Amber Wall, over which the sun rises. Standing against Amber I can look over the Wailing Wall and see the very tops of windows on the upper floor of the nearest prison block. At rare moments when an inmate, a detainee from his clothes, has climbed onto the window-sill for his own inscrutable reasons, I have actually seen a human face and with daring, and the luck of the guard's turned back returned a careful wave of the hand, even a nod of the head. Contact for him and me. A strengthening of wills.

Today all these windows are shut, and now I interpret the distant sounds of other windows pulling and banging shut. A huge human hive is muffled, blindfolded. And still I do not understand.

The silence lasts three, four hours. As when the sound

track on a film is switched on, the return of sounds is abrupt, arbitrary. And the chained six are now returning. At what moment I finally consent to understand I cannot say, since the effect of this illumination is to glue me to the bed where I have lain absorbing the silence without thought or motion. The return of the chains, heavier one moment, then confusedly lighter, I fail to place in relation to the moment of illumination. A numbed inertness, a paralysis of sensation succeeds the paralysis of thought in which the earlier hours of silence were so thoroughly absorbed. Suddenly I get up, mindless of my law which imposed no contact, nothing but essential communication with my guards. I race out to seek needless confirmation from the young warder. But he is gone and in his place I find Ambrose, red-eyed, flared nostrils, wide-pored with the stench of death. I do not even pause to reconsider my impulse but challenge him directly. 'You have hanged those men!' He nods. As if in deep need the words flow freely, in between pinches of snuff.

'Man must 'trong to do dat kin' work. If una no 'trong una no go last. 'E fit turn man head, make man run craze. Dis snuff, 'e help me. I take before an' after. Each person get in own ting. Me, na dis snuff dey help me. And afterwards, I take two bottle stout, mix am wit' illicit gin. Drink all afternoon. We get afternoon off when we do hanging squad. Some people no like am but me I no min'. When man take 'in han' kill another person, I no get pity for am. Murderer na wicked man, no sense make man dey pity 'am. Much better for worl' kill them all one time . . .'

They eat Special Diet, anything they want. Just like VIP. Very Important Pestilences like me, to be got rid of after fattening? Ambrose nods, then catches the meaning and corrects himself, violently repudiating such a suggestion. 'No, no, you no commit murder. Anybody can be political prisoner. You can be Prime Minister tomorrow.' I guide him back to the hanging ... They eat what they like, they have their own special cooks from among the trusties, the doctor visits them regularly and they change their menu as the whim takes them – games, hobbies, all the unconscious ironies that loom so important in the catalogue of the System's self-righteousness. The chains? No, they are never chained inside their own yards. Only when they come out to be examined at the dispensary. Oh, normally the doctor visits and treats them in their own compound when required but, well, it isn't really that they are going for treatment. They go to the dispensary all right but sometimes nobody even bothers to look at them. It's part of the drill. The outing is good for them anyway. This is what happens – it's simple really ...

When all the legal process is completed and the final confirmation of death sentence by the moment's authority is received by the Prisons, the transparent exercise in subterfuge begins. The doomed men know the act. Some have been in death yard nearly four years, they have been through it too often not to know. After the first dispensary outing none of them touches his food. The games are deserted – ludo, draughts – no one goes near the boards. They don't speak to one another. And the longer they participate in the black comedy the oftener they experience death, because each missed turn and the arrival of new inmates in the death yard makes each fake outing the logical turn of the older inmates. Simple law of probabilities. They are taken to the dispensary in batches, never the same. Periodic medical examination – this is what they are told – but since they are hardly ever examined and even such examinations are perfunctory, they understand what it truly presages. Only the identity of the next on the scaffold remains to be resolved. Each day may be the last. To be taken to the dispensary today does not mean a long reprieve. To be left behind is more terrifying of course – for the older ones. They know. But even to go with the 'sick' squad may be worse. It only means today is not the day. But what of tomorrow? They do not know until they return. If no one is missing then it may yet be the week after. Even a month. Months. The hangman may be taken ill.

Even the law demands only one death of its victim. These die, are made to undergo the motion of death several times over in the strange mechanism of legal torture and judicial slaughter.

A group of nine today, a different group tomorrow or next week. Maybe a successive three-day procession. Some are always left behind. Ambrose says they were not eleven each time, that the number varied every day, varying between nine and twelve. Perhaps. I thought I counted eleven each time until this morning. On the day itself it is the doomed men of course that are left behind. Their cells remain unopened. When the 'sick' gang have departed, the hanging squad enter, two warders to each man and pinion his hands behind him. A few struggle violently and have to be subdued. Some collapse and are carried only barely conscious to the gallows. Take Polyphemus . . .

The revelation did not surprise me – Polyphemus earned his first promotion as gladiator in service of the state, killing in single combat a condemned prisoner who would not walk to his hanging. A scene of elemental fury, part ritual, part medieval improvisation. One man had thrown his gauntlet in Death's face and claimed the right to a new trial by combat. Polyphemus picked up the gauntlet on behalf of state and Death.

This Bernadine waits in his cell in Enugu Death Yard. He has armed himself against death with a dustbin lid for shield and a lethal cudgel studded with metal points, fashioned somehow without discovery. The unsuspecting death-squad, confronted by the Satanic apparition crazed and cursing take to their heels. The challenger barricades himself and waits. None dare approach. Polyphemus is a mere junior warder and because he is illiterate likely to remain so for most of his life. But what is needed now is not literacy but his most impressive asset, his physique. Summoned by the white superintendent, he proves a willing volunteer, arms himself in like manner with shield and weapon and approaches. The warders tear down the barricades and retreat. Polyphemus closes with his foe, two gladiators in death struggle, the champion of the law and the outlaw in forfeiture of life. No one intervenes, no one can, such is the pace and scale, the ritualistic autonomy of the encounter. Not even the white superintendent who hovers in the wings, service revolver in hand, anxiously poised to fire an unfair shot if needed in defence of the state.

Polyphemus wins, killing his opponent by manual strangulation. But at least Bernadine did cheat the rope, thanks to Polyphemus.

But usually there is no resistance.

'We grip them by the arms – like this – and handcuff them behind. No, we don't chain their legs this time, just the handcuffs. Then the superintendent comes in. He reads each man the letter he has received from the governor and tells them, this is the appointed day. Then a priest comes in and speaks to them. Or an Imam if the condemned is a moslem. They say, prepare yourself. You took a life with your own hand and now society says you must pay for that life with your own. We set off for the hanging yard – it is right next to their own yard but they don't know it. You see, the rest are away from there when the 'time-up' ones are led away. They never know which path we took. Before the hanging yard was built in the new place they had a longer passage. And afterwards, the bodies went right through the compound and out at the main gate. Sometimes the relatives would gather looking for the corpse of their people; more often it was the relatives of the murdered man. Mind you, few relations came along to claim the body of any man hanged for murder – it was too shameful. But sometimes the relations of the murdered one would come, so the superintendent would come out and say, you see here the corpse of the killer of your relation. The state has exacted a life for a life, let all palaver end with his death.

'That was many years ago. Now, of course, there is a special entrance through which the bodies are removed by lorries. No, the scaffold is not erected until the actual morning of the hanging; that is why it sometimes takes so long, sometimes even up to three hours before we are ready for the condemned. Our part of the job is to be assistants to the hangman. We march them up to the platform, then the hangman takes over. The platform takes two at a time. When the first one is placed in position with the noose adjusted round his neck we prepare the next one. They are both hanged at once when the hangman pulls the handle. The trapdoor gives way and they both fall through. The neck breaks you see. It breaks at once, but they must be left hanging there for thirty minutes. That is what the law says. The hangman doesn't wait by the gallows. We do. There is a resting-room for him nearby and he goes in there with his assistant. There is stout for him there, he drinks while waiting. The doctor goes there too and the senior officer. No, they don't drink, mind you I have known one doctor who used a pocket flask quite openly. Nobody would quarrel with him, what for? You think anybody goes through that kind of day without some special something inside him? We could do with something to drink too but we have to wait by the bodies. Steal the bodies? No, that is not why we stay there.

'No one can steal bodies there. We wait there to guard the condemned awaiting their turn. Of course they see what is happening. They can't help it. Yes, they see the first ones to go, it's a good lesson for them. Once we hanged eleven on the same day – that's right, the Apalara murderers. They were hanged right here in Kaduna. All on the same day. No, the hangman doesn't take the bodies down. We do that. When the thirty minutes are over we go under the platform and loosen the ropes. We lower them into rough wooden coffins, then the doctor comes and makes a small cut in the back of the neck, just where the head joins it. He takes something out and puts it in a bottle, writes the name of the condemned on the bottle and puts it in his pocket. What does he take out? That's what I've always wanted to know. Some of our people say that is the thing which contains a man's life. Is that a fact?'

Kaduna 69

29

I MADE a strange discovery this morning. I'm pregnant.

For a long time I looked down on the evidence, wondering how it came to be. For there it was, firmly rounded and taut, an egg of a protuberance that had no business on my waist-line.

Considering my sex, it should not happen to me at all. Of course, stranger things have been known to happen. Sex change could creep up slowly on a man, unnoticed in such an asexual atmosphere. First the attenuation of masculine genes, then the hermaphroditic co-existence. Battle of the hormones and survival of the weakest. Or is it the stronger? Female genes are supposed to be stronger, or maybe they are merely faster in the race for the womb? Something on those lines. Anyway that is hardly the point. I have after all led a strictly celibate life for over a year.

Could it be kwashi-okor?

No. The pictures of kwashi-okor I have seen are huge calabashes which commence from the region of the lower chest, balloon evenly outwards then – a sharp ingress towards the scrotum. My pregnancy begins just below the navel, it is hard as stone, small and compact. It really looks as if I have secreted a large egg just under the skin. It is contradictory because the rest of my body is skin and bone – this is the fifth week of the new cycle of fasting. I have conquered weakness and hallucinations, there is no longer strain on mind or body. My body dwindles but without loss of strength, my mind expands without a loss of clarity. I have even recovered the greater part of my lost sense of humour.

I resolve to take a walk and ponder the strange phenomenon of my body. The act of getting up solved it at once.

I caught myself automatically expanding my belly to fill the huge gap in my trousers. The longer I fasted, the wider the gap of course and the harder my lower belly strained to fill it. I seem to have built up over the months what must be in proportion to the body the largest abdominal set of muscles anywhere in the world. My loud laughter brings the gaoler slouching round to see what is the matter. I feel like inviting him to come and take a punch at these anomalous muscles. Above them each rib is sticking out as distinct as the original rib of Adam before the fleshing over. My shoulder blades and cervix are so distinctly marked that I could be daubed in paint and pressed on a flat surface to provide illustrations for any anatomical book. Yet here, just under the navel was bunched a wad of rich, superabundant muscles, ready to step into any Mr Universe contest of the abdomen.

Why do I fast? As I move towards the confrontation from which I must not back down, it is necessary to be clear in my own mind. For the reason is beyond the letters I began to write at the commencement of this new duel. In these letters to my prison keepers I ask for books, writing material, for clothes instead of the rags on my body. I also ask for an end to my inhuman isolation.

It is March, 1969. I have been in prison eighteen months. Fifteen of those have been here in Kaduna, in solitary. In December of last year an order was signed for my release. I know, because Mallam D., my interrogator in Lagos, came to see me.

It was a strange meeting naturally, I did not at first credit the sight. He came, I remember, in the second half of December, accompanied by the Grand Seer (the new Superintendent) and Polyphemus. 'I've brought someone to see you,' he said. The visitor stepped in view: Mallam D.

'How are you? I was on my way to Kano – I've been

posted there. But I had some duties to perform here and I thought I shouldn't leave the yard without saying Hello to you.'

I do not remember what reply I made to him but it was a friendly one.

'Things are generally better now ... well, I think you'll be finding that out yourself very shortly. In fact I am here to look among the detainees. We released several of them yesterday and I'll be releasing more of them today. Things have got out of hand, well, you know yourself ... the gaols are simply overflowing. So many innocent people rotting away – for doing nothing. Anyway, well, look Wole, try and forget the whole thing when you come out will you? Consider it just one of those things that happen in war time.'

I did not want to believe what I could distinctly hear behind his words. Nor the confirmation which I could clearly read in the Grand Seer's face, grinning away in pure joy. Even Polyphemus was beaming through every inch of his frame.

I said, 'Some things one must forget. But you can't expect me to forgive or forget the fact that I was framed.'

'I am not asking that ...' And the Grand Seer very anxiously added, 'No, no, of course not. Nobody would ask that. It's not an easy thing.'

Suddenly I wondered about D. I did not expect an answer but I could at least study his face. I asked, 'D., do you know *why* I was framed?'

D. had this most unusual grace for a policeman. He could be embarrassed, visibly, undisguisedly. He betrayed emotions like a normal human being, especially such emotions as spring from moral unease. If he were white he would blush in confusion. He burst out suddenly with a counter-attack: 'But why did you try to escape? You don't know how bitter we were, how disappointed.'

I looked seriously at him. He believed it. But I had long passed the stage of wishing to denounce that lie. I could no longer accept the ethics of the oppressor. I replied, 'Let us assume it was true. I had a moral right to take what actions I could against a System so morally debased as to frame an innocent man. If escape was possible then it became my first duty. Now you answer me, do you know why I was framed?'

He said, 'Things were going on quite well. We thought everything was all right, then the politicians stepped into it.'

'The politicians?'

'Oh, Wole, you don't know what we have to put up with. I am glad I'm getting out of Lagos. And at least before I go I can undo some of the things which have been going on. If you knew how many people we've been releasing lately, in Lagos and in other prisons, it's only now we've had time to look into all these cases. I mean, hundreds and hundreds. Most of them are simply here. Nobody knows why. They have no files, nothing. They are locked up for no reason at all. Nobody knows a thing about them at the police department or in the army for that matter. Look, let's not discuss it . . . just try and forget everything.'

'All right.'

'It's all over now – well, you'll see for yourself. But please try and forget it.'

They left. I remained where I was. The visit, his words, the demeanour of the two prison officials . . . I felt I was being dishonest, not merely over-cautious but plainly dishonest by refusing to accept the plain meaning of it all.

The guard had locked the gate after them and now came towards me, expansive.

'It's true. They release about forty people from here yesterday. And that man and some other from Kaduna Security here, they siddon for superintendent office dey look every detainee record. In fact, only I no wan' tell you before,

Chief 'inself 'e tell us this morning say your own paper done come. You go see, before two or three day . . .'

That was it. In plain words. Liberty.

From those earlier crises I had learnt to clamp down on my pulse. I sensed the excited quickening just about to start and I froze it back to normality. Keep still I said, be still. Blot out this morning's apparition. Completely.

But the Grand Seer came back. I developed a deep affection for this man who allowed his happiness for another to saturate his being unashamedly. He had the day's newspapers in his hand:

'These will keep you occupied ... while waiting.' He stood for some time and then grew solemn. 'Mr Soyinka, all I have to say is, Please forgive us. Yes, even us of the Prison. Forgive us for anything we did or failed to do, for being unable to help ourselves but to keep you here.' His eyes grew misty.

'You know – and you can ask the Chief, he is the only one in whom I really confide; I trust him. He may be illiterate but he is a wise man. I discuss things with him, especially when I'm puzzled. And I told him this, shortly after I took over here. All I knew about you was what I had read in the papers, and the reports from our headquarters. But after watching you for a few months, I said to the Chief: I am sure that man is innocent. Ask him before you leave us, he will tell you it's the truth. You remember I came myself to ask you your own story, about two months after I resumed duty here? Well, it was the day after I made up my mind you were innocent. I think I told you at the time that I believed your story?' I had not told him anything of the underlying causes, only the facts of my interrogation. – 'In this job one learns to study human beings. And not only criminals. All the politicians who were imprisoned during the Action Group crisis, including Awolowo himself, they passed under me at one time or the other. I was able to study the dedicated ones among them, the mere opportunists, those who simply were there for the adventure and excitement of politics and so on. One learns something about human nature. Frankly, I was convinced you never made that statement. That was why I came and asked you. But you know, I felt that there had been a genuine mistake somewhere. I did not believe that any human being in a high responsible position would deliberately forge a false confession. I have to admit that. I felt it was all a mistake. Even now,' he continued, 'if I had not heard it directly from Mallam D. . . .' He broke off. 'I must get back to the office. Is there anything you want? I think we had better send you a barber. Your hair is. . . . Have you ever had a haircut since you came here?'

I shook my head. 'Samson lost his strength that way.' He laughed. 'Do you want one now? It really is a jungle Mr Soyinka.'

I said 'All right, send him.' What I thought of at that moment, strangely, was not my hair at all but my face. I had not looked in a mirror for over a year and the flash that came with the mention of a barber was a figure in prison uniform clipping the hair of another prisoner, and that prisoner watching the barber's progress closely in a mirror. Perhaps one of the last scenes I observed before my entry into the Crypt. I was overwhelmed with a sudden curiosity to see my face.

'I'll have the Chief bring in one right away. And your clothes?'

'There should be a spare pair of trousers in the store.'

'I'll see if they are clean. If not the sooner they are washed the better. I'll look up some old magazines and let you have those too.'

He was off. The Chief took his place not long after, a heaving seven foot of grins and sly winks and even plainer innuendoes. He kept repeating, 'Sometimes it look like time never end. But one day na one day when God hear all prayer. Abi no to so?'

The barber nodded, making all his preparations. Polyphemus placed the chair first in one corner, then in the next, asking, 'Is the sun too much here? No, I think that place is better.' He left finally: 'Yes, na so. Suddenly one day na one day.'

I sat in the chair, felt the white cloth passed under my chin, tied at the back of my neck. I reached for the mirror, slowly turned it over and looked at my face.

The hair was unbelievable. I had been prepared for it but still it took me by surprise. It was long and dense and I wondered how my comb had managed to penetrate it for so long. I took the comb from the barber and said, 'You'd better let me do that for you.'

But even as I combed it out I was looking at my face. My eyes held me riveted, for I saw in them what had been whispered in my mind since the first hint of my release. Doubts, deeper than doubts. It is not over, not yet. And the coming phase will be harder because of this false hope.

I lay down the mirror and undid the cloth round my neck. 'I'll leave my hair as it is,' I said.

I was back in my cell, flat on my bed asking, Why? Mere caution? No, it went deeper. I could not place it, no one ever can; but I knew I was not leaving jail that Christmas.

(The terms of my release were easy to anticipate – a selective Christmas amnesty.)

Even so a part of the mind was all too humanly functioning the other way. If I were released what would I say or do? Whatever I did I knew that I must pour contempt on the Christmas tomfoolery. A phrase came easily to mind and I heard myself shouting with genuine anger: 'I hope this is the last time anyone tries to play Father Christmas with justice.' And it made me much calmer. After that I shut down the optimist-function side of the mind and busied myself with thinking how I would survive in continued isolation after this cruel seep of light.

The storekeeper came. Yes, those are my trousers. Shirts? Those are what you see hanging there. Yes, the lot. Wash them or stuff them I don't care.

The Crypt was full of the false alarm. The trusty who brought my food looked on me like a man already apart, a being touched and marked by the wand of his favourite deity. The warder followed him as usual but this time, not so much keeping watch against surreptitious communications as from a desire to pontificate on providence, patience, justice and courage plus a number of items in his ill-digested piety. When he had gone I tried to eat but my appetite was gone. My premonitions hardened every second.

End of morning shift. Into the yard rushed two warders who sometimes came on relief duty in the Crypt. 'I off-duty tomorrow sir. I say make I come say good-bye in case I no see you when I come back.' Another: 'The whole of us done happy too much oga. But God dey. God see everything.' Former long-vanished warders also came. They had served two, three, sometimes four weeks, or months, then disappeared. I had thought that the frequent changes were a mere Security precaution. Now they rushed in quickly to shake hands, telling me, 'You know why you no see us again? We no like this place at all. Man siddon here for eight-hour shift do nothing. Wit' other prisoners we dey talk and play but here we dey for solitary confinement. So we all ask for transfer for outside gang.'

Then they were gone. Afternoon has its quiet hour just at the end of morning shift. The prisoners are confined to their cells and it is very silent and peaceful. I let myself drift on the silence, stretching it into weeks and months. If only I would be transferred somewhere else! A new place, new smells, sights, a new environment to milk for the shadow games of survival. Yes, perhaps one should aim for this. In the brief excursion into my future in the Crypt I came across an incurable stretch of agony, a grey fungoid spread for which the very palliatives were in themselves manifestations of that disease. There is no redemption, ultimately, from hideous boredom, no novelty that can distract the mind from contemplation of this abyss. My first twelve months had used up more than the normal creativity of a mind that received no replenishment from other sources.

Polyphemus was the first to appear baffled. He came round on evening inspection, in mufti, confident that I would be gone. It was Christmas Eve and he had been certain that I would be in my own house for Christmas. He had imagined me departing the same way I came, in a special plane, disembarking on my own front lawn on the very eve of Christmas. In the morning he came to say good-bye and wish me well, now it was close to nightfall and I heard him at the gate, baffled to find a guard still in the Crypt, and the detainee still waiting.

He scratched his chin somewhat angrily. 'Anyway, never mind, Christmas Day no pass yet, you go reach home tomorrow. Dat one I know for sure. I beg you, make you no begin worry at all at all. Small time you reach home. You dey go. Na this foolish nonsense I no sabbe; police people, dem useless.'

On Christmas Day no one came, except the guard on duty. On each face the same amazement. The beginnings of doubt. Consolation. I had long turned off.

Boxing Day. 27th. 28th. The gloom began to vanish from the staff for whom the affair had become a personal thing. As New Year approached their courage picked up again. The release must have been planned for the New Year Amnesty after all. Obvious. 'New Year's Day, you no go spend am for Kaduna.'

The Grand Seer re-appeared on the 29th. Crestfallen. 'All I know is that orders have been signed for your release. Those Security men told me themselves. You heard D. yourself didn't you?' His voice demanded exoneration. I said, 'Yes, I heard him.'

'Two men were sent from Lagos, with the order. I heard there was some problem over how you were to get back to Lagos. I think they couldn't get a plane or something. Anyway let them release you. After all you can find your own way back. Why shouldn't you start enjoying your freedom now?'

It was my turn now to console him. 'The longer it's kept, the sweeter it is in the end. Don't worry, I'll be getting out some day.'

'Not just some day. I am sure you won't be here on New Year's Day. Just the same I find it very annoying.' Suddenly his voice rose in protest. 'We want you out of here Mr Soyinka. Believe me we want you out of here faster than even you want to get out. Don't misunderstand me, we like you. I wish we could have met under different circumstances and I certainly hope we will meet again. But you are the most uncomfortable figure any prison officer could hope to have in his charge. I have never had so many memos about one single man in my whole experience. Memo from headquarters, memo from police. Secret spies from all of them. Rumours. Accusations. You simply don't know how it is. I cannot do a thing, I cannot offer you even one new plate without first writing to headquarters. And of course I get no reply. But if I do it they somehow know about it and I get a query. Believe me, at one time I even thought of retiring or asking for a transfer. The strain was getting too much. When you leave here, we are returning to normal routine.

Normal routine! If you knew how fast I want you out of here...'

And New Year's Eve came. And in spite of battening down the hatches to prevent any seepage of hope into my heart, I caught myself listening for footsteps, interpreting the opening of a gate several yards away, straining impossibly to hear any sound from the distant office or the prison's main gates.

When it was over, when the period of grace had expired, finally, definitively, I was grateful for the cessation of contact by this new-replenished humanity. Only Polyphemus came in occasionally. I could hear him at the gate demanding 'All correct?' and receiving the stock answer 'All correct, sir.' Once he did summon enough courage to come close to the cell, overcome I supposed by a need to see how I was taking it. He moved as if attached to something just beyond the entrance to my cell, made a noisy inspection of the object. On the way back he seemed to have resolved to speak to me. I lay still, looking into the net. He hesitated, faltered and fled.

After the first three or four days, the newspapers also had stopped. Once again the world outside was sealed off. There was only the long stretch of days ahead. No landmarks that I could envisage. In spite of recalling myself again and again to the accuracy of my intuition and in spite of the preparation this afforded, there was still a residue of blasted hope, enough to generate despondency.

How much time do I prepare against? A year? And all in solitary?

Not under the same conditions as before. I need clothes, occupation, *things*! I must have the minimal needs of a human being! The gaoler walked by. I had shouted aloud.

It is *wrong*. The question is not whether I can bear it or not. The issue is, should I have to bear it? If it is a minimal requirement, a need that is granted to convicted felons, then to deny me means of utilizing my mind is torture. To feed my body but deny my mind is deliberate dehumanization. To accept this meekly is a form of supineness. To accept it continuously is to accept risks of an end which even I cannot foretell. I need to exchange thoughts not merely with myself but within a community of other minds. I cannot circle indefinitely in the regurgitations of my mind alone. It is evil. These fiends are stretching my mind beyond human tolerance. I must end this reliance on myself. I must break out of the mental prison in which they have encased me.

I asked for pen and paper and wrote my first letter of demand to the Prisons. I wrote again demanding books. Writing material. Clothes. Medical treatment specially for my eyes, an end to my isolation or a transfer to another prison. The last had become crucial in my thinking for yet another reason. After the debacle of my expectations of liberty I knew that where before I had been surrounded by a mixture of fear, hostility and suspicion, that perfect condition for strengthening the resistant will, I was now enveloped in a mire of sympathy which would end by destroying me. I saw my will weakening, saw increasing acceptance of my fate, saw me drawn into this suffocating cocoon of affection and pity. But powerless. Powerless pity. Powerless kind men. Capable of redressing nothing. Nothing could be more insidiously subversive. I wanted eyes of hate and fear around me to keep me constantly alert. If I should choose to pursue my explorations of the psyche, entering again and again into that accommodating territory of release, returning to question the realities of pain and even temporality, it was necessary to have hard evidence to welcome me back to earth; the slit of animal cruelty in the eye of paid hands, the quickness of their mind to inhuman inventiveness. Those around me had turned to mere shuffles full of guilt, waiting to alleviate my plight with any gesture even with any material aid that lay within their power. But the word was power. Little lay within their sphere of affectuation. Sympathy is poor substitute; it was finally, capable of the erosion of the will.

It was a month at least before a reply came back. The Superintendent would not show it to me but he quoted a phrase from it. The phrase too had struck him, evidently, but he hardly knew why it did. The tone was scornful and jubilant. I thought, what are these people? *How* are they made? It was not even the voice of a torturer. It was the tone of the vicarious torturer, a small envious functionaire whose validation as a man came from a power exerted on inert forms and files. It was such a murky tone so despairingly human and small that it produced a flash. A young man, about my own age. He had a rather thin face and his hair receded a little at the temples. He had very dark skin and long fingers which ended in close clipped nails. The flash was over but I continued to picture him holding my protest in one hand and chuckling with self-satisfaction. I saw him obsequiously rush to his boss with it in gloating. I heard him say, 'I think it's beginning to get him sir.' His boss slapped him on the back and left him with the appropriate phrasing for a reply.

And yet there was something – excessive. Something not totally called for, not justifiable in that tone. There was a glee which went not merely beyond decency but seemed to be largely conjured up without a cause. I could not, for a start, understand the word 'yearning', could not understand that is, the right of my gaolers to employ this word. It became a minor obsession akin to that of 'humiliation'. I looked at the Superintendent, his face betrayed the explanation. I asked him:

'Did you simply send my letters or did you add a covering letter of your own?'

He had written a covering letter. Nothing wrong with

that, but I saw also what kind of letter he must have written. I recalled again the look in his eye when he paid his first visit to my cell. His eyes had come down and stayed on my ragged jeans. Full of huge rents, frayed patches. The shirt was no better. I had seen a large humanity in him at that moment, and now I could read every word of his covering letter, a lachrymose description of my condition and an appeal for amelioration.

'It is not the first time I have written them,' he continued. 'Ever since you first complained about your eyes I have written. I have even spoken to the Security people here to come and take you to hospital. But no reply. This is the first time they've bothered to reply.'

These men are not merely evil, I thought. They are the mindlessness of evil made flesh. One should not ever stumble into their hands but seek the power to destroy them. They are pus, bile, original putrescence of Death in living shapes. They surely infect all with whom they come in touch and even from this insulation here I smell a foulness of the mind in the mere tone of their words. They breed themselves, their types, their mutations. To seek the power to destroy them is to fulfil a moral task.

In some vague way, my plan to fast towards nothing was an obsessive search towards this goal. Something must be tested even at the risk of life. I must reach that point where nor mind nor body of me can be touched, move beyond the capacity of small minds to soil my being or reach towards it. It has not been fasting alone. I have let my psyche roam free, seeking them, learning to destroy them when the time comes.

Embarking on this new conflict in the only area left me in the battlefield of the will, I was impressed by the need to give it tangible shape and form. It had to be quantitative, not a brief feat of endurance whose sharp collapse would leave no choice but such indignities as forced feeding. If I could fast in such manner as to avoid the symptoms of collapse, holding up my body by gently hiving off the flesh, accustoming the body to less and less till finally – nothing. Locked within the physical orbit of their power much could be done by them if panicked. I wondered suddenly about the Grand Seer as a person in that fix.

I sent for him and asked: 'What would you have done that other time if I had ignored your plea to call off the fast?'* He replied, after much stammering: 'I am not really sure what I would do. Naturally I would continue to appeal to you to . . .'

'Would you force-feed me?'

'It would depend on the doctor. Naturally if things came to a head I would have to call in a doctor. And if he says you must be fed . . .'

'I am going to fast,' I said.

'Not like that last time please. I never want to see a human being waste away like that; never again. It's dangerous. I wish it were possible for me to talk to you about Islam. The Koran preaches that self-preservation is man's first law.'

'When I make demands, minimal demands for a decent existence, is that not also for purposes of self-preservation?'

'I have done everything possible, you know that.'

I assured him again that I knew it. 'But you will admit that it is beyond your power to do anything for me.'

Even as I spoke to him inspiration came to me for achieving a gradual fast. He continued to ask me for assurances and would not leave until he obtained a promise that I would not repeat a total fast. I assured him no, not for a start, but we might easily find ourselves moving towards it.

The idea that came to me was simple. The first week I

*My first 'token' fast after the abortive release. It was a mild, partial fast of 21 days which, however, rapidly emaciated my body.

would go one day without food, the second week two days, the next three . . . until the seventh week, and then – what?

This is the fifth week and the last day of this week's cycle of fast. I am committed to breaching the security that rings me round before the seventh, the last continuous stretch. I have made myself that promise. Someone outside must know that this confrontation is taking place, lest, if the course prove fatal an emaciated form be pulled out of a hole with a hard incongruous lump for stomach, an unlikely pregnancy that will be diagnosed cerebro-abdominal meningitis.

30

THE sirens began about four o'clock yesterday. I followed the sounds and plotted a chaotic criss-cross of motions. There seemed to be no particular direction and I amused myself for a long time with the possibilities. It was no siren of alarm or natural disaster. The Biafrans were not invading. Quite on the contrary, the feeling was all of the flurry and incidence of pomp. I wondered who it was. A foreign dignitary? A committee of the OAU? I diagnosed an international meeting, a pan-something delegation or some such kind of protocolic infliction. Some by road and some by air, some lost and stranded in the vastness of the country. That made sense. The sirens would not only guide them to rescue points but warn the citizenry that the town belonged, on the excuse of this important invasion, to the guardians of the peace. With us sirens equate purpose and a sense of direction. A vehicle travels after all from nowhere to somewhere and if a crescendoing, then diminuendoing sound can render that achievement in direction palpable, then the nation is well tuned.

The psychology of sirens has been turned into one of the most unanswerable systems of coercion not only here but in almost all our continental fraternities. Banda's thugs have made physically memorable the risks and penalties involved in sanctifications of the siren. I have watched the smoothly articulate Senghorian version in procession on the broadways of Dakar. And locally, once I saw at the cathedral junction on the Marina, Gowon's motorcade halt, his bodyguards leap out, drag and pulverize a motorist in the mud because his vehicle was slow to respond to the imperatives of the siren.*

*An episode lyricized in *Prisonettes* 'Background and Friezes'.

Not that he did not understand! Who *dared* not understand? But mechanized aids to intention often let down the thinking man, so, there he sat physically man-handling the starter and steering-wheel when the whirlwind descended on him. Fool! He should have abandoned the jalopy and taken to his heels. This was within the first few months of Gowon's self-consolidation. Later there would be no such public displays. The motorcade passed in unruffled dignity except for that small falling-off, a minute falling-off which took the culprit in charge and 'vanished' him in thin air for months, returning – if he was fortunate to return – a sadder, wiser man.

It spread. A Police Assistant Commissioner on his way to kick off the start of a football match rated himself four motor-cycle escorts and four waggonloads of riot police. At Shagamu a consultant at the University Teaching Hospital was slow to diagnose this particular symptom. The motorcade stopped and the uniformed thugs gave him a beating. It spreads.

There is, I suspect, a secret prestige rivalry between dictatorships, especially the new *arrivistes*. How many hours before I actually pass through, is all traffic stopped? Between Banda, Mobutu and Gowon there must be little to choose. I have watched them all in action. Senghor is, of course, in a class by himself.

But the sirens were not welcoming or seeing off any visitors to these shores. The sirens continued all the following day and towards evening I strolled out to demand of the guard what great occasion warranted these noises. Strange, it was again a strange face.

'Didn't you know? Gowon dey make marriage?'

'Good for him. Is it today or is all this the rehearsal?'

'No. 'E done marry for Lagos. Dis one na for we wey no see the Lagos show. After two day 'e go Zaria make another celebration.'

I didn't get it. A local custom I hadn't heard of?

'No, not like dat at all at all. The whole government come here for party. And all Lagos society. They begin for Lagos, den they come here. After, they go Zaria. Na big tour. You for see all the soldier wey den bring come parade for street. Every foot na soldier you go find. Army one side. Air Force one side, Navy one side, riot police one side . . . de whole ting. Even Prison get in on parade. Today 'e dey visit the wounded soldier for hospital, 'e an in wife.'

'And the same thing will happen Zaria?'

'Certainly. But I no know yet if 'e dey go make another party for Biafra.'

He chuckled and went away. A new tone. A sweetly deliciously dissident overtone to that wedding march which filled the organ pipes of the prestigious Christ Church Cathedral where, without being told, I knew the wedding must have taken place. I wondered if the complacent privileged élite had not misjudged this class of people after all. Were there more of him? Were even the silent ones like him?

I sent word to my prison contact: I want cuttings of everything to do with Gowon's wedding.

But before the cuttings arrived, the same warder brought, the following day, a copy of the *New Nigerian*. 'Make you look am quick. Na you people say you dey fight for common man. We siddon here wem dey suffer. We ask for increment we no get am. De arrear wey Wilnik Commission done say make den pay us 'e pass two years we no get am. Dey say na wartime, make we wait. They say everybody economize. We no fit pay school fee or buy uniform for picken. War dey war dey but dis man bring all Lagos society come Kaduna, they begin blow we money right and left for in wedding? Wetin me a get for in wedding? Na me go fuck in wife?'

He went off and sat by the gate, keeping the door carefully locked. Got up again and returned. 'I done drink too much today and I wan' sleep. If you hear noise make you hide the paper for under your pillow. A go take am when you finish. A no do dis work come kill myself. I dey go sleep. If chief catch me make dem sack me.'

I opened the paper and saw a photo of a little piece of fuhrist complacency, surrounded by what is known as 'local dignitaries' including some of the once all-powerful Emirs. But there was an even more important news item in that day's issue. Either the guard had not seen it or it had not impressed him. Umuahia had fallen. And the victorious bridegroom was announcing this item to the Emirs in the following terms: that the fall of Umuahia was unfortunately a few days late, as it had really been planned as a present for him on his wedding day!

I waited for my news-clippings to arrive. Only that item really interested me now. I needed to check it against other reports. It could have been a misquote. I could perhaps even absorb the élitist arrogance which went into the wedding extravaganza of this nonentity in the baffling process of history, I could ignore the later idiocies I uncovered – the deliberate corruption of impressionable schoolchildren whose precarious powers of evaluation had been exploited by the national educational machinery to induce them to compete for souvenirs from this hubristic insolence, I could forgive the competitive slavishness of the Lagos State Government and the naïvete of its head, Mobolaji Johnson, an amiable but unlucky miscast, who considered it a duty to immortalize this better forgotten disgrace by altering the name of a major street to Yakubu Gowon Street in honour of the wedding; I could laugh, as one of those grisly jokes by which history compensates temporal derangements in rational thinking and human sensibilities, I could laugh at the photo of Gowon at his Island Club high-society reception, a photo in which he was happily conducting an orchestra during the devastation of a Nigerian city – there was Yakubu Nero Gowon at the reactionary centre of the Nigerian leisurely classes fiddling away while the nation was burning. All this I could accept and more. Even the printing of a commemorative wedding stamp! Two years of power and most of those a history of genocide, mass hatred, destruction and civil war, yet so confidently insulated was this individual, human enough – thank goodness for that at least – to have pre-empted his marital dues by at least four months, yet so far above and unrelated to the human plight that he prints and regally launches commemorative stamps of this abysmal corruption in all the country's embassies. Again, this was really stretching it far but I found somehow that I could gloss over it. I could put it down to the not inconsiderable blunting of judgement which is the work of the slavish courtiers to be found around power and whose important existence – a crucial sensation for otherwise empty lives – can only be proven by the penumbral glow of the excesses of that central power.

But the inside of the man, the deadness of mind and sense was summed up in the final unedifying revelation: that the taking of a rebel stronghold, the taking even of the smallest bow-and-arrow defended hamlet in a civil war was not to him the sum of lives on both sides, of mutilation and sacrifice, was not even the weighty dilemma and disquieting decisions of human sacrifice but – a wedding present! A glorification of a private and a personal bond between himself and some unknown, irrelevant quantity. Nothing but a feudal dynastic mentality could have conceived such irreverence, nothing but power drunkenness could have bilged forth such grandiloquent vomit on the entire national sacrifice.

I owed much to Gowon's wedding. The guard came some hours later that day for his newspaper. I handed it over but he waited; he was awaiting comments from me.

I looked up and laughed. 'Well, what do you expect me to say?'

His voice turned abrupt. 'Wetin they say you do?'

Surprised I answered him finally, 'But you must have heard. They say I wan' buy aeroplane for Ojukwu.'

'Na true? You do am?' This transformation in him to the role of an interrogator took me slightly aback. Wondering, I denied the charge.

He said, 'I 'grẹẹ say you no confess nothing. They tell us say you don' confess but me I done tey for dis work. But I wan' know true-true whether you dọ am.'

I assured him that there was no truth whatever in the charge.

He said, 'You for do am. I for glad if you do am. Dis government service, the trouble na say, man no fit talk, das all. But if man talk wetin in eye dey see . . . I dey here when dey begin kill Ibo. I see am wit' my own eye. The ting wey dese people do, God no go forgive them for ever. And when I see dis kind bagga come dey make yanma-yanma wedding party while we siddon here dey suffer . . . anyway, God dey for heaven.'

There was a long pause; I was uncertain how to react. It came too sudden and there was the fact of his newness. Was he a Security spy come to take the temperature of the hard case? Again an abrupt question from him: 'Why you dey fast so tey?'

'It is difficult to explain,' I said.

'No, tell me. I wan' knọw. I no see person do dat kin' ting before. Week after week after week. I don hear Chief say you no be moslem, you no be christian. You no believe in God. Why you dey punish yourself? Gowon siddon dere e' dey blow we money for champagne. Man dey die for front and you too wan' kill yourself for nothing. Why?'

It was a long time since I had spoken to a *curious* human

being, an uncertain mind in the sense of notions that did not belong to his immediate needs and his range of experience. A mask had dropped, the mask of the gaoler. I read the dissatisfaction, the comprehensive even if vaguely personal awareness of necessary social egalitarian agreements as the norm for any community of human beings. I began to ask him questions in turn, seeking to obtain a measure of his malcontence. He seemed to be offering himself but I could not be certain.

He said, 'You know, when you first come, Chief address us for parade. Any time some new person come, especially important man like yourself, they must tell we for early morning parade and give instructions. He tell we say you be dangerous person. He talk for long time. He say, if you talk to this man at all, make 'e no surprise you if you find yourself inside detention. Na clever man, na big man, but na dangerous man. 'E say you make trouble for Akintola, you make trouble for Sardauna and now you wan' make trouble for Gowon. He warn we, 'e say, make you just do your job and lef' the man. But after some time, 'e go siddon dey talk, sometimes during break. 'E say, hngh, dis man wey dey for solitary, I no sabbe de man. Small, small, small, small, 'e begin talk as if 'e done begin like you. And Chief enh, before 'e like somebody, 'e done see something . . .'

I let him speak; he so badly needed to, especially about himself. The picture was familiar. Early ambitions squashed by acceptance both of social reality and his own personal limitations. A close relation dead in the war, fighting for the federal cause. He himself had wanted to enlist, had in fact been placed on the reserve list but his family had badgered his life reminding him that he was the remaining adult male of the family. That family was now expanded to include that of his dead relation killed early in the war. Yet only a few months after his death he had been chased all the way home by a mob because he lived in rented quarters filled with Southerners. He was a Northerner, at least in the old sense, but the landlord was a Southerner and most of the tenants were also Southerners.

Something did not quite sound right. In prison time plays strange tricks yet I knew that my recollection of the sequence of *those* events was unimpaired. I observed, 'You must be a man of conviction then if you enlisted to fight for the Federal cause after that.'

He struck his chest. 'Me? Never! After that I said, make the bloody baggas go fight den own war.'

There was a time contradiction which I struggled to trap. I asked him for the exact month and year of this incident.

'Na something like August last year ...'

'Last year?'

'Yes, last year. 'E no pass seven or eight month yet ...'

'Wait a minute, last year the war was already on.'

He exploded. 'Yes na de ting wey I dey tell you. 'E happen dis very last year. Na 'in vex me mos' of all.'

'Are you sure?'

'Am I sure wetin? Governor Adebayo 'imself come here when Yoruba people begin run back for den home ... 'E make broadcast for radio.'

I finally pieced the story together. Another sectional mob action organized with the same thoroughness as the 1966 ones, embracing all Southerners. The complaint – that these had usurped the positions vacated by the Ibos. Kaduna had woken up one morning to a combined army and police blockage mounted by the military governor. His prompt action had scotched the pogrom before it could begin. But there were a few killings in Kano.* The usual posters had gone up, on walls and trees, leaflets were boldly distributed by hand,

*I have since checked and confirmed the murder of a Yoruba tailor in Sabon Gari, Kano.

couched in the same language as had heralded the May and the September massacres, an ultimatum calling for the repatriation of Southerners – or else! The military governors acted fast but in several states skilled men – doctors, engineers, etc. – had taken 1966 to heart and headed South. Even the Chadians (called Godo-godo) had been affected and specially singled out. Their favourite occupations were the uniformed services – army, police and prisons.

The man spat out his disgust. 'Look inside Army and wetin you go find? Na these Godo-godo people full de Army na dem dey fight de war but our people even give governor ultimatum make e' pack dem commot for state one time or else den go smell pepper like de Ibo . . .'

Two general alarms during the civil war. The last threat was in September (a fateful month apparently) of 1968. This was when Governor Bako had called out the forces.

We talked. I felt him out, though I was already sure of him. I brought up subjects to which he could respond. Finally I asked him if he would be on duty in the Crypt the entire week. No, he replied, only until Gowon's departure. The Prisons were mounting their own parade and for that all ex-service men were needed to show off their ribbons and medals. It seemed that most of my guards were ex-service men. The following day was probably the last; the bridal show was due in Zaria the day after. Mentally, I tossed up a coin.

The decision was predictable. I had nothing to lose.

My first letter, the test, was innocuous. I sent out a poem and requested books. I said to the man simply, 'I want you to post that for me.' I had fashioned the envelope myself from scrap paper. He looked at it, turning it round and round in his hand. I could not read what went on in his mind – until he let out a long laugh.

'You mean, you make this envelope yourself?'

I showed him other artifacts. He had heard about such

things from the other guards but seeing them in the flesh – he threw back his head and roared.

'I go post am for you, and if you want write more, tomorrow I bring you proper envelope and paper.'

I said, 'I shan't forget this.'

'But make you write everything you want tomorrow. After tomorrow normal routine go start again. For now nobody get time dey search when we commot here. Everybody busy for Gowon wedding.'

I wished Yakubu Gowon many more honeymoons. And with the paper left over from the letters I began work on my celebration of the event, *The Wedding of Humbo*. It was the least I could do for an obscenity to which I owed so much.

31

WITHIN its sparse twenty-three paces by seventeen, the warders have managed to create a vegetable garden of some variety. It is *their* retreat, a refuge which shelters them briefly from duties that most regard either as a punishment for sins committed in a former life – na God wan' punish man when 'e lef' am dey do dis kin' work – or as a stop-gap until the day the Pools come home. For a few, for perhaps more than a mere few, the job is legitimization of sadistic instincts that would have found expression somewhere somehow. Yet even for these the garden has served as changing room, the robing and disrobing shrine of masquerades. I have watched them take off and put on the mask, slowly or in a flash.

The Crypt was the torture chamber, too strong a word to use perhaps but what other word best expresses the crimes that were committed and are still continued in places such as this? Euphemistically it is called the punishment cells. A prisoner would be brought in here, locked in one of the cells and let him scream till his lungs burst – no one paid the least heed. The door closes against a little ledge about six inches from the floor – you have to step over it to enter. The cold water treatment consisted of plugging the hole in that ledge and filling the cell with water. The prisoner is stripped stark naked and flung into the cell. In the harmattan season which I twice experienced even without the benefit of the cold pool, I know that one night alone in such a cell would leave cracks in the toughest will. And that is only one variety of punishment. There are the baton sessions. Five or six warders, practising sadists in private life undoubtedly, so avid was the enjoyment on the faces of those whom I watched in the early days in Lagos – these warders would set on a prisoner and beat him at selective points – knuckles, elbows, ankles, head and shoulder bones, in a rapid continuity. Once the officer in charge of the beating at Kiri-kiri even came in to apologize to me for the screams which tormented us for upwards an hour. And the whole purpose: to force the prisoner to confess where he had hidden some contraband cigarettes smuggled into the prison. The *real* purpose, of course, was simply to break his will, to have the pleasure of watching the victim, known for his toughness, break before their eyes. That session continued each day for seven days; he did not break.

Such scenes were the norm in the Crypt, before an excess of political prisoners turned 'punishment cells' into VIP containers. And so the adjoining Yard of Purgatory is the new setting for all human violation while the Crypt is transformed into a brief passage of humane restoration. I have watched the most maleficent mask crash through the gates of the Crypt still snorting from recent exertions in Purgatory, then stooping to perform a brief Pilate parody with water from the fire-bucket, turn a gentle farm sprite in a trice.

It is, of course, very illegal. Since my tenure as reigning deity in this grove the Gates of Paradise have been shut on all but the guardian angels whose purgatory it has also become. And when a signal is given of the approach of the Superintendent, the horned devil that came in with swishing forked tail and stamping hooves, flushed and winded from staging a flagellating session on the other side of the wall, this knuckler of knuckles, wielder of buckled belts, stomper on toes, breaker of bones, gladiator on baton charges, this terror of the back cells dons yet another mask, the delinquent mask, and a comic truancy is painted wide on his visage.

But the scene is mostly idyllic, a brief glimpse of saved souls tending cabbages on some Elysian field. Purged is all the violence, the cruelty, smoothed the fury on the brow of contention among recalcitrant spirits over yonder who must be broken to be similarly saved. A tap at the gate and they come in one, two, even three at a time to mark the progress of growing things. The creases of their oversize khaki shorts stand out as wings as they stoop to loosen the soil, prune dead leaves, confine some overspread tomato bush, pronounce on burgeoning groundnuts, excommunicate the lizards whose teeth marks on young lettuce often spell death. They lop and carry off bagfuls of the lush-green vines, succulent leaves for an evening stew at home.

But the guava stands supreme. It is the forbidden fruit that all are waiting to prey upon, the pomegranate of Hades whose taste will not enchain but release them from a life indenture to the prison underworld.

I could not understand it any other wise. There must be better guavas outside, better tasting and less fraught with the petty enmity that developed over the guavas. I listened sometimes to the angry rumblings that evolved as the dawn harbinger arrived and saw that another had beaten him to a fruit long lovingly watched, cherished and anticipated. And a cataclysm overtook the tree one night the blight of which was felt as no natural disaster ever affected man. One by one they came and stood silently over the violated tree.

Around it lay its unfulfilled harvest, bitten, nibbled and cast away. A Beast of Darkness, an uninitiated night patrol had seen what to him was only a guava tree. One after the other he had tried the fruits, not with his hand but with that ultimate proof, the teeth. One after another, seeking ripeness in vain, he had plucked and bitten them all, wantonly, murderously, spitting their incompleted essences on barren soil. The gate opened again and again, softly; they came in one after another to keep wake at the death of a harvest, wordlessly except to murmur, 'What kind of a beast can do dis kin' ting?' Through the slit in his door Pluto observed them and sympathized. The guava was their private tree of life, and Kali had made her visitation while they slept.

It made the action of the Grand Seer even more hard to bear, when that blow came finally. There was no premonition, no self-preparation against that blow. I was the not so innocent cause.

They had their guava and tomatoes, their groundnuts and their millets. There had to be something in it all for me. I had the compost, and I also had the sun.

The compost beds were life, for they yielded tools. They yielded metals and beads, phials discarded from the dispensary, wires and strings, bones, springs, knots; they even provided the horned dung beetles whose chilling whine was another night hazard to cope with and overcome – eerie, ceaseless, a sound of the trapped animal that seemed to emerge from a rotted sac in slow collapse. I tracked it down in daytime, harnessed it to a little mechanized creation from the compost scraps and made it pay by operating a treadmill for motive power. It was a partial success. The compost beds opened up new avenues of occupation. Gradually my fingers became yet more sensitive, my mind floated with airy unbounded designs.

The first tool is the knife. It is the primal tool, the matrix of forms and shapes. That much is accepted, but I watched it happen, woke up one day to observe the evolution of the iron age and the liberation that came from it in the cave man. The pleistocenic vegetable was shed and from its chrysalis I emerged, neolithic artisan. That first knife, made from a rusted piece cut from a metallic band was Release. Guardedly I honed it on the concrete floor, gave it a handle from a slice from one of the useless fibre stalks which supposedly held up the net. That act in itself revealed, nay, reminded me of the suppleness of its bark, the staple material of basket-weavers, and that in turn . . . the chain-reaction was endless.

I began work on Mobiles, the most soothing single creation in that dark place. From first making them spontaneously I even began to design them first. The weighted end was the empty shell of my toilet roll closed and filled with stones and gravel, covered in cigarette foil to glint in the sun. They functioned smoothly on several points, finely balanced. They danced and bucked in the wind. I was *never* tired of watching the delicacy of their movements.

And after the plain sculptured forms? The entire artistic gestalt! Light self-contained verses to fly in the wind. Single-verse lyrics plus invectives on my tormentors (in Spanish, the latter was always written in bad Spanish) I christened them poetry-sculptures, muse-on-the-air, poetrees, sculpture in verse, sculptrees, etc. I made chaplets of wood and paper, wrote out the verses and watched them fly.

In the beginning I had kept lizards. By accident I discovered a nest of eggs in the process of hatching, the babies pushing through the soil to air. Out of cigarette packets – making tunnels from the cylinders of toilet paper and the plastic bag in which the bread came I built a framework of communicating nests and tried to train them. I fed them ants and flies. This phase was now over. Deserted also were the ant colonies whose natural cruelties I exploited to stage duels to the death – one red, one black ant or teams from each group put together in a bottle would massacre one another to the last man: I named them Biafra and Nigeria.

The Mobiles became all-engrossing, the designs more complex and daring. From a hollow stalk of the sunflower plant I cut two cylinders, made a lengthwise slit in each. Next step, a length of toilet paper wrapped round a smoothened piece of stick: this bolt of parchment went into one of the cylinders. Carefully one end of that roll was manoeuvred out of the slit, then in through the slit of the other cylinder where another rounded stick was waiting, ready coated with my makeshift glue.

The stick picked up the edge of the paper and rolled it round. The Chinese prayer-scroll was finished. Linked by an adjustable length of fibre bark it served as a counterweight to the remaining complex of a new mobile. I covered the paper with poems, turning the handle to display a new verse each day to suit the mood. Other verses, framed, floated on the other arms. Sometimes the wind turned the scroll unaided, the weight remained the same as both scrolls had been balanced on the same unit. The first time I watched this happen, the unwinding of the scroll by the wind and the continuation of a perfect equilibrium, I had no alternative but to give credit where credit was due. I turned to me and said, Cave-man, you have not merely created the perfect Mobile, you have invented a new concept – Genius!

The first Mobile erupted on the guards quite suddenly. All at once there was this *fabricated* object, certainly not within the regulation furnishing of the cell. An object too that bore the marks of careful tooling and alien material. I spied on them for reactions. They moved from incredulity to admiration. Without exception they resolved simply to let it alone. The Chief Warder came, he was full of loud admiration and finally the Grand Seer came on inspection and blinked at it. The Mobiles had received official sanction.

Disaster was not far, but the early days, even weeks of the great mechanical awakening were permitted to continue in full inventive flight. When the great calamity occurred a by-product was already at hand. It began when, growing ever ambitious to take over the restlessness of the mind, I began to plan a miniature wind-turbine. In this kingdom all must serve. I selected the corner of the hut where the wind's entry was most impertinent. Harness the bastard! Already I had visions of generating a little electricity, modestly, just a few volts, or at least operating some form of contraption with the power. The goal was power. I sought more from the wind than spinning mobiles. My head was full of turbines, designs that would have honoured any museum of unfulfilled prototypes. I stood watching the liquid dance of the mobiles – I wondered sometimes if I let myself be hypnotized by them for once I found that I had spent a whole day merely staring at them, standing. The wind had been smoothly consistent on that day. Thinking of turbines, however, watching the counter-motions of the sculpture's arms on several pivots I thought suddenly: I wonder how many possible combinations there can be in the movements of those arms.

Thus was born the algebraic age. The turbine was forgotten. Nothing left but to go to the root of mathematics, through diagrams, by trial and error to spend days discovering what must be the simplest arithmetical principle on earth. I excused myself. In school, figures had been an anathema from which I was only too happy to part company after a scrape-through in school-leaving examinations. But not any more. I had newly discovered the world of numbers. Once the first breakthrough was over I began with increasing rapidity to rediscover one mathematical formula after another. Part investigation, part titanic excavation from the murky burial-ground of the labours of long-suffering teachers I tackled one idea after another, testing and retesting the achieved formula by the most simplistic count-by-count systems. I had TIME! Often I woke up in the morning to a problem and one minute later, literally one minute later the guard was tapping on the door to signal lock-up hour. I DESTROYED time. Once I wrote out all the possible combinations of six digits. In the process, I uncovered the only way that this could be done to ensure, at a glance, that there was neither duplication nor omission. The result was so obviously a plan for computed aesthetics that I ruled out squares on toilet paper and proceeded to repeat those combinations with coloured squares. (Green from leaf juice, purple from a berry, black from my ink – christened Soy-ink – and toilet paper white.) The cyclic continuum of the result next made an impression. I joined one end of the toilet paper to the other and asked, Now what have I got? It had a strong resemblance to symbols made by computers. Now how on earth do computers function anyway?

My mind was like a compost heap, teeming with life, clotted with undigested scraps, struggling to keep pace with an uneven fecundity of its tenants. It was chaos and oasis when the yard was suddenly laid waste, reverted to a desert.

I had earth, the compost. I had the sun too and that was within reach, those outsize sunflowers planted by the men of masks. Some rose over seven foot, a huge periscope locked eternally on the sun. It was the abundance of pollen that made the most impression, the windcropped powder of the sun which lay on broad leaves and filled the grooves of their stalks. The sunflower was mine in the way all other plants belonged to the guards. It was tacitly acknowledged mine for I alone had use for it. (They were not even aware that some races eat sunflower seeds.) They planted it for the colour, from habit. I saw the stalks as flutes; the knife awaited ripening.

As flutes go, they were hardly a success. I obtained notes but failed to extract music from the tantalizing tubes. They cracked at the holes or split on the mouthpiece. I created mouthpieces from every object, the mouthpiece split the stalk. In my head rippled those sweet notes that would fill the nights when the flutes achieved perfection. Perfection proved elusive: I consigned the sunflower stalks to the making of Chinese prayer scrolls, dirged a consolation over music that remained forever locked in the sun. The obvious title was *Flute Manqué* :

Rib of sunflower
You have not fulfilled
The promise of your lyric form

Notes immured
In threadings of your stalk
Haunt me still

Dream of Pan hours
In a silent wilderness
I thought to hymn

The rise and setting of
Your distant origin
And draw

The fiery demiurge to earth
On threads of woodwind spell
Yet harmonies

To keep sublime are best
Unsung

I listen
To songs that may have been

When breaths of cosmos
Stir the soil where,
Once, you stood.

The pollen did not seem of the consistency of powder. Each day and each increasing windcrop turned it into little rivulets of gold until I yielded to the urge to gather it before it flew off in the wind. I had a glass tube that once housed a tooth-brush. I reached in among the broad coarse leaves and began the slow sensuous task of gathering in the pollen. It went further. Each morning my first task turned to gathering the pollen that had fallen in the night, shaking stamens into the tube before the wind dispersed them. And the last task at night. Lovingly I picked impurities from the pollen. Slowly the pollen mounted towards the desired goal – a solid bar of gold. It would take time to build an airless packed pollen bar to match the sensuousness of the glass tube. Insects and other alien minutiae were painstakingly ejected, the tube was shaken firmly to rid the grains of all air-pockets. In time it would have made a perfect golden bar: I had that time but alas the sun was close to a full eclipse. And the pollen did not seem to move.

Part of the prison technique for keeping inmates subjugated is the shock disorientation technique. Nothing is done as from one civilized being to another. If a search has to be made then it is made in an atmosphere of the storm-trooper. Explanations are never given for anything; the inmate must be kept off balance, left to stew for a while and ponder the significance of the latest eruption. Then and only then the officials appear, again *en masse*, in a new role of Inquisitors.

And thus they came in that morning, warders and prisoners, armed with axes, shovels, hoes, picks and matchets. Down went the lime shrub, down went the sunflowers, down went the millet, up came the tomatoes, groundnuts, lettuce and garden egg. The guava tree was not merely cut down, the picks went into operation and dug deep into the ground to unearth the last inch of roots. For some reason however, the other squad was some minutes behind. I saw what was happening and I knew that the fanning of a tornado through my cells would only be a matter of seconds. Without recognizing my action for what it was I swept up all the sheets of the latest thing I had been working on, secreted a few nibs in pre-selected caches, drained off the series of 'maturing' ink sparing only one bottle, then came out to watch the work of demolition.

They broke into the yard a few minutes later. This time there was no attempt to examine anything on the spot. They came with baskets and pails, swept everything including my spare clothes into their containers. The pillow was taken, the mattress prodded, the half-completed mobiles (abandoned for a demented Time-Space Research project) placed – carefully I was compelled to admit – into baskets. Tools, all the precious tools carefully refined over the time – swept off. I had made no effort to save the golden bar and strangely, perhaps because it was in the tin cup with the fork and spoon, this was passed over. Polyphemus led the squad. On departing he gave a last instruction to the harvesters – 'Everytin , everytin must be remove.'

Later the Grand Seer himself arrived. His sharp eyes immediately caught the tube of pollen. He ordered it removed, searched the cells himself more minutely and recovered one or two overlooked pieces. Then he went away without a word.

Not one growing thing remained in the yard. Every last shred of leaf had been removed.

I moved my chair outside, not caring to wait for the certain resumption of close patrolling watch, the greatest mind-driller for a prisoner. A butterfly came in search of vegetation that used to be there. A bird flew in and departed seeing nowhere for caterpillars to hide. Only the ants were busy; they erupted from myriad holes bearing away a harvest of fallen seeds. Finally there was no living thing walking the earth.

32

Why do I fast? I do not mean, why do I fast now? I have settled that in terms of continuing conflict. But why do I fast at all? Why have I, at any given time, suddenly decided – I must now do without food for some time? Perhaps I ought to settle that in my mind before I am trapped in a fatal demand of my own self-indulgence.

Yes, self-indulgence. A sensual self-indulgence. It is important to separate the area of will-power from the drugged immersion in rainbow-tinted ether. For I suspect that it is the truly sensual that take easily to fasting.

I have read of, but never experienced even a nearness of the sensation of freezing to death. I understand that after a while the body ceases to feel pain, sinks blissfully into sleep. Rest. I think fasting must be like that. It begins with that critical hump which is in fact a very brief passage and occurs during the first three days. The body either succumbs at this point or afterwards condemns the very thought of food. I find it best to provoke this hump as early as possible. When the decision to fast is taken, I dwell on the next meal in my mind, I let my body crave it and I let the food come to me. I am hungry. I open the dishes and sniff, I dwell on the tasting, the mastication, the swallowing. I salivate. I dwell on my body's satisfaction, the heavy body-contented sleep that must follow if I fill my hunger from this plenitude. A fierce protest commences in the pit of the stomach and I let it rage. Armed with the power of my veto, I stand aside and enjoy the violent conflict, waiting for my cue to thump the gavel. The moment arrives and I cover the food with a slow deliberate motion saying: This taste cannot die. I have known it and will know it again. Taste is selectiveness, choice. I am denied choice and thus all taste is rendered non-existent. Pleasure also is choice; it is fulfilment and choice. My existence is a crippled one, it debases fulfilment by restricting fields of fulfilment. To take pleasure in the granted area of fulfilment is self-betrayal. To eat without pleasure is to betray my nature. From now on I will not betray my nature.

Sometimes a day or two later the stomach devils come out again to play. But I view their antics with dispassionate interest. Food cannot tempt me but I wonder sometimes what I would do if I had, within reach, vitamin pills. I do after all entertain fears of the gut-walls collapsing, of unfed enzymes atrophying and dying, of perpetual damages done to the body by excess. I know it is wiser to take a glass of orange juice a day but I am not capable of the compromise. Orange juice is too close to food. Vitamin pills on the other hand do not seem insiduous saboteurs of will-power; that test has luckily never come. So I accept only a glass of water each day, sipped at intervals. I ensure that I do not exceed the one glass a day.

The body achieves, of course, true weightlessness. I am blown about by the lightest breeze, by the lightest lyrical thought or metaphor. The body is like an onion and I watch the flesh peel off, layer by layer, layer by layer. And this is the risk, it is this condition that begins the danger of self-indulgence. For, by the fourth day the will is no longer involved. I become hungry for the show-down, the moment when I must choose between death or surrender. I resent even the glass of water and begin to cheat. Each day it gets lesser by a fraction. Once, for a whole day I did not drink at all. In the morning I said, I shall drink at noon. At noon I began to cheat, procrastinating until I decided I shall drink an entire cupful when the sun goes down. I lay in bed until dark, then said, I did not see the sun go down.

What do I do all day? I watch light motes in the air. When

eyes are shut a whole universe of colours fills the dome of darkness behind the eyelids. In extreme fasts the open eye is treated to the same display on a lighter, vaster scale. The air is broken up in swirls of coloured dots. Each speck of dust in a sunbeam is a fiery planet in the galaxy, its motion sedately plotted, imbued with immense significance. In the muting of sounds which overtakes the senses the mind drifts easily into transcendental moods, wiping out environment, reality, fragmenting slowly till it becomes one with specks of dust in ether.

Only sunsets prove unbearable, for while sounds are muted, colours are intensified, and the sunsets turn raw, cannibalistic, fanged and blooded as if the drooling demon of day is sinking its teeth in the lap of a loud lascivious courtesan, reeking of gore. Not so the storm-clouds with their copper rims and light golden depths hinting of caverns beyond the passages of dieties. The stars fade into nothingness; only the silence exists that brought them forth.

Rejoicing, I watch my body waste. I identify but do not prohibit the human satisfaction which comes from the pain and fear, the concern and incredulity in their eyes as the gaolers prowl round, on orders to report the slightest hint of weakening. Something in me, a glee I recognize as profoundly human laughs and condescends when a warder stops and says, 'Please, this is not possible. You must stop.' The Grand Seer enters . . . 'I have come to beg you. I ask you to think of your family, your wife, your children.' I protest – but I am well and strong. 'You cannot see yourself. I can. We all do. You don't know what you look like. You are a living skeleton.'

It is strange, but the effect they all have on me is to resent even that cup of water. Each time the Grand Seer has turned up I have thrown the rest away. His concern adds to the growing sense of superhumanity. I need neither drink nor food. Soon I shall need no air.

The hallucinations, the brief fainting spells in which walls, earth and sky move suddenly about me I accept and control. And so I know it is no illusion when one night I detect the motion of a terrestrial object among the stars. Seeking beyond stars into that pool of silence I fasten suddenly on this fluid speck, sedate and self-assured in its predetermined orbit. Another hallucination? The passage was brief since I could only follow its motion through my barred window. Yet I am so certain that I wait again the following day and the next. And remember its identity. A heavenly body but a human satellite. The immensity of the moment – the moment of certainty – becomes imperishable. Locked and barred from a more direct communion, a human assertiveness has reached me through the cosmos, a proud, inextinguishable promethean spark among dead bodies, astral wraiths, failed deities, tinsel decorations in barren space. Sign, probe and question I accept you, incandescent human dare. Extension of my restless eye and mind I claim you and absorb you. I transmit you, pore of my skin, electronic core of my will, prowl . . . prowl . . .

Tenth day of fast. By day a speck of dust on a sun-beam. By night a slow shuttle in the cosmos. Night . . .

A clear night, and the moon pouring into my cell. I thought, a shroud? I have returned again and again to this night of the greatest weakness and lassitude, to the hours of lying still on the stark clear-headed acceptance of the thought that said: it is painless. The body weakens and breath slows to a stop. Gone was the fear that a life-urge might make me retreat at this moment. I held no direct thought of death, only of the probable end of a course of action, I felt the weakness in the joints of my bones and within the bone itself. A dry tongue that rasped loosely in the mouth. I felt a great repose in me, an enervating peace of the world and the universe within me, a peace that truly 'passeth all understanding'. I wrote . . .

I anoint my flesh
Thought is hallowed in the lean
Oil of solitude
I call you forth, all, upon
Terraces of light. Let the dark
Withdraw

I anoint my voice
And let it sound hereafter
Or dissolve upon its lonely passage
In your void. Voices new
Shall rouse the echoes when
Evil shall again arise

I anoint my heart
Within its flame I lay
Spent ashes of your hate –
Let evil die.

No one came on the eleventh day. I thought the gaoler when he peeped in my cell looked wary, even frightened. I mistook the cause. It had happened. It was happening, happening even then. I understood now why the Seer had laid waste their paradise. I understood when they stormed into my Crypt the following day, the twelfth, questioning and threatening. I wedged myself between door and wall for support, seeking to disguise my weakness. It was a long way, a long height from which to cast down my gaze and understand. The sounds, the words, the gestures were plain and yet remote. The presence of strange faces, and the Grand Seer among them concerned me crucially but did not touch me. I saw and pitied his bafflement. They paused often waiting, pauses of increasing desperation. I watched them hang upon my silence yet I could only think, But what is it? What do you want of me? Why should you want of me?

I need nothing. I feel nothing. I desire nothing.

Were these new kingdoms which that sage hermit sought, the kingdoms of nothing? Or did he speak, as being replete in his own being, spurning all exterior augmentation?

33

In the Beginning there was Void. Nothing. And how does the mind grasp it? As waste? Desolation? *Nothing* is cheaply within grasp from what *was*. But as the fundamental nought, the positive, original nil? As the immeasurable drop into pre-thought, pre-existence, pre-essence? But then, the mind that will conceive this must empty inwards from a lifetime's frame of accumulated references, must plunge from the physical platform into primordial abyss. Within which alas, lie the creative energies which 'abhor a vacuum' even more than Nature. The cycle must commence again.

Still, there being nothing worse to do, Pluto tried to discover tunnels even from the dead netherworld into deeper bowels of Void. At the best, it was mesmeric: the mind's normal functioning seized up, the day eased out in a gentle catalepsis. At worst it lay within that darkest ring of re-creative energies, revolving on its axis, turning on its spoor in the gossamer dust of infinity . . .

Which existed and had always *been* – Life, that is, which God did say Let there Be. Why? For it had always *been* within his protean mind, within form that was not formed, motion that did not move, time and space which existed not, yet were all severally and wholly contained, rolled and moulded within that great amorphous origin, pulse, breath, androgynous source of matter and of essence. Until, suffering, I do not seek, I find – he delved within and ordered: let there *Be*! Tangibly, visibly, olfactorily, audibly . . .

What then, what was this need to materialize in poor second-mould copy such merely outward manifestations of the pure Idea! Why break the invisible chrysalis of essence, that one unassailable Truth? Truth, because there was no copy, no duplicate, no faulted cast, not even a bare projection from an alien mind of that pure idea? For there were no *other* minds. No faker. What was this need to turn materialist? Uncertainty? Ego? Narcissism? Reassurance? Loneliness, said the Holy Writ. A fear that thought was Nothing, and a fear of Nothing which could only be allayed by the thought made manifest.

When at first the pigeons came, Pluto held their arabesques of wing-bolts high in the air, burning as incandescent tracers long after their creators had departed. Yet, fearful for when the seasons might change and the pigeons migrate and come no more he moved at once to wean the mind from dependence on such fortuitous aesthetics. A stone lay on the ground, worn smooth and oval shaped, subtly creviced as if by human hands, faintly reminiscent of a shuttle. Inert, yet he imbued it with the tapestry of fates, of seasons, pierced to core and crowded its infinite lethargy with infinite creativity, coming away from that stone with only its pure luminous essence. For finally the loops and arcs of the pigeons did disintegrate, the quicker for being witnessed being only an activity in Time. The feathery designs did crumble and lose their formal rhythms, falling back to earth in showery sparkles. And it rendered the Crypt darker than before.

Not to create or think is best. The pauses leave the Crypt a little darker than before. Creation is admission of great loneliness. Turn the mind to a loom of cobwebs, rest the time-smoothed shuttle in its home of timelessness.

I need nothing. I seek nothing. I desire nothing.

Not even loneliness. A mess known as the world was created to cheat the loneliness of the one pure essence. So witnesseth the Holy Writ, faking it a virtue.

The fat somnolent spider, the abhorrent blob who messes up the walls with fly-traps and egg-pouches unwinds in clean geometric filigrees suddenly, at will. And it gathers dust and filth, is soon filled with foul repellent flies. A mind must be the shuttle and the loom but in dead repose for in the home of death the living *is* sole creator. And what agitates and moves, what manifests itself is surely the work of that mind. Dawn, noon, night and man-made satellites. Lest the spirits of the underworld suspect him and unmask him he shall wear vestments of and as the dead, embrace the outer form of death, chill his mind to that inaudible beat of death inertia. A shuttle in repose, as in the darkness of an old woman's hands, whose heavy lids drop lower and lower even as she weaves the death shroud of the old, the swaddlings of a new awakened world, her tired earth-departing hands sinking slowly on her lap. Why then spin and gather dust and filth when the pure unsoiled form reposes in the mind?

I need nothing. I seek nothing. I desire nothing.

But that hermit did not speak in void and his words were spoken to a living soul. Nothing ... nothing ... nothing, that is, nothing besides what lies about me, besides this brief fulfilment in the chance of renewed affirmation, simply nothing ... nothing ... nothing. And if he had not replied the questioner, if he had not spoken, if he had turned simply away and plunged for refuge deeper into his luminous (or camouflaging) unconscious, even this act of re-affirmation, this 'nothing needed' was – besides your questioning dear Incident. For *that* did happen. Your own need, your humane curiosity, your voice, your doubts, your presumptuous charity. Besides sky, earth, grain, life and the living – the *choice* of the free will to need nothing, seek nothing, desire nothing. I know the hermits. Not even Malarepa was truly in a nothing existence; he *actively* dodged and rebuked (and forgave or revenged on) friends, disciples, relations and apostates. Not even John the Baptist.

His spirit moved among the laden clouds, across the dark

gestation of waters, across the waters restless, lonely. A dragon-fly, a twig-legged water insect, insubstantial ray of matter, probing clues where the slow mutation had begun, exciting those inert gases that moved towards the first amoeba, nudging, prodding, pleading, this light immutable catalyst. I create, I re-create in tune with that which shuts or opens all about me. Dawn or dusk. Darkness or light. Concrete bars and iron gates.

A murmuring rose from the gate in the Wall of Flagellation. He saw it was the anachrones, and their eyes were on his restless spirit among the clouds, and they sank their heads again and shook them, staring at the waiting land ... Dare we plant? Will the Seer wait again until close to fruition then give the wanton order for destruction? Do you think God has punished him enough for that wicked deed? They looked at the barren spot where once the guava stood. A sigh broke from among them.

... Oh ye of little faith. But they were shadows not substantial men. Their apprehensive utterances spoke, true, in undercurrents of hope and bridged a gulf, a new rib of humanity pushing upwards from their barren soil. But anachrones he called them yet, saying, they were formed before their minds. The mind is time – and on that flash he rested now the problem of Infinity at last. The mind is sole coefficient of time and space. Muffle it Pluto, muffle it in thick impenetrable cotton wool.

A wet print on my forehead. Rain.

34

FINALLY the heavens take a hand. Literally. I smile. Am I now supposed to believe in Providence? For in bright sunlight, seated outside staring at flies, a black light object floated down and settled down barely a foot away from my feet. I looked up and there, just disappearing into the horizon were two crows whose cawing I had heard above my head only a few moments before. I had not even deigned to look up at these creatures whose status in the winged world I rated only one rung lower than that of vultures. It did not fail to startle and impress me; I grasped the potential of the strong-quilled feather before it was one minute old on the ground. I let it lie there the entire afternoon thinking, I really ought to believe in Divine Providence. In the huge prison yard alone – my world did not go beyond this and there was no thought of that outside world, the unbounded scope of the bird's freedom – but even within the prison it is an act of deep benevolent selection that the loose feather should drop off over and into the tiniest yard, at the feet of one whose need was surely the most desperate.

I begin, when I finally absorb this gift, to whet my thumbnail on a stone. At night the thumbnail fashions the quill into a nib. I unearth the store of ink that has escaped detection and pause. I add this little miracle to the thousand other claims of God and Divine Providence. It is a cold collected exercise that lasts into the dead of night. There is no quickening of the spirit nor upliftment of the soul. The arguments are old, nothing of great note beyond the fall of a much-needed quill. And finally the worn mind-treading is encroached upon by an impatient tribute to the kind, forgiving crow. It is the first task of the quill, scratchy as the crow's cawing, but it writes –

Fire
Of antimony in the sun
Dark mane curvetting
From stables of unspoken prayers

He dropped
His lone gift from the sky
A rain of fiery coals – for he
The lyric eye had scorned –

And flew
His raucous way. But newly
Sounds the raw theme of your haloed throat –
As trumpets at the lofty breach in walls
Of immolation

(*Crow Quill*)

35

ALL souls congealment. All souls meet in grey-ghosts All Souls' Day. And Night. All souls day after day, union, airless vault and cathedral gloom. Grease clouds of candles but not one flickering flame, not one tinted saint in leaded windows. Lead pall, cloud mounds, heavy feet of mourners, grey shrouds, a shudder of souls in graveyard rituals.

Damp and suet sounds, an old worn record played in mournful chambers of a flooded gramophone wheezing through rusted ports, a dead seep of dead voices, webbed feet suction in a weariness of motion, a fitful drowning slap of nerveless feet in slime caverns. And a damp of saturated sponges to soak up gleams of light.

The sky is an eyeless, finless fish, dead swollen, thrown up on a swamp, a grey inert mass ballooned out to obscure the sky of life. Flabby, a dead hulk without odour without stench, opaque imposition filled with an infinite shadow of itself, grey sluggish undertow, an enervating bulk of deadness. It yields, this raw latex screen to a weak pressure from the blunted edge of thought and rolls back ponderously into place. Nothing pierces the amorphous hulk, nothing breaks its skin of eternal somnolence. And the rallies of the will are brief, short-lived spurts of futility. It is the day of leprosy, of nameless ulcerous deeps and underbred horrors.

Time passes through a congealment of carrion air and water, drifts through a cosmos shorn even of shocks and fire, cleansed of disintegrating noise, cleansed vapid of the landmarks of memory. Nor freefall, nor the harrowing disquiet of eternal flickers moves to warm the numbing of fingers, teeth, ears, eyes and the grope of tongue for relief in a clarity of sound. It is not the rich all-conscious subsumation of individual measures but a watery stagnation, a loss of anchor in the encroaching miasma, a defeat of tenuous links by nothing. From her lofty negation of all direction, time has turned a slippery circuit of fouled imprints, crumbling at the railhold of momentary bearings, sinking into slush, gradual subsidence, enfeebled churn in a hushed and mottled void.

Dim caves, sombre gleams diffused in cracks of sea-walls raised against the marshes. Listless forms pass beyond a distant cave mouth. A lizard flattens on the wall helpless in the drip. A moat around the pot-holed lettuce bed pocked with deadwood slops down eroded channels on the slopes of a ragged hillock. Resignation stares dumbly from the eyes of the lizard. A damp gong tolls in and out of the rims of consciousness, strokes of lassitude which waken nothing, not even echoes.

Lead sheen on the roofs, a deceptive glaze seems to trickle down in grey leaden drips long after the rain has ceased. A rucked zinc sponge sucking moisture from the air has replaced the vanished horizon and the swallowed sky. It sits, a frozen slab, a squat oppressive presence lacking, like my world this day, hold or definition in non-existent space.

36

THE predatory rounds begin with the rains. A short fierce burst one evening and a drum of hailstones. It is the end of harmattan. The hailstones fall for an hour, then the wind sweeps off on its southward run. A deep moist earth is left behind and a crisp sweetness in the air. From a long hibernation they emerge, beetles, flying-ants, sausage flies, moths, a violent flock of fragile wings battling the lone bulb on the pole. It is a blind and fierce riotous whirr from the long silent sleep. Like water-skins at a new resurrected oasis, the ducts of all life begin to swell. Stings. Claws. Dried-up talons acquire tension, stings swell in readiness and carapaces take gloss. Life arms for the long round of predatoriness.

Enter Lord of the Jungle. He is excessive, this regal spectre, this sneak-shark among restless minnows. Alas, it is too true, he has but one eye! I have heard him before, even caught glimpses of his ambiguous being. But only as a shadow in the night, a feral blur terrified of Kronos, monarch of time-lapses in the underworld. For him I was as lethal as the boot he often felt, the angry kick of Ambrose as he nosed around left-overs. He has learnt a pecking order from the noble overseer of leavings, Ambrose, learnt to nudge a slow head, then one foreleg after the other through the drainage hole, alert to sound or smell of hostility, then a flash along the wall into remote darkness leaving a toll of moulted fur on the iron grating. With the rains King Leo comes into his own, bolder and degenerate, a one-eyed king in the insect world. I view the shaming spectacle of feline degradation.

A cat, wild or tame, moves with majesty unequalled in the animal world. A lordly alternation of muscle pivots on the shoulder and a constant flow of the elastic pulse even in its moment of freeze. In the dark a cat is a vibrant furry presence, awesome behind its emerald burns, hypnotic in darkness . . .

Tyger, Tyger, burning bright. . . .

Oh Blake, poor Blake, you should see King Leo! Into this jungle of walls where we all are bound by every trick of survival, with his sparse but exact and proportionate frame strides Leo majestic from nose-tip to a vibrant questing tail. But only in left profile. His right is a sinister piratical ruffian with an opaque eye-patch mockery of its buccaneering ancestry.

Stalk. Crouch. Spring. The bag – a beetle. Or a praying mantis. But nothing is worse than the sound of its lordly feast. A crunch of gourmandizing relish and – I swear to you – a distant smack of the lips after the last wing of the insect is demolished. This one-eyed sorrow after his nauseating smack of the chops mentally caresses his belly; this can only be conjecture but I swear to its truth. I raise my eyes to the roof to erase the spectacle.

On the roof-beam, another predator stretches out in wait. The wall-gecko, eyes of beady lamps held in steady fascination of the unconscious victim. A head high-lighted from the bulb throws him right back to his ancestry the brontosaurus. Massive glittering Ancient Mariner eyes. One by one the flies come to him unresisting, they come within the orbit of those magnetic eyes, his jaws open and he sucks them through.

His mate begins a slow crawl to the praying mantis, the eyes are headlamps on an armoured tank. Now she lies still on one plane of the beam but this plane is at right angles to the mindlessly rocking mantis. His problem is that angle, how to whip round it fast enough to strike before the mantis is alarmed, yet retain a constant grip on the beam. Below, tiger, tiger burning feebler continues his majestic stalk of beetles. Suddenly two close-linked objects land on his good side – gecko and mantis. Scared, Leo leaps backwards in flight. The gecko, never at home on level ground, recovers instantly but races up the wall leaving behind a green-white parachute badly roman-candled from the mantis's arrested flight. Leo from a safe distance is reassured, nevertheless he goes through all his stalking motions even for this crippled prey. Stalk. Stalk. Crunch. Crunch. Smack!

The gleaners work incessantly. Stinkbugs, flying ants, cockroaches, dead and dying beetles overlooked by the pirate are dragged by tireless armies of ants into subterranean recesses. They march over raised banks of fine sand, marshalled by the outsize-headed soldiers. A pile of unwanted wings lie just outside the doorways to their caverns, lifting minutely in the movement of breezes like ghost-watchers to underworld passages. The flutter of wings diminish around the lighted bulbs. Drowned in the fire-bucket, sucked in by geckos, gobbled by the pirate, dead from their own whirring mindless exertions, a noisy prodigality of flight power roused by the call of rains diminishes to a last lone insect crawling on the bulb. Finally the last corpse is borne away on invisible shoulders to unseen larders, a lone wing is dropped on the doorway pile for later building schemes.

One object, a paradoxical moth has kept away from the festival of light. Fat, powdery, complacent presence on the wall, it has kept to that one spot, heedless of the fuss that went on all around it. The gecko's eyes are hooded at last, the bulge of its underbelly spreads over the beam in gross satiation. The night round of the first rain is over.

37

DAYTIME brings the man of infinite jest, the male lizard. An outsize papiermaché head in obviously artificial orange colouring. An indigo costume all the way to the tail is again tipped a faded orange. Undignified in hunt, lacking even the failed majesty of the pirate, he runs helter-skelter after a fly only to make a full about turn and engage in an inconclusive flirtation with a randy female. She taunts and leads him on with her raised tail and steaming orifice, back hunched in a mixture of anticipation and caution. He will come back to her again but at the moment a butterfly has flitted past, miles over his head. He cocks his head to one side then to the other, rolls one eye after another in seeming hope for a morsel that was never remotely within reach.

They copulate incessantly, the crypt has become an orgiastic spectacle of sex. It would be a lizard sanctuary also but Ambrose, when the spirit of boredom overtakes him, hunts them down with stone and baton, sometimes slaughtering three or four in a single afternoon. I question him. No, he does not hate lizards. He piles up the bodies and proudly points at the day's bag.

Orangehead now performs his parody of the gecko. He scrabbles up the lemon shrub flattening against a branch, gecko-style, ruins the brief ambush by dashing to the next branch to keep in plane with the butterfly which continues wisely to hover beyond reach. He actually hides his head beneath some leaves, wise to all the tricks of camouflage. Forgotten naturally is his scaly dirty-blue hide and the flagrant orange of his tail. The butterfly has long disappeared. Orangehead, his vision completely obscured by an all-too-perfect camouflage, continues to wait.

He comes down finally, takes consolation from the new lettuce probes which he nibbles with a kind of nervous enjoyment. And then – mistaking the orange among the green for a flower from that distance? – a butterfly descends to just an inch away, realizes its error and gathers itself for retreat. Too late. Antenna to wing-tip, Orangehead munches this godsend, certainly no fruit of his skill or cunning, head darting nervously in every direction. He picks up a fallen wing fragment, then returns to the lettuce.

There are reasons, undoubtedly, in folk-lore why the lizard constantly nods his head. Or the praying mantis. Whatever ancestral trauma plagues the lizard still, will, I hope, be exorcised some day at some great lizard meet. The spectacle now of a tribal gathering of senile geriatrics sunning their scales, indulging their sensuous underbellies on the rough tickle of the wall face, nodding their squashed pumpkin heads drunkenly balanced as on a float in some rustic pageant robs him of a place among the higher predators. When he 'flattens' it is only a child playing hide-and-seek.

On the wall-tops, however, Orangehead is a beast in massive transformation. Transformed and transported back to that hidden pre-glacier kingdom among fierce thistles of bottle splinters in all tones of aquamarine, amber and green, an amphibious monster rears its flat-iron head reaching easily to highest treetops when he rises on forelegs surveying skies and marshy wastes. These blunt-ended conical heads blend with the cubist monsterland, a landscape of green gradations in the straight-edged cactus varieties, prismatic growths thrusting their jagged points to form a bristling skyline. A sudden wedge of orange and blue-steel makes angled runs between the dense-packed prisms. From this skyscrape comes the weirdest music of the vault, an oriental tinkle of hollow tubes as the scales of the lizard strike the glass keyboard at high speed, already mostly loose in their concrete bed. When a duel takes place among the monsters – always part strike, part flight and chase – the melody is long sustained, a true music of the spheres moving through sun filters of subtle tones, harmonizing as the scales hit simultaneous keys in an elemental struggle.

The sun has sunk level with the wall, gradually it lowers out of sight. Its muted rays are now in tune with the concert, a symphony of the twilight hour of the giant lizards, the dawn of the first ice-age.

I am seated at the death of the world. A red and copper sky with its blue-grey depths reflect the distant hidden primordial marshes. The glaciers have begun their surreptitious growth, huge icicles are sprouting from the sheer side of the valley, a cold army of cones thrusting ever outwards in remorseless bid for life that is poised towards a final stillness. Amber, green, aquamarine and pale yellow prisms, they hold the dying sun, weaken and bleed it through a thousand refractors.

A hunter, Ambrose the Anachrone enters, creeps along the wall. The giant lizards have rushed to the safety of ice thistles where they know he cannot follow. They do not understand him but already they fear Man. A soft mournful delicacy rises strangely from their flight, a series of wistful notes from luscent organ pipes. As Man pursues them, leaping up and thrashing with the thong of a smooth club, more glaciers are dislodged and fall into the valley depths with a sorrowing tinkle. Now Ambrose is wild. Up and down the walls he runs forcing them back and forwards along the icicle spines. A fellow hunter herds them back when they flee for refuge to the other side. A rapid succession of notes, tympanic rasps, a frantic run of scales into sunset. Ambrose misjudges a gap in the glass, lets fly a flint. High against the sky explodes a deadly discord in new colour impulses, a chromatic disintegration dazzles and deafens, showering down in primal damp fragments of the sun's last rallying percussions.

Lazarus rises, enters the inner crypt and awaits the rolling of the stone into its night position.

38

AT some point the games which I played with mathematics must have gone too far. I moved into greater and greater absurdities and plunged at some point over the brink of rational principles into clearly unhealthy regions. My recollections of this phase remain hazy and a little frightening.

From the mere fascination with Time as measure, as beast of burden, womb and grave, Time began to weave new fantasies around the figures and symbols of my algebraic exercises. It began, I think, with an idea that Time ought to be *integrally* related to its companion in Infinity – Space; it required only the discovery of the right mathematical principle. That this was well within the scope of human achievement was entirely beyond dispute, it was indeed only a question of time before its discovery, and time was a commodity in which I was generously endowed. I could not, alas, recall the formula for Einstein's Theory of Relativity but consoled myself with the thought that it dealt with too narrow an aspect of Time. From the point of view of time consumption it was an ideal problem, being quite insoluble; for a mind already infected by tendencies towards sustained, exclusive concentration, the idea of relating Time and Space, mathematically, within the concept of Infinity, was a most dangerous fantasy.

I was always on the verge of a breakthrough. Hours of sleep were lost during which time had been far more healthily consumed. Even now I am still uncertain how it came to an end; the frantic obsessive scribbling at night and increasingly careless calculations in daytime, the miraculous flight of time, erasure of reality, concrete surrounding and all environment, intolerance of food and the loss of the consciousness of my own person. This conceptual conceit burrowed deep and wide in my compost mind, burgeoning into poisonous tubers which burst from time to time and spread corrosive fumes through passages of my mind.

It ended somehow. And one day, long afterwards, I rummaged in my cache for some lost verses and discovered acres of toilet paper, cigarette packets and other precious surface covered with equations which I could not understand, symbols which I could not relate to any concept or quantitative value, with no recollection whatever of when or how precisely they came to be written, at what stage in the meanderings, least of all when or how I came to hide them. Terrified I destroyed the more alarming pieces and commenced a watchful period on my actions, thoughts and impulses, scanning the guards also to detect any sign or change in their way of regarding me.

39

FOUR creatures enter. Microbes but endowed with the gift of questions. Seeking what?

My mind is a cotton-wool consciousness, absorbing all, creating nothing. In the deathness of the Crypt I sit motionless in the sun and wait.

The seekers are gone; they came questioning, probing, insisting. You are seeking the bird that is flown. I need nothing. I seek nothing. I desire nothing.

Shouts. Threats. Cajolery. Such persistent microbes. And some all-important paper flutters in their hand.

They dwindled. Until at last only the Grand Seer came. Do you think you are playing fair? You are protecting someone but have you thought who you are destroying in the process? You had a courier. We know he is one of the . . .

Guardian angels with flaming batons? Even the gates of hell may be breached. The bird has flown, nor will it now rest. Can you put salt upon his tail?

I have been kind to you. I have bent over to make this place more livable. I took pity on your plight and gave you privileges . . . Privileges! At last he made a breach. My rage is divine but I pay him attention. And I remember him. The worthy one, not the Grand O, that smiling emptiness. I listen :

'You have repaid my trust with treachery. You are telling me now that I made a mistake to have been so humane. You know in what condition I found you here. I felt that no human being should be submitted to such conditions. I eased them up where I could. I have had nothing but queries. I can show you the file, it is all full of queries. I don't know what spies are here or who spreads around rumours of the latitude I've given you since I took over here. An investigating group was even sent from headquarters, they came with stories that I was permitting you to move among the other inmates, that you were holding classes and teaching subversive philosophies. I asked them to go about and talk freely to any of the warders. I invited them to go immediately, unaccompanied to where you were held and to judge for themselves. They refused. I have been persecuted over the treatment I have given you. The last letter from them warned me strictly not to let my kind feelings overcome my sense of duty. I wish I could bring the letter to show you. It warns me to carry out instructions about you to the letter. But I have not allowed it to interfere with my concept of what decency should be. You are a human being. You are an intelligent being. You should be treated like one. Well then, I appeal to you as an intelligent being. Is it fair to me that in protecting a man who has deliberately betrayed his office you should destroy my own career and get me into trouble? You say you are a fighter for justice. I ask you, is that justice?'

Casuist! Damned casuistic functionaire. Damn you! This hell a privilege?

He left, and in high passion. In this new state of being the law-giver calmly examined the claims of justice. I have to make a new set of commandments; I have the time. Whoever thinks time is a tyrant must learn patience – like me.

But all too soon he was back again. This, Pluto could not understand. He seemed so restless, a fluttered hen. What was this immense problem which he catalogued so breathlessly? He grew more human at each visit and this began to make some impression. For the Grand Seer was as immaculate outside as within his keen, observant mind. The buttons of his uniform were brassoed, his pips shining, his belt, his cap seemed manicured by a brace of servants and his individual swagger-stick a pleasure to behold. A devout inward man who loved the Koran. And now he came without his cap, his buttons were undone, his suit sagged on him and it seemed that his trousers needed a belt or braces. There was no swagger-stick and his pointed shoes were dusty – with trampling between door and door, surely. Whose doors and what offices? Finally, he was unshaven; the stubs on his face were at least two days and suddenly it came clear why his uniform sagged – the Grand Seer had lost weight!

I have come to ask you if you have changed your mind. Will you give me the information I require?

Pluto came up to earth, to a contemplation of a human being. A human being crying to be saved, yet asking in return for the damnation of another being. Open-mouthed he stared and wondered, experiencing again the shock and thrill of the human dilemma. Even in this abysmal place, shorn of identity, of volition, maimed and chained and ciphered out of human activity, to be called upon to choose between two human fates. Who dared impose such moral debt? Into the cycle once again of human safety-seeking predatoriness. Betrayal. Substitution of the sacrificial lamb. The lesser for the greater. The voiceless for position. But there was no judging, no condemnation where fear was so great and real. Suddenly it seemed to me that this problem was small, contemptibly small, that it required only a mundane imagination. I laughed. Why, it is still the same old people that bother us, the same old tyranny.

He said, 'I don't understand you. But I had better tell you that these people are now convinced that I smuggled out the papers for you. In fact they are desperately looking for the original because they want to check if the paper came from my office. I showed them all the paper we seized from you, showed them your bottle of Soy-ink or whatever you call it. But they still think I've been abetting you in all this smuggling. They cannot see how you could have broken through the security arrangements. I tell you, there are moments when I am nearly persuaded that they are right, because I can't see how you did it! We even search the warders before and after they come on duty. Who helped you Mr Soyinka? Just tell us who did and I promise that nothing serious will happen to him.'

A strange sound just then – what was it? A long vanished sound, a trigger towards human re-identification.

Mr Soyinka? Yes, I had forgotten. I am still Soyinka of the human race.

'All right. Give me time to think it over.'

He threw up his hands. 'But what is there to think over? These people are after my . . .'

'Please! After all we have been on this for quite a few days. Now I only ask a couple of hours . . .'

'How long then? How long?'

'Two hours.'

'All right. It's eleven now. I shall be here at one. And I'll bring the Security men with me so that they can hear it with their own ears. I don't want to hear it by myself and then report it to them. They are capable of accusing me of planning it with you. I'll just tell them that you have asked to see me at one so as to confess everything.'

'I haven't said anything about confession.'

'Mr Soyinka, let me say something. I hope, I sincerely hope that when I am detained I am put in the cell right next to yours. Yes, I shall specially request it. Because I want you to see me everyday and be forced to think over what you have done. I shall ask those men to accompany me here at one. I only hope that your sense of justice will prevail.'

About the gate where excitement had gathered – in such moments of crisis no guard not on duty in the Crypt dared enter it – the anachrones communicated through the chinks and summed up the situation as divine vengeance for the Superintendent's destruction of the harvest, forgetting or simply unable to conceive that the razing of the grounds was related to the first, early hint of a breach in the prison walls. I heard the small human tone of anticipation, the thrill that comes of the fall of another man.

It had happened. What was more, I sensed and had no doubts whatever of the effect of my messages to the living world. It was time to end my fast. The fight was over, the struggle for a humane confinement. I called my guard away from the chattering at the gate and sent word to the cook.

It was absurdly simple, once the passion of that kindly human had pierced my long detachment, the gradual fungus of indifference which spread and covered the skin of feeling even to that extent of blurring recognition for a while. The law-giver went to sleep and the fox emerged, wondering how these hounds of injustice could create and pursue a dilemma that need not exist. The prisoner-fox now sniffed the air, abandoning his winter hole.

They came promptly at one, two Security officers, the Superintendent, Chief Warder, Cadet and a few more senior warders for witnesses. The Security man was beaming.

'Well Mr Soyinka, I am so glad to hear that you have decided to cooperate. I assure you that the man will simply be given a warning . . .'

I cut him short and made the announcement. 'A night patrol man smuggled out the note for me.'

An audible sigh rippled, yes, literally, rippled through the gathering.

'Can you tell us his name?'

'I don't know it.'

'When was it? Do you remember?'

'No.'

'Approximately. Just give us the idea, three weeks ago? Four? Five?'

'One loses all sense of time here. After a while you hardly distinguish between one week and a month.'

Simpletons! Did they think I would be caught by that one?

'Can you describe him?'

'Difficult. It was after lock-up so I couldn't see him in full.'

'How did you get acquainted?'

'By talking. He used to ask me if I was all right and so on. About the third day it struck me he might prove useful in that direction. He had a kind voice.'

'Was he young or old?'

'Difficult to say. Sort of middle I would say.'

'Can you describe his face? You must have seen his face above that frame.'

'Oh there isn't that much light in the corridors you know. And he always had his cap on. That throws a shadow over the face. If you look at the light bulb . . .'

'But surely you must have got to know him pretty well. You couldn't just trust letters to a man you had just met. You must have talked a lot. He must have struck you as being utterly reliable. Really, Mr Soyinka, you don't expect us to believe you gave your messages to a total stranger.'

'Why not? There was nothing dangerous in what I wrote. Just a human desire to communicate with the outside world. I took a risk. He could have been planted.'

'But you saw something of his face. A vague outline at least.'

'O yes, I did.'

'What tribe was he from?'

'We spoke broken English.'

'But surely you . . .'

'I am no tribalist. A man's tribe doesn't interest me.'

Gestapo and Prison held brief consultation. The next proposal could be anticipated by a drugged idiot.

'Well, suppose we arranged an identification parade, could you pick him out?'

'Easily . . .' I chewed and savoured the moment out of all proportion. I had not had the chance for a very long time to score against the Gestapo. So I let the excitement die down, then added '. . . *if* you had arranged before then for me to see an optician. I have been demanding treatment for my eyes for a year. Now I couldn't recognize even my own father.'

'Mr Soyinka . . . !'

'Now listen. You wouldn't want me to pick on an innocent man would you? Ask the Superintendent. He shares my views on justice.'

40

HOW do I describe a clean, virgin sheet of typing paper? A tabloid of space, untouched, unmarked, without fold or wrinkle? What shall I term its equal that this sensation may be fully grasped? A spring? An oasis when hope is gone and the tongue is glued to its roots? As wine? No, not wine, not even wine after years of deprivation can compare with the smell and feel of a quarto sheet of paper in its inviolate purity. As a much junior sibling then who one loves dearly, loves to see in fine prints and little silver earrings, as a little sister dressed for communion, fragile and vulnerable, holier than the mother of Christ and more adorable. But it was not one sheet alone, it was hundreds. And there I sat, compelled to number them one after the other ... 50, 51, 52, 53, 54 ... 103, 104, 105 ... 207, 208, 209.... It hurt. I wrote in the tiniest possible writing in the corner of the page. It was also stupid. This idea of numbering was to ensure that I did not use any of this paper for illegal messages. An officer stood over me while I performed this criminal philistinic chore. From 219 I moved backwards to 120, a slip that might seem natural enough if detected. It was not detected. At the end we attained the number 375. I asked him to report this figure to the Grand Seer because the packet did claim 500. I said, I didn't want to mention it until we checked, but did you notice the wrapping was torn? He had hardly left when I began to sort out the chunks which were twice numbered. I need not have hurried. The figure was accepted.

But I have not yet described the beauty of a quarto sliver of purity. As a vast expanse of shore after days of shipwreck when one is sole survivor? Perhaps. But then, the flotsam existence must have lasted so long as to create doubts in this wretch's mind of his human identity. He must have regressed through the earliest amoebic origins of man, identified himself with the various oceanic mutations and been washed ashore, a mere ectoplasm needing the reassurance of his imprint on the sands. Yes, yes, I think we approach a barely adequate metaphor. But the *smell* of this virgin ream did not belong to any such adult experience. It belonged purely to childhood – the fresh baking smells in a bakery, the sweetness of a heap of mown grass after rain, lemon leaves and grandmother opening her tin of snuff. The feel was the first taste of adolescent lips.

There was not only paper. There were pencils, and pens. Biros of all colours. A file, a box file if you please! Not one but two. There was CARBON paper! CARBON for the making of duplicates! Wait a minute, if carbon comes, can – I did not dare conceive it – can *that* be far behind?

That finished me off. A TYPEWRITER! And soon. Permission had been given but she wanted to know what make I wanted.

A typewriter. I had lost count of the number of times I said, if only I had a typewriter.

And the books. And journals. Fresh minted books, they seemed to have come straight from an oven round the corner. Books! I saw these objects – books! But a prisoner is not a human being. The act of being a prisoner is in itself not even a process of but an instant metamorphosis. He is no longer human, he approaches, I think, a new invention, the human radar. He grows eyes where they do not belong, his body surface becomes indeed a mass of eyes. While the Grand Seer busied himself reckoning the list of journals and books I would carry back to my cell, I was turning two, three journals into one. We called out the name but three journals or three books went into the pile. Polyphemus was assisting so the process was not difficult. While they busied themselves about my clothing, I had several pens tucked out of sight.

My wife had come from the Head of the 'E' Branch himself. There was no time limit specified for the visit nor was the number of permitted visits stated. She was to stay overnight in Kaduna and check on my health and all other widely publicized complaints. I did not want to see her again. In prison peace is a state of isolation which cannot bear too much encroachment by the living world. I asked her to go back and not return. But I had also requested a pair of slippers – these she was to bring back the following day and leave with the superintendent. We parted.

One hour after she had left the prison, a squad came in and swept out every item that had been given me. *Everything!* I had expected them. I could not explain it. It could only have to do with living so long in the minds of these torturers, plotting their pettiness, being oneself partially destroyed and eaten by the evil in them, just to be able to anticipate. Great as the temptation was I had not even switched on the radio. The guard had patrolled and repaced himself a hundred times over, throwing unsubtle hints about his favourite programmes, what would be on at that moment on what station . . . I ignored the fool. Most difficult of all was to ignore my own cravings, to stop myself tuning in to a little world of music for which my being had thirsted so long with a passion new to me. The radio was untouched when they came. I heard the footsteps from afar and I knew what it meant. I secreted a few more items by taking even the inside out of the recorded journals. I tore them out. And I knew also that this would not be a thorough search, they were merely coming to remove items lately allowed to an unsuspecting ass. I shoved them casually under the mattress.

I permitted myself a grand speech denouncing the treachery and demanded to see the Grand Seer.

The Grand Seer duly appeared. One look at him and I was

filled with pity for his role. It was the Instructions. That faceless anonymous begetter of all dastardy – instructions! But I could not get over the sixth sense which had held out such warnings in his office. I asked him, did you have those instructions while my wife was there? While I was with her in that office?

He admitted it.

I asked, were those the instructions too, that you were to keep me fooled? That entire charade, the listing of items – books, paper, journals – was this part of the orders from headquarters? That you should raise my hopes then deliberately smash them and return me to a vegetable existence? Was that performance strictly for the outside world?

He began to protest ...

You staged a farce! You wanted my wife to leave satisfied that I was now receiving humane treatment at your hands. You went through a performance which lasted nearly two hours. You made sure that she saw me go off to my cell laden with books and paper. Even a radio. Then your goons come here and sweep it all off. I want to know Mallam A., if these were part of your instructions.

The Grand Seer surprised and shocked me. The subterfuge was entirely his own idea. He had received first of all a notice from 'E' Branch and from his office in Lagos that my wife was to see me and bring these items for me. But another letter had arrived from his headquarters on the very morning of the visit, instructing him to see that not one alteration was made in my condition.

Confused about what to do – he had decided to do something on behalf of his superiors. A dutiful Civil Servant, Mallam A. had become over-sensitive to the recent bad publicity given his department over my affair. This loyalty to his department dictated that he must, by all means, let my wife go away feeling satisfied with my new conditions of detention. His orders from the headquarters were in fact *not* to permit the interview. But here, fortunately, he had two directly contradictory instructions. I was also a detainee to whom the Police had right of access at any time. My wife arrived accompanied by a Security official; Mallam A. had no choice whatever but to have me brought out for the visitors. To himself, however, he had quietly formed the resolution to retrieve all the items brought by my wife as soon as her back was turned.

My note was slipped into my wife's hands as she stepped out of a taxi before the Prison Gates, bearing the slippers. This time the prison torturers had overplayed their hand. She flew back to Lagos and sought out the Head of 'E' Branch. To him this was a mystery. What exactly was the Prisons' concern in all this? He assured my wife that he did not have, had never held any objections to my having books or writing material. He had no objections to my being made as comfortable as possible. He swore that he imagined that I had been receiving the same treatment as any other detainee. Finally he expressed surprise that I had been held in solitary confinement all this while.

I believed, and I still believe him. There were many things which Yesufu did not know even in his own department, least of all of the political Gestapo arm, run by Yisa Adejo. What Yesufu did do, and with immediate effect was to put the Prisons in their place. And in stating this it is essential to distinguish between the bureaucratic sadists who inhabit the headquarters of that department and are indeed agents of the more sinister government activities, and the overworked prison officials, many of whom are balanced, humane and efficient creatures. It is essential to recognize the natural sadists who gave most of the instructions concerning my treatment in prison, who issued orders countermanding the instructions of 'E' Branch in August '69 and who served on the same committee of mind demolition as Kem Salem, Yisa Adejo, and Giwa Osagie. On *all* matters that affected me in detention, this evil triumvirate had much to do and say.

41

'GET ready,' Polyphemus said, 'we dey go hospital.'

The convoy was made up of eight cars; five belonged to Security, three to Prisons, one of which was the Superintendent's own car. I lost count of the number of prison warders and the legion of plain-clothes police that the cars eventually disgorged. As the first car pulled up in the parking-space before the clinic – late afternoon, a time selected specially as being the least crowded – all four doors flew open and out they swarmed, filtered through the steps, floors and corridors of the building and vanished through key-holes. I was greatly gratified by the performance; it was a long time since I had been entertained by sleek choreography albeit of the police variety. Gently but firmly the eye specialist reduced their number in the consulting room to a tolerable level.

The poor warders contributed by the Grand Seer to this great outing, to the first unwrapping of the mummy, these poor palace guards were outshone, outpaced and outmanoeuvred by the dervishes in mufti. He had lost the earlier argument outside the prison gates when he insisted that such a massive security turnout was not only unnecessary but embarrassing. His rickety Land-Rovers were no match for the suave Peugeots of the Security squad. Even his own private saloon shrunk somehow from the power redolence of the Secret Service.

Five days and two visits later, still embarked on the series of examinations ordered, it appeared, by the Great Man himself, my accessories of power had shrunk to a mere prison Land-Rover and a police car. I protested at this loss of status, threatened not to cooperate unless my rating as a dangerous man was raised to its earlier level. The officer promised to mention the matter in appropriate quarters.

By the fifth visit, the last, my down-grading reached its lowest ebb. No vehicle came from the Security, and only one personnel was supplied. He came on foot. It was then the turn of the dentist and we went in the coughing saloon of the Grand Seer accompanied by the plainly bored Secret Service agent. I complained to the Grand Seer that the Security people were beginning to take me for granted. But my humilitation was not yet complete. Seated in the dentist's chair, the lights failed suddenly. I expected the policeman to leap into action, pull out a gun and order me to keep still, or fling himself on me in anticipation of a sudden move. Instead he simply moved outside the surgery where there was still sufficient light to read his newspaper by. He even closed the door! It was sad no longer to be considered a dangerous man.

The Grand Seer remained gloomy at the belated attention given to my health. Conscientious and sensitive to the image of his department he continued to lament, 'This is what we should have done from the first, then we wouldn't have had all the abuse from the foreign press and even from some of our own people.'

Cardiograms, blood pressure, blood samples, urine tests, reflexes ... on the second last visit to the hospital it rained. The deluge was a strange unreal awakening. I had forgotten wind and flood as denizens of open spaces.

This was clean spring water, energized in endless cosmos, not mere cold venom from an iron-ringed hole in the sky. Until now I had locked out all intrusion of this new extended space into the mind, branding it alien and dangerous, inimical to the future that lay after the brief excursion into a simulated liberty. I denied recognition even to the presence of women in the streets as we drove through, denied that my body had made physical breach of the prison walls. Submitting at last to public pressure in this one respect, the graceless men might seek revenge in other ways for the one surrender. My outing therefore remained an ambiguous omen. I refused to take pleasure in the sensation of breathing a less restricted air.

Until the rains crashed through the barrier of insulation. An exhilarating storm, it penetrated all defences physical and mental, crushed the capsule to release the wild sweet scent of liberty. I gave into it, turning it to the strength of a thousand combative resolves that rushed out one after the other. Soaked to the skin, lashed by wind and rain as we fled through the long unprotected corridors of the hospital I was struck suddenly by the phenomena of this wild, free yet governed motion of the elements and us, and its contrast with that first death march into an artificial tomb. And, with the gaunt figure of Polyphemus racing far ahead of us, clutching his robes to him in a losing battle with the wind, I experienced a conviction as sharp and certain as the pessimist intuition of the turn of the year only, this time, in a positive revelation. It had to do with liberty but not with the gaining of it. It was a passionate affirmation of the free spirit, a knowledge that because of this love, my adversaries had lost the conflict. That it did not matter in the end for how long they manoeuvred to keep my body behind walls, they would not, ultimately, escape the fate of the defeated. At the hands of all who are allied and committed to the unfettered principle of life.

Appendices

Appendix A

The (Real) War Profiteers

Extracts from

AN ADDRESS OF WELCOME PRESENTED TO
HEAD OF STATE AND COMMANDER-IN-CHIEF
OF THE NIGERIAN ARMED FORCES
MAJOR-GENERAL YAKUBU GOWON

BY THE CHIEFS, COUNCILLORS AND PEOPLE
OF IKOM DIVISION ON THE OCCASION OF
HIS EXCELLENCY'S MAIDEN VISIT TO IKOM

dated 20 February, 1971

Your Excellency, our loyal greeting!

We, the chiefs, councillors and people of Ikom Division, feel greatly honoured to be visited by our Head of State and Commander-in-Chief of the Armed Forces, Major-General Yakubu Gowon here today. This is a unique occasion because it is the first time in history when we have had opportunity to welcome a Head of State in this part of the country. We are happy to know in person, the man who had redeemed us from the wicked hands of the 'lords' of the former Eastern Nigeria and are gathered here today to pay our respect to you. Our happiness knows no bound and our affection no limit in expressing our gratitude to Your Excellency for making this visit possible in spite of the very bad road you had to pass through with members of your team. This is the occasion we have long expected and we are gathered here to pay our homage to Your Excellency.

2. MOLESTATION OF THE CIVILIAN POPULATION BY THE SOLDIERS:

Citizens of Ikom Division are known to be peaceful and law-abiding. We are proud of this because there has never been any case of rioting or lawlessness in Ikom from the colonial days up to the last civil rule. When in 1967 the civil war broke out, we rose up as one man and fought side by side with the Army of Liberation. Realizing the sacrifice the soldiers made for our sake, we have never had any ill-intention towards them. But the high-handedness of some of these soldiers has astonished us and left many gasping for breath. To cite a few instances; may we mention Mr Dennis Okparaku Edim of Okanga who in 1968, was shot in his house for no cause whatsoever, Mr Ajom Agvor who was killed at Nkum, in 1969, for refusing to allow his school-daughter to be raped and Mrs Aggie Ntue, who was stabbed to death. Recently, a third year student of Ikom Secondary School, Master Agbor Nohor, was beaten to death when the School was besieged by a group of armed soldiers. Their only reason was that the school authorities had denied them the use of the secondary school compound for cattle grazing. Apart from this, the students, the tutors, and even their wives, came under the most ruthless type of treatment, with many books and other valuable property destroyed. In all these cases of death, the culprits have never been brought to book to serve as a deterrent and make the common man feel that the law protects his freedom from inhuman treatment as obtains in other parts of the country. Then there are the daily cases of men and women and sometimes children being beaten up indiscriminately, wounded, and detained in the Army cells after an ugly hair-cut for no just cause (see caption and photographs of some victims attached). We are pleading that Your Excellency should use his good offices to guarantee our freedom to move and to live without fear, so that we can contribute our quota to the building of this nation. Life is becoming intolerable for us as a result of treatment we receive from the soldiers daily. In the whole of the South-Eastern State, Ikom is the only town whose Road Check-Points have never been removed since the end of the civil war. There are three Road-Checks within the town and *two* at the boundary with the Cameroons and the worst of these atrocities on the civilian population emanate from there. These soldiers plunder such commodities as palm wine and even food-stuffs from the pedestrians and cyclists as they pass through the Check-Points. Some have refused to pay for food or drinks purchased and the sellers have often been beaten up when they insist on their pay. Some civilians have been made to carry their bicycles over their heads and run for fifteen or more minutes at these Check-Points. How terrible!

Appendix B

Extracts from

A REPORT OF ACTS OF INTIMIDATION AND VICTIMIZATION AT IKOM DIVISION OF TBE SOUTH-EASTERN STATE DURING THE STATE GOVERNOR'S VISIT TO THE DIVISION

dated 11 March, 1971 and sent to Yakubu Gowon at Dodan Barracks, Lagos.

5. His Excellency started off by asking Mr Ogar whether he took part in the writing of the address of welcome in view of the fluency with which he read the address. Mr Ogar denied taking part in the writing of the address and was allowed to go. His Excellency then turned to the Chiefs, whom he abused as being 'foolish and illiterate chiefs who allow yourselves to be misled by riff-raffs'. The Chiefs denied ever being misled, and admitted that the address of welcome was true reflection of their feelings and wishes, which was why they signed it.

6. His Excellency then turned to the members of the Committee that drafted the address of welcome and after a barrage of questions to them he ordered soldiers to flog Messrs H. E. Eyaba, aged 42, the General Secretary of the Ikom Divisional Farmers' Union, and Philip Ntui, aged 36, a private businessman. These two men were immediately stripped and laid before His Excellency, and in the presence of His Excellency's entourage, the local chiefs, and pressmen, were given about fifty strokes of the cane each. The two were later detained on the orders of His Excellency. The Governor further directed that the other member of the Committee that drafted the address, Mr Raphael Tatey,

who incidentally was not there, should be looked for, arrested, punished and detained the same way as the other two. He instructed that efforts should be made to prevent Mr Tatey (who incidentally has managed to escape to Lagos for safety) from sending a copy of that address of welcome to the Ogoja Community League in Lagos, which he said, would make a book out of it.

7. Messrs Eyaba and Ntui were later taken by the police to Ikom Joint Hospital, where they were treated for severe wounds sustained during the flogging episode.

GOVERNMENT BY FLOGGING

8. Your Excellency, we are sad to remark that for your honest, law-abiding citizens to be so flogged publicly, as if they were rogues, is not only shameful and degrading, but is in conflict with the principles for which you stand. The flogging incident mentioned here and other similar acts are fast becoming a pattern of the South-Eastern State's Government. We recall that some time ago one Mr Hogan, a Federal Officer on duty at Calabar, was similarly flogged and his hair scraped before he escaped to Lagos.

Appendix C

THE MAN DIED

(*Extracts from personal statements*)

'We were assigned to cover a party thrown by Chief Oni. We refused to carry out this assignment on the strength of a prior information from the Governor's office banning Press and Television photographers from giving any coverage to parties he would be attending. A superior officer at our station then gave us assurance that the Governor had waived the ban for this particular party.

So we went.

At the party we sat around in a corner away from everybody else, until a Chief Olusola requested us to start filming. The party was in large sitting room. At the time of the arrest we were working away from the Governor – although the Governor's wife was dancing with the Oni man. Suddenly the woman walked off the dancing floor and lodged a complaint with the Governor about the Television boys insulting her. Meanwhile Chief Oni was angry for being so treated, that is, left standing on the floor.

Next thing we knew was the A.D.C. to the Governor shouting. "Where are the boys from Television House?" We stood up and he then said, "Get out of here – immediately."

Well, we packed our equipments and trooped downstairs. As soon as we got downstairs we discovered that the Governor himself was there too – waiting for us.

Whatever his wife told him we never knew but he was so agitated that he went shouting all over the lawn about how rude we were, etc., etc. He then ordered us to be taken straight to his house. We were taken to his house and there we were, under gun-point, till he came about a quarter of an hour later.

When he came he said, "Take them away and give them a thorough beating and then bring them back here to me in the morning. If any of them tries any tricks gun him down." Fortunately the officer in charge was a man of God and so instead of taking us to the barracks he took us to Iyaganku police station. We were ordered to strip and the Mobile Police boys were jumping on us with their heavy boots. At the time we were made to lie on the concrete floor.

After the beating we were thrown into an overcrowded cell of hardened criminals...

...at nine o'clock the following morning we were returned to the Governor. The first thing he said was, "Did you enjoy your punishment?" To which only one of us (the oldest), a driver answered yes. The Governor then said we could return to our office where the General Manager would be telling us more about his decision.

Back in the office the Management, without hearing our own side of the story ordered us suspended.'

The accounts of the other (living) victims corroborate this account in detail. The following report is given by a member of my research team on the one who died:

The family of this man never knew anything more than that he was beaten, sent to England, and that now he is dead. *From his colleagues and friends I have managed to get this rather sketchy account of what really happened to to him:*

He was one of the four people from Television House who were beaten up on the orders of the Governor. During the beating he got his ankle smashed. Responsibility for his hospitalization and treatment was refused by the TV Management on the grounds that they were not responsible for his 'accident'.

He was taken to Adeoyo Hospital for treatment. When the hospital failed to achieve a lasting cure he was transferred to the University College Hospital. From the U.C.H. he was taken to a Missionary Hospital in Ogomosho. After going the round of hospitals in the West, he was sent to England.

Funds for this treatment were purported to have been raised by either the Ministry of Education or the Ministry of Economic Development. Nobody is definite as to the precise Ministry.

In England his amputation story began. First, below the knee, then above the knee, then the whole thing – from the socket – was chopped off. The wound was badly infected (gangrene) and soon his lungs became impaired. The English people could no longer help him, so he was sent back home – as a bad case. He was only six weeks at home when he died.

LEE ABBEY INTERNATIONAL STUDENTS' CLUB, COURTFIELD HOUSE
26/27 COURTFIELD GARDENS
LONDON : S.W.5

WARDEN: The Rev. Christopher J. Hayward, M.A.

TELEPHONE: 01-373 7286

Mr. Wole Soyinka,
c/o The Guardian,
192 Gray's Inn Road,
LONDON, W.C.1.

4th December, 1972.

Dear Mr. Soyinka,

I was most interested to read in "The Guardian" a week ago about yourself and your new book "The Man Died". It was particularly interesting to see in the article mention of Segun Sowemimo, since many of us here in this Lee Abbey Hostel, came to know Segun extremely well while he was in England.

I wonder if you knew what happened to Segun after he left Nigeria. It was a long and very tragic story of continual and worsening illness. Segun came to live here about three years ago following the amputation of the lower part of his left leg at Roehampton Hospital. He learnt to walk using his artificial leg and very courageously attended college. He was well known and well liked here and it was sad for us to see how his suffering increased. Eventually he became sick to the point where the doctors could do no more for him and it was then that arrangements were made for him to re-join his family in Nigeria. I suppose that I was one of the last to see him in England.

I kept in touch with his family and heard on occasions from his father and his aunt, but it was not very long after his return to Nigeria that he died.

It may be that you know the complete story of his time here in England and that none of this may be new to you. However, whatever may be the case, I should be most glad to welcome you here and to meet you if you would ever like to come to visit us here at Lee Abbey.

With every good wish to you, particularly as you make your decision whether or not to return to Nigeria.

Yours sincerely,

Chris. Hayward.

C. J. HAYWARD
WARDEN

Index

INDEX